The Woodsman

by Stephanie Varah

Published by JJ Moffs Independent Book Publisher 2019

JJ Moffs Independent Book Publisher Ltd
Grove House Farm, Grovewood Road,
Misterton, Nottinghamshire DN10 4EF

ISBN 978-0-9957881-8-3

Printed and bound in Great Britain by Clays Ltd, Elcograf S.p.A
Typeset by Anna Richards
Cover design by Tors Benham taken from original artwork and Green Man woodcut by Ruth Atkinson.

For Mum, Dad and A.J.
with deepest love and gratitude.

Time is,
Time was,
Time is not.

(Sundial motto)

Prologue

There is something magical about moonlight. Cloaking trees and gardens, fields and houses in a silvery glow, it transforms the ordinary to unexpected, mundane to mysterious. On a clear, still, moonlit night anything is possible, anything imagination creates. On such a night it is possible to discover a world long forgotten, where cavaliers gallop over the countryside on headstrong horses, and village people gather round a fire to feast, sharing simple food together. In the moonlight, echoes of merrymaking and music drift on the air, notes on a breeze, laughter floating through branches of trees – sounds half heard, whispers dancing in the corners of the mind …

Moonshadows

It was not a good idea. It was one of her many ideas, most of which involved him somewhere down the line, whether he liked it or not. His sister was big on ideas, and brain cells; he was lacking in both. This would probably explain why he found himself crouching uncomfortably in the cold, head buried in the shrubbery, on vole patrol.

It was hard work, maintaining the splendid proportions of an impressive 'spare tyre', something his nimble, feather-light sister would never understand. All available mental capacity was invested in finding the next meal. A casual mention of a family of bank voles taking up residence in the garden had been enough to whet his insatiable appetite; pride in his ability to rustle up a quick snack had got the better of him. She knew him too well. Knew he would fancy a bit of supper before surrendering to a long, dreamy sleep, but there had been no sign of life in the undergrowth for hours, and bed was fast becoming far more appealing than a midnight feast.

He shifted his bulk restlessly, there had to be an easier way to get a bite to eat. Waiting motionless like a statue he was starting to get really cold, the night air seeping into his flesh, stiffening his bones. And, though he didn't like to admit it, he was getting increasingly more nervous of the strange shadows being cast over the garden by the full moon. The holly tree in the corner, usually a safe haven for stalking a potential snack, rose towering over his head in a sinister, dark pillar, magnified to monstrous proportions by the brilliance of radiating moonbeams. Its shadowy, spiny branches leaned menacingly towards him reaching to entwine themselves around his body and drag him into their murky depths. He shivered and retreated to the relative safety of the nearby wheelbarrow, peeking around the tyre as he tried to assess his chances of safely reaching the house. He knew he would need to summon up all his energy and make a dash across the lawn, dodging the ghostly shapes thrown into his path reflected by the old stone garden wall. Speed, he knew, would be vital – something he aspired to but never quite accomplished due to the size of his undercarriage. But there was something else. He was convinced he was being watched by a pair of searching beady eyes – this fact alone should provide the additional acceleration required once he broke cover from behind the wheelbarrow.

It was way past bedtime. Irritatingly, he knew his canny sister would have long since drifted off into blissful oblivion curled up in front of the stove. He realised with a sinking feeling that she had done it again – she was inside, victorious in her strategy to commandeer the warmest side of the bed whilst he was outside getting colder and more terrified by the second. Why wasn't he as bright as her, and why did his stomach always dictate his every move?

He was contemplating these important questions about life, trying to summon up the courage to make his move, when a particularly large moon shadow flitted past projected on the garden wall. He froze, a statue marbled in the moonlight, small wisps of breath on the night air the only clue to his presence. His spine tingled – surely imagination was getting the better of him but he could definitely quite clearly hear a low rustling noise coming from the flower bed – an oversized vole perhaps? For a fleeting moment, fear overcome, his tummy took control, a vision of supper swimming before his eyes. Suddenly the moon disappeared behind a cloud, the garden swathed in darkness as if smothered by a deep dark blanket. Then, a sudden flash as the moon reappeared – something glinted momentarily, dazzling like metal caught in a silvery mirror and he realised with a jolt his imagination was perhaps not working overtime after all – he was not alone.

★

It had been one of those perfect summer days. Endless blue skies punctuated by the occasional white fluffy cloud that looked like it had been sketched on to a living canvas by some invisible artist. It had been the day of the village street fayre. Crowds of excited children and their doting parents had rummaged through brightly decorated stalls, bought endless jars of chutney topped with jaunty gingham lids and savoured fresh strawberries dipped in chocolate. There had been valiant attempts at pot smashing, hook-a-ducking, coconut throwing, and wood turning. Families had clambered around farm machinery, taken dray rides, drunk gallons of tea and consumed thousands of ice creams – they had also been transported back in time to the seventeenth century.

A band of musketeers and pikemen from the grandly titled Sir Henry Radley's Company of the King's Own Lifeguard Regiment of Foote had marched down the main street between the pink stone-walled cottages and 'invaded' the village. Villagers and visitors alike had gathered expectantly along the sides of the road around the band of men, summer shorts and dresses contrasting wildly with the red and burgundy breeches and old fashioned stockings worn by the Royalist regiment.

For a moment the modern world ceased to exist – an ancient presence was alive in this quaint and beautiful setting. A hush descended – hairs prickled on the back of the neck. The only sound the snapping of the colourful Royalist standards in the afternoon breeze as the village slid imperceptibly back in history. A sudden cry of "God save the King" shattered the silence and preceded an ear-splitting musket volley startling the onlookers and smothering them in clouds of wreathing grey smoke. An acrid smell of gunpowder hung on the air like burning pepper. In the space of a heartbeat, time stood still. For seconds nobody moved. The stunned crowd held their breath, suspended in the moment.

Then, in an instant, reality returned bringing with it the twenty-first century and all its gaudy trappings; baseball caps, oversized handbags, fluorescent-coloured ice lollies and all. Ranks of infantrymen meanwhile took up their positions – children looked on in awe and wonder as the gallant men staged a pitched battle in the street angrily brandishing fifteen foot wooden pikes made from the mighty ash tree. Those plotting against the King were singled out and 'hanged' from a nearby tree in a frighteningly realistic

4

gruesome re-enactment that sent shivers down the spine. For a finale, the gunners wheeled out a battered cannon firing a thunderous volley over the heads of the gaping crowd rattling mullioned windows and teeth in perfect harmony. As the smoke cleared the delighted, slightly dazed crowd burst into rapturous applause somewhat relieved to be in one piece. What a spectacle it had been.

The weary troopers marched away to their quarters to quaff ale and demolish chunks of rustic bread round their campfire. Curious children watched in fascination as archers fashioned longbows from lengths of young, green yew with their bare hands and women prepared a hearty meal in sturdy cast-iron pots suspended over glowing embers. The onlookers gazed on the living history display spellbound by the timeless simplicity, intrigued that people once managed to survive without gadgets using only natural resources and human endeavour.

As the fayre drew to a close, Sir Henry Radley's Company assumed their everyday identities. Pikemen became bank managers and tax inspectors. Muskets were replaced by mobile phones. Only one of Sir Henry's men seemed a little bemused by this transformation remaining in breeches and hose, pulling his heavy, rough cloak close around his neck despite the balmy evening air. His eyes had an unsettled faraway look as he melted quietly into the background.

*

The time had come … it was now or never. Sitting motionless under the welcome haven of the wheelbarrow for what had seemed like an eternity, he had watched the silver glow flash around the garden like a bad-tempered sprite, getting nearer all the time to his rusty refuge. He realised he was holding his breath not wishing to reveal his presence on the cool night air. Then he saw the cause of the crazy scattering of moonbeams; it was a substantial metal helmet. The helmet seemed to be attached to something – it looked far too heavy to be bobbing around by itself. The helmet was crookedly sitting on something's head and it seemed to be just at his level, aiming straight for under the wheelbarrow. The creature attached to the helmet was crawling on all fours in quite a laboured way being hampered in no small part by a heavy, brown cloak and an extremely long, vicious-looking stick with a point on the end. All rational thought (what very little existed in his food-obsessed brain) rushed out of his mind as he sprang forward to sprint across the lawn. At that exact moment the pointed stick and cloak seemed to wrestle with one another completely wrong-footing their owner. There was a loud whooshing noise and the helmet parted company from its moorings, somersaulting through the air in a perfect, symmetrical arc to land squarely on top of him with a muffled clang.

This was not what was supposed to happen. By now he should have been negotiating the open window, tiptoeing quietly to his long-awaited bed and drifting into a deep sleep – his second most favourite pastime. Instead, he found himself imprisoned in the gloom under a mysterious, and none too fragrant fusty, old hat from which there appeared to be no escape. There was no possible way that he could lever off the helmet. He imagined he would never again watch the world passing by from the lofty branches of the gnarled, old apple tree or chase his sister up the woodpile. She would probably be quite pleased but he could see a major problem looming – how would he get anything to eat? This was turning into a nightmare; perhaps he really was in bed and having a bad dream.

Just when he could bear these terrifying thoughts no longer there were sounds of scuffling close by and the helmet was suddenly scooped up into the sky. A chilly blast of air gusted over his body. A pair of bright, inquisitive, blue eyes twinkled at him in the moonlight framed in a friendly, weather-beaten face adorned with an extravagant, curling moustache.

"My dear fellow, let me liberate you at once from your most dreadful plight – it would appear my helmet has grown wings. Amos Longwood at your service, my friend – and who pray are you?"

2

Dreams

Racing across the field he felt alive with energy, exhilarated. All around him nature assailed his senses. Pounding the dry, scorched earth he left a heady, musk-scented dust trail hanging on the warm evening air. Midges danced in the fading rays of sunlight streaming through branches of the copse as he flashed by with effortless grace – a red streak against the dark, twisted trunks of the ancient trees.

The thrill of the chase was his only quest in life; he lived for those breathless moments flying across the fields, crashing through the brittle undergrowth of the old Long Wood scouting and raising the next target. With an athletic build, lean and muscular, he was designed for speed. A smooth, gleaming red coat, the colour of peaty malt whisky, gave intensity to his dashing appearance. A strong, handsome, intelligent face, large, soft brown eyes, silky ears and jaunty white socks on his hind feet were the finishing touches that, in all, made Tal quite a striking fellow – qualities which had not gone unnoticed by some of his female admirers in the village.

He was gaining on his quarry. If he lengthened his stride he would soon be in striking distance but needed to put on a spurt before the hare crested the looming ridge and gained speed on the downward side. Lifting his head to catch another drift of scent, he adjusted his path – his whole being intently focussed on the chase like a missile locked on its sights. Nerve endings straining, taut with anticipation, blood rushing through his veins, heart bursting … a few more strides, almost there. Baying a triumphant hunting cry he put on a final burst of speed … *Clangggg!!!*

A metallic, ringing noise shook his eardrums as his head thumped heavily against the dog grate in the fireplace. Looking around sheepishly, bleary eyed, he realised his paws were scuffling frantically, not through dark, earthy, leafy glades, but horizontally against something soft. He was dreaming again on the fireside rug, claws scratching on the hearth as he ran, not getting anywhere. Dreaming about the chase was nearly as exciting as the chase itself, even if it was somewhat embarrassing to others who were wide awake and not in the dream. Nevertheless, he relished abandoning himself to a good snooze, allowing dreams to spirit him away from the cares of the world, especially after the unusual events that had disrupted their routines that particular day.

There had been a terrible commotion that morning. The most unbelievable occurrence had taken place. Bungy had not touched his breakfast! He had been beside himself, too preoccupied, babbling on about a ghostly encounter in the garden and flying helmets. And as the tale was told and retold, Bungy's heroic attempt to outflank this unwelcome, marauding visitor grew in exaggerated daring until, eyes wide with astonishment, the others had listened captivated and Bungy had fluffed up with such self-importance, fit to burst, breakfast had been forgotten.

At first Tal had assumed the stupid feline had been at the catnip again. Guaranteed to remove all trace of rational thought, the billowing clouds of blue Nepeta were paradise, it seemed, to his friends. They would spend hours lazily rolling and lolling in the soft, downy leaves only to emerge, eyes glazed, incapable of doing or saying anything remotely sensible. But, this trance-like effect was only achieved when the leaves were warmed by the sun; Tal decided it was safe to assume that as Bungy's 'adventure' had occurred at night – the catnip wasn't to blame.

So, had he been dreaming, or was Bungy telling the truth after all? Real or fantasy, something had happened that had put him off food and that was unheard of. On this basis alone there must be something worth further investigation so they paid more attention to the story, getting more and more intrigued until it was decided that a plan was required.

All eyes turned to Pie. Pie was Bungy's sister. A fact that was extremely difficult to believe going on external appearances. Pie was the prettiest, sleekest and shrewdest cat in the neighbourhood. Slim and graceful with markings resembling meat and potato lashed with gravy, she had earned the unflattering title of Pie. In reality, her tortoiseshell hues of apricot and coffee tinged with black were most striking and endowed her with the ability to melt into any background, disappearing without a trace. She had enormous owlish, piercing green eyes, a most superior air and cunning brain. Bungy had not inherited these sophisticated genes. Mostly white with haphazard grey splodges, a wide grey line under his chin giving him a lopsided clownish grin, Bungy had always been the ugly duckling of the family, with an inability to think beyond the pantry door.

A plan – definitely Pie's department, she had all the ideas. The best approach, it was agreed, was to lay a trap for this creature luring it back to the garden so that Bungy's wild assertions could be well and truly verified. But what kind of a trap could possibly contain the wild, untamed beast Bungy had described? More to the point, what substance could possibly entice such a monster to even venture near their invention? They racked their brains – a deafening silence prevailed for some time. Tal was getting restless. He was fed up of all this *thinking*; he needed some action. He was getting perilously close to missing out on his morning run across the fields. Making a feeble attempt to contribute, he offered to scout around the garden for unusual smells. With that he promptly escaped to the unbridled freedom of the waiting countryside.

When he got back a plan had been hatched involving a length of clothes line, an old clay planter and the rusty wheelbarrow. *A plan destined for failure*, he thought. Putting his reservations aside he gave his report. Despite earlier scepticism, he had to confess there was something different in the air; traces of a distinct earthy aroma reminiscent of wood smoke, felled timber and drying leaves lingered around the garden. Logic had to dictate that the farmer next door had been thinning his trees and burning the brash but a quick look over the wall confirmed that the trees were just as they had been the day before. How strange, perhaps he was losing his touch. All these mad stories of apparitions in the moonlight were evidently getting to him – he was becoming as crazy as the others. Resigning himself to the inevitability that he would somehow be involved in this madcap scheme, he gave in and listened patiently to Pie's detailed explanation.

Something with a strong, interesting smell would be strategically placed under the upturned barrow which would be held in a slightly elevated position by the washing line, secured loosely to the apple tree and held in place by an old plant pot. The barrow would be raised just high enough for a tantalising drift of scent to escape and lure the unsuspecting creature to feel inside. As soon as the creature's arm reached out for the bait, the planter would be pushed off the branch releasing the barrow which would fall on top of the target trapping it underneath. Masterful. Tal had to agree it might just work. Hold on though – how would the planter be dislodged from the branch and what bait could possibly be that irresistible? These finer details Pie had so far elected to omit. Bungy had been valiantly trying to pay attention to his sister but was starting to feel the effects of an empty stomach. A loud grumbling noise reminded him he had not eaten his breakfast so he slunk off quietly back to the pantry as his sister held court. This turned out to be a big mistake. The planter, it seemed, would be helped off the branch by a willing volunteer. Bungy, it seemed, had been volunteered in his absence.

As for the interesting bait – a roasted chicken cooled conveniently on the Aga within an athletic Lurcher's reach. What could be simpler? At this point Tal realised that he would not be enjoying those succulent scraps tonight, he so longed for as a garnish to his dreary, dry everyday meals. If he refused to help with the plan, he could still have chicken for supper. One look from Pie gave him the answer. If he didn't help out, his nose would be a pin cushion. He sighed and gave in.

As night fell the plan came to life. Pie assumed the role

of leader and dished out orders to her reluctant troops. After much huffing and puffing everything was in place, except the all-important lure. Where was the chicken? More to the point, where was Bungy who was central to the success of their endeavour? It was safe to assume these two important elements of the scheme were together; whether the plot would be operational if Bungy wasn't located in time was another matter. It had, she realised, been a mistake to give him responsibility for fetching the tasty fowl but she really didn't want to desert her position in charge; she was enjoying herself. Time went by and Bungy had still not appeared. It was starting to look like her brilliant plan was going to be ruined, as on many occasions by her brother's insatiable appetite, when he rounded the corner licking his lips, a half-eaten carcass bouncing along behind him on a tatty bit of string. Oh well, miraculously there was half left – it would have to do.

As they took up their positions the garden was flooded with moonlight. The man in the moon stared down on them escaping from the last of the inky, blue clouds to cast his clear, white light around. It was very still and quiet. Eerily quiet. Bungy peered through the branches of the apple tree convinced with every rustle that he was being watched. A gentle breeze stirred around him bringing a familiar smell of wood smoke drifting to his nostrils. Snatches of a faint, lilting melody floated by him and he was certain he caught the sound of distant laughter from very far away, as if funnelled through history. Tal sniffed the cooling night air. He too caught waves of dry, smouldering leaves yet there was no smoke to be seen anywhere. Pie was too preoccupied to notice. They waited and waited. There was no sign of writhing monsters, not even a passing vole.

The night wore on and Bungy felt his eyelids drooping. His earlier highly alert state of readiness had worn off and sleep was creeping stealthily over his body weighing down his legs like a stone. Before he had time to think, gravity took over, his body sliding waywardly off the branch dragged by some invisible hand sending him hurtling rapidly towards the flowerbed. Landing on all fours he started nonchalantly to wash his face as if nothing untoward had happened, secretly hoping that Pie might not have noticed his ungainly departure from his post, but she had witnessed the whole sorry episode. Giving him a resigned look, she announced that it was probably better to abandon the plan as it was obvious that her brother was deluded after all and no such creature existed. She strode haughtily off towards the cottage door, nose and tail stiffly in the air. Bungy wasn't sure whether this was a good outcome or a bad one. On the one hand he was free to head for the cushioned softness of his beloved bed, but on the other he was leaving a half-eaten chicken in the garden and, no one would ever believe him again.

Defeated they trooped back to the house and settled down to let gentle waves of slumber wash the night's events away. The moon shone down like a magic lantern, silvering and silhouetting the garden whilst indoors contented muffled snores and rhythmic breathing were the only sounds to be heard. An owl hooted mournfully as it surveyed the countryside from the weathervane of the old dovecote behind the house. The haunting cry echoed into the distance just as a fleeting, dark shape emerged from the building's shadow and darted beneath the owl's lofty perch.

Alert, the creature swivelled its head to track the cause of the disturbance. There was nothing to be seen, but hunting instinct told the owl something was out there.

The next day, all was apparently back to normal. A queue formed at the pantry door for breakfast and daily routines fell into place. Bungy, feeling slightly hurt by his sudden fall from the spotlight, had decided he was not cut out for adventure – there were no regular mealtimes. Wandering into the garden to find a sheltered spot in which to sulk and heal his wounded pride, he remembered the half-eaten chicken; perhaps there were some compensations after all. Everyone else was too busy ridiculing him to think about dismantling their trap; the bait should still be intact. Licking his lips in anticipation he waddled off towards the old wheelbarrow. That's strange, he was certain they had left everything as it was, Pie insisting they reassemble the trap to investigate what had gone wrong before they went to bed, but the wheelbarrow was firmly planted to the floor – the chicken presumably trapped underneath. The world was, it seemed, against him, then he remembered the planter designed to be a counterweight – if it lowered the barrow, it could also lift it again – all he had to do was to pull it back up the tree.

Several hours of grunting, tugging and pulling later the planter reached its destination. All that remained was to find a suitable anchoring point to secure the heavy pot and the chicken would be freed from its iron prison. Bungy savoured the moment picturing himself nestling comfortably into a sunny corner behind the woodpile and tucking into the chicken with relish. Smacking his lips he tasted the succulent sweetness of the moist, tender meat and drank in its smoky, roasted aroma. He realised he was dribbling – he could wait no longer. One last hefty heave and the wheelbarrow rose slowly off the springy turf – he zigzagged down the tree like a crazy squirrel and peered into the gloom. It took his eyes a moment to adjust to the murky darkness. Perhaps the sun's glare was making the adjustment harder but he couldn't see the chicken anywhere. He looked again, straining his eyes, willing them to identify the rounded form of the long-awaited delicacy but there was absolutely no sign of anything edible. Bemused, he scoured around the entire gloomy depths of the upturned barrow now convinced that some magical force was at work and had spirited away his prize. Dejectedly he made for the opening, dazzlingly illuminated by the warm sunlight, to go back outside. Just as he crouched clumsily to squeeze under the rim into the overwhelming brightness something caught his eye. A small, golden object sparkled in a stray sunbeam. On closer inspection it appeared to be what looked like a brooch in the shape of a tiny braided knot. Intricately woven golden strands interlocked with one another in an exquisite pattern – it was really quite beautiful

The chicken had most certainly been appreciated but by whom?

3

Time

A gentle orange glow bathed the octagonal walls. A living mural of crazy, black shapes thrown by the modest wood fire, fanned by shadowy draughts creeping through rows of nesting boxes, flickered and danced over the bricks. A small pile of dry sticks hastily gathered that evening crackled and spat, sending sweet-smelling smoke spirals up into the rafters. Amos Longwood sat cross-legged close to the fire relishing the welcome warmth as he licked the remaining morsels of chicken from his fingers, wiping them clean on his rough brown cloak. He was feeling slightly more normal now he had found shelter, warmth and, most unexpectedly, a delicious meal to stave his nagging hunger. He decided though that 'normal' was far from an appropriate description for his current situation.

In the blink of an eye all the things he knew, understood and treasured, his friends and faithful companions, his entire world, had mysteriously disappeared – the natural order of things had completely changed. He seemed now to exist in a strange, new reality the likes of which he had never before experienced in his lifetime. He was totally and utterly displaced, as if he had stepped through a door in time.

He had tried desperately to rationalise and explain

this strange occurrence, reassuring himself that it was some temporary lapse of consciousness, a figment of his imagination, a bad dream, or even an hallucination possibly caused by the potion he had been taking for his bruised toe, the one he had injured stumbling over his pike – when was that? He couldn't remember … time was, he realised, something he took for granted.

Time was intangible, uncontrollable yet constant – an unseen presence that governed his day from sunrise to the long evening shadows that led to the depths of night. He always rose early as the first pale blush of dawn spread across the watery sky. When the sun reached its zenith overhead, he knew half his work was done and a simple lunch of crusty bread, honey and rough wine was to be enjoyed. And, as dusk approached, he and his sturdy pony Hector would wend their way back to the village with Bruce his faithful hound bounding ahead, scattering the geese which grumbled honking as they fled down the hill to the lake. An overwhelming sense of sadness washed over him as he wistfully recalled his daily routine and pictured himself in the clearing outside his rustic woodland shelter from where he tended the King's forest. His heart sank as he contemplated the fact that he may never again see sunbeams slanting through the canopy, or smell the dry, musty leaf mould disturbed underfoot when he and Hector trudged up and down the forest paths collecting timber.

He longed to stroke Bruce's rough ears, feel his comforting warmth on his feet in front of his rustic hearth. To the outside world Bruce was a warrior dog. Strutting confidently along, cheekily defiant, Bruce was always on patrol, ready for action, head and tail high, fur bristling, quick eyes missing nothing and noting everything. His wiry, golden fur singed black on the ends, looked like Bruce had been sitting too close to the fire – a narrow escape. This only added to Bruce's unruly, untamed look and infamous reputation – locally he was known as the Lion Dog. Other dogs in the neighbourhood gave Bruce a wide berth, even though he stood only a foot high from the tip of his nose to the ground. In truth, under this fierce exterior, Bruce was as soft as a brush. To Amos he was Bruce 'The Lionheart', devoted, loyal and brave. *Where could Bruce possibly be?* Amos wondered, getting more despondent by the minute.

Endlessly replaying the last twenty-four hours in his mind, Amos tried to make sense of what was happening. He remembered he was stacking felled ash ready for delivery to the wood turners who would fashion it into the much- feared Royalist pikes when he had heard the cry go up, "For God and the King!" He remembered pausing, as he had done on many occasions, to watch the officers of the King's Own Lifeguard of Foote go through their daily drill. It always filled him with pride, and it has to be said, a little wistfulness as he looked out on the assembled standing army with colours and standards fluttering gaily in the breeze. A much-revered regiment and one Amos would dearly have loved to join. The King though had other ideas and insisted that no one could be charged with that most serious responsibility of managing the royal estate other than Amos Longwood – why, he even had the right name for it. Despite this being a great honour and essential to the campaign, Amos longed to experience the seething press of battle and smell the gunpowder in the air. He recalled daydreaming for an idle moment, as he had many times, imagining himself in the jostling melee, muskets blasting, warring cries and clash of sword surrounding him. Then, all at once, he had found himself in the ranks, fifteen-feet of solid pike in hand, marching behind the Banner Royal hoisted by the standard-bearer. He had fallen in with fellow troopers, so close in step he could feel their breath on the back of his neck. They had marched for a short distance then performed their pike detail. Amos had tried faithfully to follow but found himself more and more distracted, uneasy, at the most peculiar sight unfolding before him.

Instead of rolling green fields gently melting into the dark tree line of his beloved forest, he saw stone buildings – where had the trees gone? But the strangest thing of all was the clothing and behaviour of the onlookers lining a hard, grey metal village street. The only thing Amos could liken it to was a troupe of travelling jesters who had been summoned recently to entertain the King and his royal guests. They, like the assembled crowds in front of him, had worn strange, garish costumes, the likes of which he had never seen before. The men, women and children surrounding them now were apparently all members of a strange club that was made to wear dark circles over their eyes, perhaps to keep their identities secret. The comic routines of the King's jesters had caused great hilarity at court and stirred the guests to a whooping shrieking frenzy. A bizarre thing had happened yesterday whilst the regiment went through their paces; the assembled crowd had whooped in delight and applauded their every move. Why hadn't they recognised the importance of drill practice and taken it seriously? It was not entertainment; it was to ensure survival on the battlefield. The villagers usually showed great respect for the King's regiment and stood reverentially until the detail was completed. Who were these odd people?

Things had then taken the most surprising turn when the regiment came to the end of their drill. As the ranks dispersed the troopers had mingled with the odd individuals in the crowd and proceeded to remove their Royalist uniforms, changing into the same strange attire as those gathered to watch. Only Amos remained in his trusty brown cloak and faded breeches. At this point he had become so bewildered he assumed he was definitely asleep and having a very bad dream. Swiftly removing his helmet so as to appear less conspicuous, he had drifted away into the background to find a place to come to his senses, stumbling upon this old dovecote just behind the area where the troops had mustered – tentatively pushing at the heavy wooden door it creaked open to reveal a dark and pungent interior.

He had only ventured out of his refuge at night. During daylight hours there were unfamiliar, frightening sounds that passed by; some low and droning, others loud and rumbling. Peeking through the slats in the dove house he had witnessed something so unbelievable he had pinched himself to make sure he was awake. Enormous, gleaming blue shapes being propelled by something – he had no idea what – lumbered along held up by massive, black wheels that slowly rotated as the growling giants went by. A roaring noise grew in volume as the shapes gathered speed. Never before had his eyes looked upon such a sight. These cumbersome creatures were spending a lot of time rumbling up and down the field behind his hiding place tearing up the landscape as they trundled along like giant termites gouging grooves in rotting timber.

The most terrifying sight though had been the bright, yellow monster as big as two woodland shelters sporting a row of menacing, spinning spiked teeth longer than three Royalist pikes put together. This beast thundered over the field making a loud, anguished howling noise chewing up anything that got in its path and spitting out the remnants in a whirling cloud of dust as it crawled by. Amos cowered in his refuge until these leviathans disappeared over the horizon, longing for nightfall, when the only sounds that could be heard were the screech of hunting owls. The locals, he noticed, were dressed most unusually in bizarre garments, most impractical for tending livestock or the land. It truly was a peculiar place in which he found himself, yet somehow the countryside looked oddly familiar.

His one close encounter with the new neighbours since his world had changed had been with the round and startled creature, which had the misfortune of being imprisoned by his helmet, from which he had most violently parted company. Funnily enough, he sensed an instant connection with the frightened animal which his instinct had told him he should cultivate. He had absolutely no idea why, but something in the back of his mind linked this innocent being with getting home, and that was all that mattered. Amos decided he had to try somehow and communicate with the little fellow under the helmet; he had a feeling it was his only chance.

Slipping out of the dovecote at dead of night, Amos stole quietly like a ghostly shadow across the nearby garden where he had first encountered the unlikely ally. All was still. He gazed heavenwards at the dazzling array of stars, relishing the fresh night air after breathing the heavy, bitter aroma of bird droppings all day. Warmed by the sun in the confines of the ancient dovecote, the cloying smell clung to his whole being. It had become so powerful he was certain that anyone within yards would be completely overwhelmed and make a swift retreat – an unpleasant yet useful deterrent, perhaps. He soon found the old wheelbarrow which had yielded such a pleasant surprise, still upside down next to the apple tree – a splendid example of a typically old English tree he noticed. Heavy with apples the size of small cannon balls, the tree formed a perfect graceful arc, its gnarled, lichen-crusted branches woven into a delicate lattice umbrella. Amos loved trees nearly more than his nearest and dearest relatives, and had been known to disappear into the forest to avoid noisy family gatherings preferring the cool, green solitude of the ancient woodlands he lovingly tended. He felt at one with nature and often talked to the trees as he and Hector traversed the forest rides. He thought a conversation with the apple tree right now might be a wise move before he put his plan into action.

He needed to make contact – the only way he could do this was to use the tree as a messenger. He would etch a sign into its majestic trunk to alert the creature to his presence. It was something he would never usually do to a friendly tree, but he was desperate – he was sure the tree would understand and want to help. Fishing in his breeches for his whittling knife he suddenly remembered the gold, knotted pin, a gift from the King for many years' loyal service; he could stick this in the bark instead and preserve the natural beauty of this fine specimen. Despite his desperation, he hesitated momentarily. How could he possibly part with this most treasured possession? Would the creature even see his signal and, if it did, would it know what it meant? Wasn't he just grasping at straws that, like his hopes, were being tossed aimlessly into a void at the mercy of the wind? His thoughts became befuddled, descending into a spiral of dark indecision. At that moment a spectral shape swooped by, creating turbulent ripples in the still night air, startling him out of deep preoccupation. A haunting *'tiwit twoo'* resounded from high in the tree as if the owl were saying *'stop dithering and get on with it'*. His woodland conscience was right; doubt dissolved and gave way to a much stronger resolve to survive – to find his way home. The pin would have to go – the King, he was sure, would commend his ingenuity and be grateful for his loyal servant's safe return.

Rooting in the depths of his pockets Amos turned out bits of leather, a small length of ragged nettle rope and a few left over grains he'd saved for a bowl of pottage. His heart sank again. What he would give for a steaming bowl of his favourite chunky vegetable stew right now didn't bear thinking about. His taste buds threatened to distract him again from the task in hand. With a mammoth effort, he wrenched himself back to the present and rummaged more deeply. After several more minutes re-examining the pathetic contents of his pocket, he realised with a sickening feeling that his beloved pin had apparently disappeared, possibly when he tripped over his cloak yesterday. He would have to craft a sign after all. Retrieving the knife from his other pocket he thought of an appropriate symbol – he would make the King's mark, a twisted knot, in memory of the missing token. This sign would have no meaning in such a foreign world; no one here would know its true significance, and there would certainly be none of the so-called 'roundhead' Parliamentarians around in this strange land that might find the secret symbol and pose a threat.

The thought of an enemy presence sent a shudder through his being. How could he be in such a tranquil place when rural England was torn apart by the turmoil of Civil War, dividing family against family and family members against each other? The only threat here, as far as he could see, was the danger of being exiled, thankfully not one of Parliamentary troops rampaging around the countryside, looting and plundering all before them. He wasn't sure which was worse.

An unexpected shiver crept over him – he sensed a presence close by. Turning cautiously to look over his shoulder, Amos nervously scanned the garden – the owl perched high above him followed his gaze, peering into the shadows. Amos felt his heart beat quicken; he must complete this task and return to the relative safety of his temporary home, as quickly as his fingers would allow. Turning to the broad trunk, he whittled away at the rough bark, fashioning a crude knot with three entwined twisted coils. Satisfied with the rushed handiwork, he dropped to his knees into the flower bed and crawled along the edge of the garden wall towards the dovecote, cloak dragging along the ground behind him. As he turned the corner reaching the edge of the field which housed the old building, he lost sight of the garden and didn't see the owl suddenly stare intently into the night, body taut, senses highly tuned on a form emerging from the shadows, gradually taking shape.

A lone, dark figure hurried across the lawn, hunched and furtive, looking this way and that, as it ran to the base of the apple tree. The owl peered down through the branches at this clandestine intruder. A matted head of thick, closely cropped black hair was all it could see. Shifting branches to a better vantage point, the owl disturbed the intruder who craned his neck and looked with cruel, searching eyes directly at him. An evil-looking man in a uniform from another time stared fixedly at the wary owl – a piercing, lingering look of someone possessed, driven. After what seemed like an age, the man feverishly scoured the trunk of the ancient tree, intent on a quest. He eventually spied the knot crafted by Amos and smiled a thin, cruel smile – he had been right in thinking that the Royalists were on to something; he would watch, listen and wait. Time would yield the answer. The man ran back to the shelter of the woodpile where he had discarded his heavy cloak, weapon and characteristic pudding-bowl shaped, Roundhead helmet.

4

Tree Talk

Life was slowly getting back to normal after the annual summer fayre. Bunting neatly rolled and packed away, coconut shy and bowl-a-pig unceremoniously relegated back to their dingy corner of the draughty barn until their once a year appearance in the limelight came round again. Mellow tones of brass band were now replaced by the heavy, monotonous rumble and drone of tractors passing up and down the tiny village street every ten minutes. Things settled back into the natural seasonal rhythms that governed daily life in the small farming community, as they had for hundreds of years. Living in harmony with the landscape and at one with nature, this was a haven caught in a timeless other universe, detached from the busy outside world.

The village consisted of one narrow lane stretching away into the fields lined with ivy-clad, pink and grey limestone cottages topped with red pantile roofs framing tiny, mullioned windows that glinted in the sun. It nestled quietly amongst gentle, rolling countryside fringed by ancient, waving woodlands. A place steeped in history; centuries old. A small pond at the end of the lane with a tiny duck house planted in the middle made an exclusive residence for a couple of house-proud ducks who spent the day sunning themselves on their terrace, and taking it in turns to attentively stand guard.

At the heart of the village stood a small, charming stone-built hall which had served over the years as malthouse, schoolroom and even makeshift mortuary at times of war, but these days more often resounded to much merry making and music, doubling up as the operational nerve centre on the day of the village fayre. From here, lost children were reunited with anxious parents; mountains of cakes were consumed washed down with gallons of tea and the vicar rallied villagers to take up their positions at allocated stalls. When the day was done, and the village again retreated from the outside world, a communal feast was held on the village green for weary helpers under jaunty bunting and starry skies. Behind the village hall, proudly placed like a sentinel in the middle of a large, undulating field stood an ancient, red-brick octagonal dovecote. In times gone by a vital resource – providing a constant supply of pigeon meat to feed the hungry locals, and rudimentary gunpowder, a useful by-product from the droppings, to fuel their weapons in times of unrest. Now the dovecote stood in splendid isolation, a welcome roosting post for passing doves and an historic symbol for the village – a reminder of a bygone era.

Beyond the duck pond the lane became a bumpy track meandering gently into the glorious countryside beyond. From here it was possible to disappear within the surrounding woods into a very different world. Those at home with nature were at home here. If the track, fields, woods and buildings could talk, they would tell a stirring tale. They would speak of castles, squires and noblemen, of buried treasure, and a ragged army of ordinary men –

country folk called to arms, forced to choose sides. They would tell of a land divided, and the brooding presence of Oliver Cromwell.

The visit of the Parliamentarian army leader at the height of the English Civil War was the village's claim to fame. Legend has it that Cromwell was entertained here by one of his most distinguished, high-ranking officers, Sir Randolph Knight, who owned the local manor house. This was a Roundhead stronghold; supporters of the King strayed here at their peril. It was hard to imagine the ordered ranks of Sir Randolph's cavalry trotting through this peaceful place en route to head off an anticipated Dutch invasion in East Anglia. The tribulations and miseries of war seem completely at odds with the present-day tranquillity, but their echoes remain in the branches of the trees and grains of soil. Passions ran high between supporters of the Parliament and the Royalist supporters of King Charles the First, etching themselves into village folklore. It is said that when the full moon bathes the tiny village the distant sound of hooves and marching men can still be heard.

All of this historical nonsense was of no consequence, however, to a significant number of village inhabitants – those of the furred variety. A thriving community with its own unique perspective on local life existed unseen and unnoticed to the untrained eye. On a daily basis a whole other world of experiences, dilemmas, challenges and victories were being played out in the animal world. Every day held an adventure, and every creature had their own distinct personality. In a rambling, stone cottage next to the dovecote lived three such characters, each highly individual, together, a potent hot-pot of free spirits. They enjoyed an idyllic lifestyle of creature comforts – trees to climb, wild and interesting territory to explore, warming fires, cosy beds and food on demand … well almost. For Bungy, the hungriest cat in the neighbourhood, this last point was debatable, food was not as instantly accessible as he would like – this was a constant bone of contention. He discovered, however, that by being a persistent nuisance, sitting in front of the pantry door tripping people up and whining incessantly, he usually got a bit more to eat just to shut him up. Unfortunately this was a highly labour-intensive strategy and he often ran out of steam, waddling off to lie down for a while to recover. He was sure his two companions didn't understand him.

Tal kept to himself as much as possible. He lived to escape to the wide, open countryside, and to run like the wind chasing anything that moved. He adored scouting around in the wood for the scent of a passing hare and locking sights on his prey like a homing beacon. Once he reached the searing heights of excitement there was no stopping him as he disappeared over the horizon, only to return much later gasping, chest heaving when the chase was over. At all other times he was the most placid, quiet, uncomplicated creature imaginable, curled in his bed sound asleep – his one sole aim in life, to avoid the prickly claws of the bossy, opinionated feline with whom he had the misfortune to share a home. A true classic Lurcher, Tal was either at full speed or at a full stop, and would do anything for a quiet life.

Pie was a cat who knew her own mind. Beneath her sweet, demure and innocent exterior lay concealed wilful cunning and impudence – a proper minx, yet completely enchanting at the same time. With one eye constantly on her next move, she was an infuriating, yet highly successful, combination of ingredients that yielded her all the right results. Between the three of them, life, inevitably, was never dull, but everyone knew their place – behind Pie. So it was a most unusual turn of events for Bungy to be in the spotlight. Things had gone suspiciously quiet on that front but the chicken had disappeared so how could that have happened? Pie had pondered on this for a long time and concluded that Bungy was either eventually losing his mind, and they with him, or he was a magic cat.

It was a well known fact that magic cats see things others don't, and despite her better judgement, she was beginning to believe that her brother might after all fit the criteria.

So it was that the village provided a most serene and beautiful fabric around which the threads of these three unique lives wound themselves into the tapestry of daily life. As summer blazed its parting rays, the sun-scorched, tired earth surrendered the greedy crops it had sustained for so long to the mechanised teeth of the combine harvester. A dusty haze seemed to hang permanently in the air, and the tiny cottage window panes rattled constantly as tractors lumbered till late in the evening up and down the village street.

Bungy was hot and bothered. Summer was not his favourite season, and the harvest mites sent him into a frenzy of constant scratching. He was not a happy soul. Only in the cool, late evening air did he feel peace at this time of year, so seeking tranquillity he ventured out into the garden stretching luxuriously, feeling the coolness soothe his itchy skin. He sighed.

This was more like it. No disturbances, no noise just

the promise of a possible light supper and the freedom to mooch around without the other two providing a running commentary, filling his head with their ideas. Before he set out, he had made sure that the shiny, gold object he had found under the wheelbarrow had been safely hidden in his bed under his blanket where the others would not venture. One golden rule they had between them was that individual beds were off limits …

Feeling invigorated, he bounded up the old apple tree to get a good vantage point for hunting. The moonlight cast exaggerated shadows around the garden sending a frisson up his spine; visions of his recent unwelcome experience swam in front of his eyes. He told himself firmly that he needed to move on and face his fears, as he climbed to the highest possible branch that seemed to point a long, bony finger into the inky blackness like an ancient fingerpost. He must have crouched there a while, silently scanning for unwitting mice and voles commuting between the flowerbeds so he could plot their location. Not much action here. Becoming slightly bored he scrambled halfway back down the tree, his claws gripping the crusty bark avoiding the knots, particularly the deeply scoured, twisty one that he had not noticed before, but which looked remarkably similar to the pattern of the shiny object he had found. He was making a closer inspection then stopped dead in his tracks. Directly below him, a tangled, bushy mass had appeared which was attached to a tall figure with a weather-beaten complexion, twinkling blue eyes and a very grand moustache.

A million frantic, irrational thoughts, ideas and options flashed tumultuously through his mind, all at the same time making him quite dizzy, as he quickly appraised his predicament. He was well and truly stuck this time with nowhere to go, other than the top of the person's head. The stranger looked up at Bungy with a kindly smile and slowly settled himself in the crook of the largest bough at the base of the tree whispering softly,

"Do not be alarmed, my dear fellow, I seek to befriend you, I sense we are kindred spirits."

Much to his amazement Bungy understood the stranger's words. Feeling slightly braver and reassured by his gentle tone, Bungy addressed the unkempt man.

"I know we have already been introduced, but you will forgive me for forgetting your name in the frightening circumstances I found myself. Who are you and why are you still here in the garden?"

"I am Amos Longwood, Keeper of the King's Forest," Bungy noticed a note of pride in his voice, "I am lost here, a long way from my home, and time, it seems. I have taken refuge in your dovecote, only daring to step out at night into a world I do not know. I sensed you may be able to help me in my plight, so I made the King's mark on the tree and you have come to my aid."

A lot to take in, thought Bungy. He'd only come outside for a breath of fresh air, and again found himself embroiled in some weird goings-on; *what was he to do? What would Pie do?* he found himself thinking irritably. He couldn't think on an empty stomach. He decided a plan was required and that he would have to get the others involved so he could make his escape back to the sanctuary of the cottage.

"There is little we can achieve alone – my companions will have much to offer and need to hear your story," Bungy stammered, wishing desperately for the comfort of his bed, and the familiarity of an old existence which suddenly seemed to have evaporated in an instant. Why was *he* the chosen one? Why had things suddenly become more complicated than they needed to be? How could he, *they,* possibly help this apparently desperate individual, who had just magically appeared out of thin air?

As he tried to swat away these pressing and annoying questions which buzzed around his head like a cloud of summer midges, he noticed the back door of the cottage swing noiselessly open. Pie, dropping effortlessly off the window ledge, nimbly swung on the handle and released the catch, allowing herself and Tal to enter the garden. Having woken to a disturbing silence devoid of Bungy's droning snores, Pie had been watching her stupid brother apparently become stuck in the apple tree. Deciding she should show some sympathy after the disturbed few days he had experienced, she executed her now famous door opening technique to go to his rescue. Tal, knowing that he should probably have pretended to be asleep, had opened one curious eye and found himself under the steady, expectant gaze of an impatient Pie, waiting for his moral support. So, he found himself stepping out on to the dew-laden grass, following Pie's tail which stood rigidly to attention like a battle standard.

They arrived at the base of the tree to a most amazing spectacle.

Bungy, balanced on a branch halfway up the tree, seemed to be conversing, yes, having a conversation, with a tall, bedraggled, whiskery individual draped in what looked like an old curtain. Pie immediately assumed her leadership role by springing to an adjacent branch, slightly higher than Bungy, to assert her position. Tal could not believe his eyes, but his nose was reminding him there was a familiar scent emanating from the stranger's presence – something he had smelled before. A subtle aroma of wood smoke and dried leaves.

"This is Amos – who is lost and needs our help ..." Bungy volunteered by way of introduction. Pie could contain herself no longer and butted in.

"Please explain yourself, and the reason for your secret visits to our garden, we are not accustomed to invasions of our territory."

Bungy looked uncomfortable at his sister's stuck-up approach but needn't have worried. Amos smiled gently and wrapped his cloak tighter to his body against the chill night air as he began to speak.

"I am Amos Longwood, Keeper of the King's Forest, I—"

"Just which king exactly are we talking about here?" interrupted Pie in a superior tone.

"Why ... King Charles the First," answered Amos.

"There are no kings around at the moment, you must be mistaken. There are only kings in history." She sat back smugly, preening her whiskers.

"Well, I can assure you that King Charles the First is alive and well right now in 1642 and I am his loyal servant," came the reply.

Pie looked agog. Bungy, hearing all this talk about kings, fluffed himself up self-importantly, getting more interested in the stranger as the conversation unfolded – after all, *he,* Bungy, had been chosen by the *King's* servant.

Tal looked on in disbelief, but suddenly became aware

of echoes in his distant memory. *Clank! Whoosh!* ... ancient blacksmith's bellows. *Hisssss!* ... molten metal hitting cool water. A village scene of wood fires, rickety handcarts and ruddy-faced country folk flashed through his mind then was gone. He shook his head, flapping his ears as if to dislodge the invading memories.

Amos continued to speak in a quietly determined manner and relayed his memory of pausing on the hillside to survey the brightly coloured fluttering standards and the ranks of infantrymen marching past like tiny toy soldiers, then discovering that he was in the midst of a parade, apparently performing before a bizarre crowd of people like a visiting jesters troupe. The others listened enthralled and astonished until Amos' tale concluded with his chance encounter with a rusty wheelbarrow, and a startled hungry cat. The night air closed in around them; fingers of mist threaded through the tree branches and caught them in a chilly grasp. A powerful silence hung in the air, broken eventually by the mournful *'Hoo-huh Hoooo'* of the ever watchful owl above their heads.

"We have to help Amos find a way back." Pie broke the spell with customary bossiness. "I'm not sure yet what we can do but we need a plan!"

Used, by now, to Pie's *'I'm in control follow me'* attitude, the others knew it was futile to resist – besides they had all been touched by Amos' plight and it was a long time since a good adventure, a *mission* even, had presented itself. Pie was warming to her role, "We need to start with a map so that Amos can discover whether he recognises anywhere locally. If he arrived here from nearby, it's probably not far to go back again."

Bungy was having difficulty understanding Pie's logic, desperately hungry, and, yet again, parted from his bed in middle of the night. As a pale, pink blush spread in the eastern sky, framing the dovecote in a rosy glow, they all agreed to meet again by the tree the following night, hopefully in possession of some kind of map. There was no going back; the adventure had begun ...

5

Passing Ghosts

'*Cock-a-doodle-dooooo!*' bellowed the haughty rooster, his cry echoing around the farmyard and ringing in the ears of the lone man lying straddled across straw bales trying to sleep. The man, jolted out of his reverie, sat bolt upright, a startled expression on his face. Heavily built with close-cropped, dark hair and shifty, glittering eyes, he was not a man you would warm to; he was a man of purpose and steely reserve. The man stretched stiffly and winced – another cold and very uncomfortable night spent with the chickens, but at least there was shelter and grain to eat. However, it had not been an entirely bad experience. Lurking in the shrubbery he had overhead snippets of a most interesting conversation between what he assumed to be one of the King's servants, a woodsman by the look of his handiwork, and an unlikely band of creatures who seemed able to understand what the old man was saying and … better still, they had volunteered to help by finding a map, probably *the* very map he sought. So, it had been useful. He was most pleased with his night's work – he was a step closer to finding and claiming the trove of Royalist silver that would fund the continuing Roundhead campaign against the King and his supporters.

Spying on the woodsman had been an easy mission so

far, and now it seemed the whereabouts of the fabled treasure on the Croft field was going to be revealed by a bunch of crazy animals. He couldn't believe his luck. Events, though, had taken a very peculiar turn lately, finding himself trapped with the woodsman in this strange and different age – some kind of witchcraft or sorcery could be at work, or was it an illusion perhaps, conjured somehow by the wily old man to put him off the scent – assuming the doddery old fool knew of his presence. The country bumpkin would have to work harder than that to deter a master from his work, a man of supreme talent, a high-ranking officer answering directly, no less, to the campaign leader.

Despite this unpleasant diversion, like a true soldier, he had stuck faithfully to his mission. Exceedingly proud of his unswerving commitment to General Cromwell and his unquestionable prowess in remaining undetected as an intelligence officer for the Parliamentarian army, Samuel Strong, or Samson, to his fellow puritans in Cromwell's army, was strong by name and by nature. One of Cromwell's elite men, he was used to coping in extreme circumstances although, he had to admit, time travel was a new challenge. Glowing with self-congratulatory pride, Samson turned his attention back to business, instinct told him another meeting would take place that evening and he would certainly be there. The prize was his for the taking, and glory would follow. Time now to build up his strength; what he needed most was a hearty breakfast. Scanning the chicken house with cruel searching eyes he set about haphazardly rooting around for eggs causing great commotion amongst the hens which squawked indignantly as he tipped them roughly off their nesting boxes.

Tal awoke to a cacophony in the hen house. Another fox at large he assumed, or territory wars – he didn't understand the pecking order. Not paying particular attention to the disturbance which happened quite regularly, he stepped out of his bed performing a graceful forward bow stretching out his long back legs with all his might, tensing the impressive leg muscles until they hardened like iron. Then, pointing his aristocratic nose at the ceiling, he stretched the length of his graceful neck right to the tips of his ears which stood obediently to attention as the stretch reached its full extent. Heaving a big sigh Tal relaxed, morning workout over. He looked eagerly out at the new day through the tiny cottage window; the sill at perfect Lurcher height allowed an unrivalled view from a sitting or standing position. An uninterrupted romp around Fox's Folly Wood, somewhere he'd not explored for weeks, was on today's agenda – he relished the prospect of some serious scouting, possibly a good chase, but most of all, putting some distance between himself and those batty cats!

Tal noticed to his relief on the way out his fellow adventurers sound asleep in perfect symmetry, forming a 'yin' and 'yang' tangled ball of fur in the centre of their bed. He paused fleetingly to admire the artistic shapes they created and marvelled at how peacefully sublime this moment was in contrast to the absurdity of the last two nights. He was almost convinced that by the time he returned from today's expedition, complete normality would have been restored. With that happy thought in his heart he moved swiftly through the back door and escaped to waiting green solitude, paths long untrodden and perhaps a surprise.

The sun was still low in the sky, but already the promise

of a golden summer's day bathed in heat hung in the air. The dew-soaked earth struck cool and fresh through his pads as he loped contentedly along. All around him the fields lay bare, roughly cropped to stubbly, geometric lines, where once a waving sea of barley danced and shimmered on the south-westerly breeze. To his painful cost he had once discovered the savage, razor-sharpness of the stubble, mistaking the beckoning open expanse for a racetrack – a lesson well learned, his paws throbbed at the memory as he jogged down the meandering path towards a line of trees marking the outskirts of his destination.

Fox's Folly Wood had earned itself a certain mystique. A local legend decreed that to enter the old wood it was necessary to gain permission from the fearsome 'rhino' which protected the woodland creatures and tree spirits that lived there, if you believed in fairies that is. Much to Tal's surprise the 'rhino' had gained quite a reputation in village folklore and the legend along with it – so much so that local children had made up a rhyme which had become the password for safe passage:

Can it be true? But did I see
A rhino staring back at me?
Deep in the woods a menacing eye,
I'm sure I saw a rhino as I passed by.

The 'rhino' was nothing more than a fat, old, hollow tree trunk stripped of its branches, apart from one short, curving, pointed bough resembling a horn. The trunk had been blown inconveniently across the path many years ago in a violent storm and blocked the only way into the wood.

Just below the 'horn' a hole in the bark formed a sinister watchful 'eye' which had an uncanny knack of following you around. The barrelled shape of the dead trunk lying in wait amongst a green sea of choking briars was most definitely, to anyone with an ounce of imagination, a sleeping rhinoceros ready to charge at unsuspecting passers-by. Behind the 'rhino', the woods were so dense it was impossible to see more than a few feet inside beyond the 'sleeping' grey bulk. This only added to the impression of guardianship – there was no alternative, exploring the woods meant getting past the evil eye. Although he had been this way countless times before, Tal always gave the unsettling trunk a wide berth, even though his Lurcher instinct and very reliable nose told him this creepy 'custodian' was just another part of the forest. He also knew the deepest darkest depths of the wood held hidden secrets – nature protected itself, only revealing its mysteries to those who respected its ways. The deep, green corridors in front of him disappeared into impenetrable blackness, wending who knows where. Strange, his fur was prickling with, he wasn't quite sure … anticipation, that was it, *anticipation* … not fear surely, even he was starting to believe the silly rumours. He stopped and shook himself violently from top to toe, ears clapping like castanets against the side of his head. It did the trick. The dark thoughts disappeared. Lifting his head he drew the heady, earthy scents around him deep into his lungs, nimbly side-stepped the old tree and strode purposefully out of the light into the cool waiting depths.

He padded along, eyes adjusting to the gloom. Alone in the towering, green cathedral, gnarled and twisted spires of mighty wild service trees – grizzled ash, tangled alder and haunting yews – closed in on him until he felt like a tiny toy dog. Humbled by the scale of these giants, Tal sensed a change in the air, an aura, a *presence*. He had entered a hidden kingdom with different rules. No one could ever tame nature; the trees were most definitely in charge. Taking care to be on his best behaviour, it took a few minutes before he could relax and feel the drifts of wild garlic that brushed around his feet releasing their pungent aroma. Way above his head a solitary buzzard soared in lazy circles, climbing on thermals ever higher towards the sun, its distinctive mewing call echoing in the azure expanse of sky glimpsed briefly through the lofty canopy. Tal sighed, a more perfect experience he could not imagine.

Feeling more comfortable every step in the company of woodland friends, he wandered blithely along in a state of pure bliss, allowing his mind to empty completely. So immersed in the moment, almost in a trance, Tal failed to notice a persistent rustling noise approaching in the distance. It was his nose that alerted him to a new scent coming towards him on the breeze. He headed quickly for a nearby fallen trunk anticipating a chase and crouched down to wait for the creature to reveal itself. In the deafening silence he could hear his heart pounding excitedly. The rustling continued but seemed to be remaining in the distance making it difficult to identify the culprit. A sunbeam streaming through a gap in the branches arrived conveniently in time to illuminate the bustling shape from which came a bright golden glow. Tal stiffened, alert, then his heart sank as he realised with dismay that the golden coat belonged to none other than Bruce – right then his perfect bubble went *pop!*

Where possible, Tal always gave Bruce a wide berth – Bruce could best be described as a *'street dog'*, far too cocky, and with ideas way above his size. Bruce had done everything, been everywhere and enjoyed throwing his weight around. Bruce sent everyone running for cover, quite a feat for something that resembled a short wire brush.

There was evidently something very interesting that Bruce was investigating in the bushes, his next claim to fame no doubt. Tal weighed up the situation and decided all he could do was to try and leave the wood in the opposite direction so as not to alert Bruce to his presence. He stood up gingerly turning quietly away.

"Well, it's the lone Lurcher out lookin' for a chase no doubt ..." the chirpy voice made him jump out of his skin. "Long way from t'village today?" continued Bruce getting into his conversational stride. "Thowt it was just me that had t'wanderlust ... heh? I know these woods like the back of me paw, lad – I can give ye a tour if ye likes ..." A brief pause for breath then he rattled incessantly on ... "I've bin comin' darn 'ere donkey's years, that stupid rhino nonsense bin quite useful in keepin' t'rabble away, I've 'ad the run o' t'place ... any roads ..." Tal knew it was pointless trying to interrupt and sat down resignedly, his beautiful dream and quest for peace shattered. "Ah thowt ah'd seen everythin', well ah've seen more 'an most folk as ye know, but there's allus more te see it seems. Tek that there bloke mekkin' horseshoes, swords an' all, that were summat ah'd never seen afore ..."

Tal had shut off, allowing his mind to explore the mental daydream of what he had hoped to do. Swords? Had he heard right? Bruce was prone to wild exaggeration –

must be a Bruce-ism.

"An' that chap cuttin' them massive poles wit spikes. Would ne want te be on t'end o' one o' them! Best thing is layin' next t'woodfire, allus blazin' it is, mind it 'as to get hot fer t'cookin' pot ... did I tell ye ..."

Tal was suddenly paying attention. Wood smoke, swords ... was this another tall tale? He needed to interrupt, find out more, but Bruce was in full flow. Drawing himself up to full height, Tal let out a long, baying howl that rang around them reverberating off the trees. Bruce stopped dead in his tracks. "No need te be so rude, lad ..."

"Did you mention swords and a wood fire?" questioned Tal feeling very assertive all at once, for some reason adrenaline was working through his veins.

"Aye, I gets to sit in't blacksmith's shed an' watch 'im work, tha can see too if tha likes?" *For once Bruce has gone too far,* thought Tal. *This is my chance to call his bluff and show him up as the bragging show-off that he really is.*

"Well, how could I refuse, Bruce, sounds fascinating, please lead on."

Assuming the air of an overbearing tour guide, Bruce raced off in the direction of the stream which fringed the wood and bordered the long, lakeside meadow. Tal trotted behind, picturing the moment when he would at long last get his own back on the bragger Bruce; he had gone way overboard this time.

The hot weather had taken its toll. The stream was no more than a gentle trickle in a parched, crusty bed. They crossed over easily stepping into a small, dark, cool dell crowded with rotted overhanging branches curtained by choking ivy. There was something different again

45

about the air here, a subtle change in the atmosphere, like walking through a shimmering heat haze. Ahead, Bruce blurred momentarily, his outline hazy, indistinct, and then he disappeared. Tal stopped dead. How could that be? He was there large as life one second, gone the next. There was no alternative but to follow and hope he could find him. Pushing through the ivy and stepping out from the dell on to the meadow beyond, Tal blinked in disbelief. He had walked on to a film set – *The Legend of Robin Hood* by the looks of it.

All around was a hive of activity – people in period costume. Women in long, heavy dresses with lace bodices, frilled blouses and bonnets, pulled children along in small, wooden carts with roughly hewn wheels. Men in wide breeches, their worn leather waistcoats tucked under heavy belts, hacked at giant logs with rough axes, sleeves rolled up exposing strong weathered arms, heads protected from the sun by floppy, felt hats. A small bustling community, a small village in fact, was alive in front of his eyes. Makeshift tents formed a semicircle round a large wood fire over which hung a substantial iron pot. Behind the tents stood a ramshackle shelter in front of which was a large black anvil, and Bruce.

"There ye are, lad. What took yer so long? Tha looks like tha's seen a ghost!" Tal sat down beside him completely bewildered. Bruce seemed totally unruffled by the whole experience, positively at home.

"Where are the cameramen?" asked Tal.

"What ye on about, lad, lost yer marbles?" said Bruce indignantly.

"We've arrived on a film set but there's no crew, no one filming ..." mumbled Tal.

"I allus thowt Lurchers had more brains, it appears not … This is *Langhald*, the local village."

Tal's appearance seemed to be causing some interest among the villagers as a hum of conversation started to buzz on the air and fingers pointed in his direction. Then a cry went up.

"Elias, shift your lazy bones, come see what has arrived in the village – your lucky day, sire!" one of the village men shouted in the direction of a particularly scruffy tent on the end of the row.

The canvas flap was abruptly drawn back from inside by a dirty hand the size of a small garden shovel. The largest man Tal had ever seen stooped low to exit the tent, grunting as he unfolded his immense frame to its full height. *It's a human tree*, thought Tal, as he craned his neck to get a closer look. The man was indeed the size of a small oak, long, gangly limbs spread outwards from his trunk like branches as he stretched in the sunlight, blinking in the glare. One of the shovel hands gripped a gnarled thumb-stick made of twisted hazel contorted into grotesque whorls which almost appeared to be an extension of the man's arm. He looked like he was wearing scraps of sacking held together with hefty leather buckles. Across his enormous chest was slung a leather satchel, from the top of which peeped scraps of animal hide and the handle of what Tal guessed to be a fearsomely large hunting knife fashioned from deer horn. He was extremely unkempt, hair matted and greasy, skin weathered almost like bark. A large black felt hat adorned with an extravagant plume of pheasant feathers sat close on his head, the brim low obscuring his eyes. Not best pleased to be disturbed from his bed the man barked at the small assembling crowd of inquisitive villagers.

"What in heaven's name is so confoundedly urgent that I need to be so rudely aroused from my slumbers?"

"A fine specimen of hound, sire," came the reply. Tal realised uneasily that suddenly all eyes were on him – "Delivered to your door without you having to lift a finger."

The 'tree man' turned slowly like a graceful waving ash; it was almost possible to imagine his bones creaking like branches flexing in the wind. Lifting his head the man fixed Tal from under the dipped brim with a critical professional eye, appraising him in one sweeping, piercing glance from the tip of his ears all the way to white hind paws.

"*Hmmmm* ... not bad," murmured the man, his voice a low rumble as from the roots of the earth. "Not bad at all – a fine working dog 'tis true," muttered the man in more mellow tones. "Indeed a good find – I can put him to work right away." A perceptible collective sigh ran through the small group as everyone relaxed, breathed once again. If Elias Murro was content, all was well with the world.

During this exchange Tal had been rooted to the spot with fear, not daring to move, be more visible – he was in enough trouble already it seemed. Frozen with fright, his brain stubbornly refused to think of an escape strategy. The man turned and lumbered in his direction, feathers in his hat stirring in the summer breeze, stick beating the ground. Tal's head swam. Everything seemed to blur and shimmer as the man in sharp focus drew closer, almost in slow motion. Horrified, Tal thought he was about to black out. Fuelled by adrenaline, all the blood in his body rushed to his muscles – his whole being preparing for flight. The man was one step away, long, bony fingers reaching for the scruff of Tal's neck, the sour, rancid smell of decayed flesh and gusts of stale breath assaulted his nostrils, turned his stomach. Somewhere deep inside Tal heard a voice screaming ... *"Run! What are you doing? Get out of here!!"*

Just as Elias's blackened fingers reached out, something wonderful happened. Feeling put out by not being the centre of attention, Bruce had decided it was time to show off and began to race around the encampment, slaloming crazily in and out of the tents in dizzying circles, to demonstrate his speed and agility. For Tal it was as if someone had fired a starting pistol, shaking him awake – his limbs unlocked and became supercharged. Without stopping to think of the consequences he rocketed towards the edge of the clearing, praying he was heading in the general direction in which he'd arrived into this surreal 'neverland'. Fleetingly it struck him that he had absolutely no idea whether he could return to the wood where he had started out, and whether it actually existed at all. Perhaps this was a parallel universe. Random mixed-up thoughts flashed through his mind as fast as his feet were transporting him away from the villagers shouting and waving their hats in the air, in anger or jubilation he didn't really care.

Pelting along the meadow at breakneck speed Tal burst into the dark dell, cleared the dry stream bed in one massive stride and hurtled out of control into the cool welcoming familiarity of Fox's Folly Wood. He slowed his pace fractionally but didn't stop to draw breath until he reached the relative safety of the 'rhino'. Chest heaving violently, he flopped behind the old dead trunk and tried to make sense of what had just happened. He had never before been so grateful for Bruce's vanity and resolved to be more accommodating if he ever saw him again. *If he saw him again!* Tal couldn't imagine what might happen next time! – probably better to give Bruce an even wider berth and not visit this wood for a while. He looked over his shoulder towards the stream; all was still, quite serene. The peacefulness could not erase the terrifying memory of Elias Murro which would haunt him for a long time to come. For some irrational reason, Tal had the distinct feeling that their paths would cross again. Stepping from behind the comforting shelter of the dead tree he turned for home, and didn't stop running until he reached the cottage doorstep.

6

Counting Chickens

Pie was very pleased with herself. It had been a most productive day she thought smugly, stretching luxuriantly on the warm lead flashing of the conservatory roof, her favourite sunbathing spot. Only she had the nerve and sure-footedness to make the precarious climb across the ridge tiles, teetering along the gutter on the way and clambering masterfully up the slippery slope to the place where she could nestle undisturbed for hours – pure heaven.

It was quite amazing what could be discovered from eavesdropping on sunny window ledges she mused, rolling over to warm the other side of her tummy. Weaving in and out of the legs of useful people and being persuasively kittenish was also a good ploy for listening in on interesting conversations, absorbing and methodically filing all relevant information in her strategic brain. Pie had honed these theatrical skills to an art form. Combined with the things she learned from watching the television, carefully positioned a foot away from the screen following images from right to left then left to right, she was, in her opinion, pretty much unbeatable as a spy.

Basking in a warm, self-congratulatory glow she turned her mind to the coming evening – how surprised everyone would be when the information she had gathered was revealed. She would save the best, most sensational bits till last for greatest dramatic effect; particularly the acquisition of a local map which would be a revelation – it would be a moment to savour. She had to admit there were some quite astonishing titbits of information that had made her fur tingle and whiskers twitch. Perched on the windowsill of the village hall, nose pressed against the cool glass, she had learned a lot from the local history group meeting about village folklore. Legends which, on the face of it, seemed quite far-fetched, but having encountered Amos and heard about his life, she could see how everything might just begin to fit together. The legends had almost certainly grains of truth at their heart but mystique had grown over time until they had become embedded in the soul of the place.

Pie's eyelids drooped heavily as the sun baked the glass roof. Cocooned in the heat she had reached baking temperature and was helpless to waves of slumber drifting over her body. Sighing contentedly, she dropped into deep sleep and a vivid dream in which she was the first feline intelligence officer at MI5 with an important undercover mission to track down a missing shipment of succulent, wild salmon hijacked en route from Scotland. Only she could save the day.

Bungy had been doing his own research down at the hen house. Some kerfuffle had caused bedlam amongst the chickens this morning the like of which he had not heard since a fox had been on the rampage last year. The farmer had shown the sly intruder both barrels of his shotgun and peace had reigned once more. Today's cacophony had rallied his old hunting instincts so seeking a change of scenery, and possibly a bit of brunch, he had wandered down to the farmyard. He needed a diversion, felt like he needed to get back on track, back into the groove of everyday life after a very odd few days. He had given the chicken run a wide berth for a few weeks after a narrow escape on his last visit from the slobbering jaws of Basil the St Bernard. Basil was the size of a small donkey and had a bad drool problem. Despite his size, Basil always managed to hide somewhere out of sight then launch himself at the last moment on unsuspecting intruders, teeth bared, slimy tendrils of dribble flying sideways from his flapping jowls, as he pounded across the yard like a miniature steam train. It was risky but Bungy felt confident his timing would be spot on. Just after noon on a baking hot summer afternoon, Basil was almost certainly going to be fast asleep in the cool shade of his stable which doubled as his outdoor residence and surveillance post.

Sure enough, as Bungy rounded the corner approaching the farm, deep resonating snores rumbled and reverberated around the walled yard. Two giant paws the size of dinner plates flopped lazily out of the stable door. Peering cautiously into the gloom, Bungy could just make out the giant horizontal bulk of a sleeping St Bernard doing a good impression of a beached whale. He tiptoed past the door feeling quietly triumphant and unusually brave. Maybe recent events had given him more courage; he was after all *'the chosen one'*. The door to the hen run was open – most out of the ordinary. *How peculiar*, he thought, perhaps being 'chosen' provided special dispensations, like open access to chickens … something told him he was not that lucky. Stepping lightly on to the straw carpeting the floor, a familiar dry aroma filled his nostrils. Dust motes stirred and danced in the beams of sunlight straying through the slatted wooden frame as his paws disturbed the scratched parched earth. He stopped abruptly. Instinct was telling him something wasn't right. A strange smell – quite out of place in the hen house – drifted towards him. Crouching into a stalking crawl, low to the ground, belly scraping the dust, he advanced slowly towards a darkened corner of the run following his nose, whiskers quivering with anticipation – the last few steps taken in slow motion, a freeze-frame sequence of tiny movements. Stealthily, silently, hardly breathing, he became invisible, disappearing into the gloom.

An ear-splitting squawk broke the silence tearing into his head like a knife, the surprise sending him catapulting backwards. A terrified bantam crouching nervously in the dark bolted to freedom bowling him over, upside down, legs akimbo, into a stinking fresh pile of droppings – most undignified. Still reeling from the shock he picked himself up, trying to look composed, nonchalant. The alien smell was stronger here competing with the pong of the chicken muck. Looking around he realised a large pair of heavy leather boots had broken his fall. The boots, evidently leant carefully in the corner for safe keeping, were now splayed in front of him at abstract angles on the floor after the collision. A closer inspection of the boots' interior revealed the source of the penetrating smell. Someone had been wearing the boots for a prolonged length of time in the summer heat and the result was overpowering. Bungy took several large steps backwards to clear his head. What on earth was a pair of important-looking boots doing in a village hen house? Something to report at the meeting tonight – the others would be equally surprised. Completely side-tracked and quite put out by his discovery, Bungy felt the only sensible thing to do was to go and have a lie down to recover his senses before the rendezvous with Amos and, more pressingly, to vacate the chicken run before the owner of the boots came looking for them. Amos especially would be interested to hear this news, which, he was sure, would definitely eclipse anything the others might have found out – a feather in his cap you might say. Being the chosen one had its advantages; fate was on his side. Feeling slightly dazed and overcome by the cloying scent of droppings and reeking hot leather clinging to his fur, he slipped out of the hen house. Now, a spot of grooming and a good wash was required, followed by a siesta – that should do the trick.

As he peeked gingerly out towards the yard assessing his chances of successfully bypassing Basil the slobbering mountain, Bungy was unaware of the piercing dark eyes following his every move. Samson Strong had also taken advantage of the afternoon lull to stretch his legs and escape from the smelly compound. His feet particularly were enjoying their freedom from his over-the-knee cavalry boots – the chemistry between the leather and his skin had produced a potent stench almost as bad as those infernal feathered beasts sharing his lodgings. His hot toes relished the deliciously cool water in the watering trough – he had lingered there for a dangerous length of time enjoying the balmy summer afternoon. A petrified chicken's shriek shook him back from nostalgic reverie in time to catch sight of the round grey and white splodged creature leaving the hen house. Samson knew he should exercise more care. If the stupid cat could see the old woodsman, he could most certainly see the Parliamentarian officer. Being discovered at this point in the operation would be disastrous to his mission. He must remain unseen to stand any chance of learning the whereabouts of the hidden treasure which was so important to their cause, and would probably mean the difference between victory or defeat for the puritan army. Fortunately he had hidden his helmet, sword and carbine behind a large straw bale at the opposite end of the run, but his boots ... it seemed his overheating feet could have given him away. Bungy's portly frame waddled out of sight. Maybe the bumbling feline would put no store by his discovery; on the other hand ... Samson knew he would have to wait until the evening gathering to learn the outcome. Angry at his carelessness, he threw himself upon the straw bales and bad-temperedly whittled away at a piece of yew, his knife flashing in the dappled sunlight reflecting in his dark, glittering eyes.

Tal arrived at the cottage door breathless but relieved. Sprinting along the lanes in the sweltering heat, he desperately tried to regain his composure. He had also decided not to recount anything of his bizarre experience in the wood with Bruce, as he didn't want to draw any further attention to himself; he wanted to blend in and most of all have a quiet life. He knew without any shadow of a doubt that if Pie had a smidgen of an idea there was anything unusual in the vicinity, she would expect a full investigation, and he would be smartly despatched back to the scene from which he had fled. This was unthinkable. Tal had seen how poor, unsuspecting Bungy had fallen blindly into tricky situations contrived from Pie's ideas. In fact, this whole *time travelling woodsman*' scenario had materialised in their back garden just because Pie had given Bungy an idea. Feeling completely vindicated in his decision, Tal headed towards his favourite corner by the Aga and flopped on the rug, physically and mentally exhausted – he could fit in a few blissful hours of sleep before he was expected under the apple tree to listen to Pie's pronouncements. He was sure his story was safe; it would never see the light of day.

The meeting time arrived and the three adventurers assembled at the base of the old apple tree. It was a balmy night but the wind was high. Expectancy and anticipation swirled in the air around the waiting group like the clouds scudding past the face of the moon. Gusts of warm air riffled inquisitively through their fur and tugged at their ears. Over their heads the ancient branches, laden with large juicy apples just reaching their prime, creaked and groaned under the weight of their burden.

"If one of these apples scores a direct hit on my head, I won't be able to remember anything that happened to me in the last month!" grumbled Bungy, "never mind reporting on the last few hours." He looked anxiously up to the lattice canopy feeling very small and vulnerable.

"If you weren't so well endowed, you might not be such a sitting target," retorted Pie, as ever, unsympathetic to her brother's predicament.

"It's more a question of scale and probability," Bungy argued. "There's far more apples than us, and the longer we wait under this tree like sitting ducks the more likelihood of one of us," (*probably me*, he thought) "... being marmalised!"

He thought he had been quite witty at this point, then realised marmalade was made from oranges not apples. Pie was just going to point out this fact when a movement in the garden brought an instant hush. Tal felt his fur start to bristle from the base of his tail up towards his ears; looking at the others he saw that they too had taken on the 'bottle brush' look, senses on high alert.

With a *swoosh* of his long heavy cloak as it brushed over the ground Amos arrived out of the darkness.

"My friends, I bid you good evening. I am a little delayed as I have been making preparations so we can talk more in comfort." He gestured towards the dovecote barely visible against the night sky. "Let us escape this probing wind and enjoy some shelter. Come. Join with me as I would meet with fellow villagers in my time, around the glow of embers, to share tales and feast." Bungy liked this idea a lot, particularly the bit about feasting, and shot away to the field before the others had time to blink. He hadn't stopped to think about the accompanying perfume of pigeon poo, so for the second time today his nose reeled at the acrid smell which greeted him as he stepped round the door into the octagonal dove house. The others followed at a more leisurely pace intrigued to finally see inside the ancient monument which had guarded their home for as long as they could remember. Once their noses and eyes had acclimatised to the smell and the gloom, they were pleasantly surprised at the cosy sight which greeted them. A fire crackled cheerily set in a ring of small stones on the earth floor, the sweet tang of warm pine filtered gently into their nostrils. Suspended over the fire supported by an ingenious tripod of sturdy twigs was a small bowl in which a thick broth bubbled gently.

"I have put my last grains to good use and made a pottage to share with my new friends," smiled Amos proudly. Bungy peered over the rim of the bowl and eyed the grey and cream lumpy liquid suspiciously. He was not known for refusing food but it usually came from a reliable outlet such as the pantry or pre-packed from the bird table. Well, he would give it a go; it did smell rather good, he would just have to shut his eyes ...

Samson Strong peered through the thicket where he had been waiting now for what seemed like a very long time. He was convinced he had overheard an arrangement to meet again under the apple tree the following evening. The gusty wind was driving him to distraction, blowing the long, spiny holly branches against his face, despite pulling his heavy round helmet down as far as he could, the branches nipped against his nose and cheeks. Damn those infuriating creatures! – so unpredictable and irritating in equal measure. Just when they are supposed to do one thing, they do the opposite and don't turn up. There was no sign of the woodsman either. It occurred to him that he had misheard the conversation. What was happening? His super-efficient, meticulous approach to spying was deserting him – it was not a good omen; 'time travelling' was playing havoc with his rationality. How could anyone be expected to keep to their senses when dark forces were at work? He consoled himself that even General Cromwell, he was sure, would find it a challenge. He had never yet been beaten by any assignment, and this one would not be the exception. In fact, he was certain that if he were victorious and located the treasure, especially in such extraordinary circumstances, he would be a national hero, the officer famed for successfully steering the course of the Civil War to a Parliamentarian conquest. A vision appeared in his mind of Cromwell presenting him with the highest honour, inviting him to become second in command, in front of row upon row of foot soldiers and cavalry men, standards fluttering, trumpets blaring a fanfare, as he processed through the columns of men to kneel at the General's feet. A flash of adrenaline surged through his veins, fuelling an even greater desire to succeed – he felt superhuman; nothing would stand in his way. His senses keened, eyes and ears highly tuned and refocussed, he carefully parted the branches once more. Apples swinging wildly in the strong summer wind, boughs sighing and groaning, the great tree was a solitary presence – no other living beings in sight. Samson Strong would not be deterred. His resolve hardened. He would track and hunt down the King's servant starting at first light. For the cause … and for glory …

At that precise moment, one of the fattest apples parted company from its branch in a mighty gust of wind. Tossed high in the air, it rotated as it spun like the moon, catapulting in orbit around the earth. Samson looked up in time to see the heavy fruit fly into space almost in slow motion. Before he had time to think, gravity took over and the apple plummeted towards the ground hitting him smartly on the head – a blow that sent him momentarily dizzy. He swayed in the bushes then collapsed, falling forwards flat on his face poleaxed and in full view of anyone and anything. The elements and nature were trying to tell him something … don't count those dratted chickens just yet.

7

Living History

A companionable silence descended on the small group gathered around the warm glow of the fire. Outside the stout red-brick walls, the wind whistled wildly around their cosy refuge buffeting the old building. The pottage had taken effect and eyelids were drooping. Amos looked around at his new friends sprawled in an array of relaxed shapes near his feet, apparently oblivious to anything and everything. He wished he could be like them and abandon his whole being to the moment, completely immune to light, sound, to time ...

He cleared his throat theatrically, *"Ahem!"* No response. He tried again with more gusto, *"Ahemmm!!"* Pie, instantly alert, sat to attention. Realising she had nodded off when she should have been leading the meeting, she feigned nonchalance, pretending to meticulously clean her paws. When she was satisfied that the charade had given the right impression, she poked Bungy in the tummy and gave Tal a cursory pinch on the nose.

"Mr Amos, your pottage has powerful properties which are evidently hard to resist!" she began, stifling a yawn. She shook her silky fur from the tips of her ears to the tip of her tail, trying to wake up. "Er ... perhaps we should have stomach." She glanced across at Bungy who had resorted to propping himself up awkwardly against the wall, just to stay vertical. Putting on her most superior air, she positioned herself in the centre of the group commanding attention. Tal raised his eyes to the ceiling, *for goodness' sake … always craving the limelight,* he thought to himself. Stretching his sleepy limbs, a burp escaped noisily just as Pie started to speak. She gave him a withering look. It was going to be a long night.

Surprisingly, Tal's boredom, however, vanished as Pie got into her stride. Proudly describing her detective methods and the wealth of information she had unearthed, the others listened attentively, becoming more engrossed as details emerged. There was a lot to take in and a lot more to the village history than they had ever thought possible. Some interesting characters had once roamed the landscape bearing fascinating, flamboyant names; Crustacia, Agnes Randywfe and, Bungy's favourite, Galfridus Langhald. *Langhald* … that sounded familiar, thought Amos fleetingly … but even the time travelling woodsman was not around in the year 1379. Pie continued, warming to her audience. An endless stream of jumbled facts and folklore tumbled out in no particular order, leapfrogging haphazardly around from century to century, superstition to myth. There was reputed to be an infamous ghost, the 'Green Lady'; strange mushroom rings had been found on the lawn of a bungalow (what the dickens was a bungalow? thought Amos); an overzealous verger had nearly burnt down the beautiful little church; and the village had once been home to the oldest serving postmistress in the country, at the grand age of ninety-four. The surrounding fertile acres of arable land were apparently littered with pottery, broken glass and coins – there was, Pie paused for added effect, talk of treasure being found on the Croft field. Some curious 'metal detecting' villagers had found some interesting objects there; belt and cloak buckles, musket balls and a miniature gun – a *Petronel* to be precise.

It was as if Pie had swallowed a history book. Amos was finding it hard to stay focussed. Whilst most entertaining and mildly informative, he couldn't see how any of this local knowledge was going to help him in his plight. Soon the words started to lose their form; they drifted towards him like shapeless scraps of paper blown by the wind down a very long dark tunnel, a tunnel through time into which Amos allowed himself to be slowly and quietly drawn.

The word *'musket'* pierced Amos' straying consciousness like a searing arrowhead. In his dreamlike state, he had missed a highly relevant fact. Why would there be musket balls here? Pie had moved on.

"A famous horse race was alleged to have first taken place in 1776 on three large, oval fields near the wood and ..." She sounded like a guide from a stately home. He desperately needed to hear more about the *'treasure'*. As he tried to interject and halt the torrent of information, Pie paused for breath and to build some dramatic suspense. He sensed she was working up to her finale. "I have also discovered that our pretty, little village played a strategic role in the English Civil War!"

Amos expected her to take a bow. She looked triumphantly around the group waiting for a reaction, a gasp of surprise, any small indication of the importance of this exciting discovery and recognition of her prowess as an investigator.

Bungy and Tal, initially intrigued, were by now unimpressed and had reached saturation point, memory banks full, attention span zero. Looking shiftily sideways at each other, they shared the same unspoken thought which passed silently between them … *Is it time for bed yet?* Knowing there would be repercussions afterwards if they didn't respond, they adopted suitably impressed expressions to keep the peace. Amos, on the other hand, looked like a man receiving an electric shock. Sitting bolt upright, eyes riveted on Pie, earlier frustration now galvanised into complete and utter concentration he let out a cry,

"The English Civil War!" he exclaimed. "My fellow countrymen are this very day fighting for the Royalist cause, supporting King Charles the First after he raised his royal standard on the 22nd August 1642 and declared war on Parliament." The others stared in astonishment at this outburst.

"A most bloody revolution causing turmoil in rural England, dividing family against family and family members against each other, is raging as we speak. Now I discover I am trapped in time somewhere of consequence in this campaign which may have significantly influenced events!"

For a moment they all sat in stunned silence, processing this startling information, trying to work out what it meant. Did this mean Amos' presence here might affect the course of history? A ridiculous idea which flitted nonetheless through everyone's minds, but was not said out loud. Was this why a stranger from another time had arrived in *their* village – at the very time of the outbreak of this bitter conflict, but over three hundred and fifty years too late?

"Tell me more about your village and its place in history."

Amos fixed his gaze on Pie who was now starting to wish she hadn't built up her part quite so much. Remaining cool, assuming her most intelligent pose, she took a deep breath and ploughed on relaying as much as she could remember from eavesdropping on the village hall windowsill.

"Well, it seems that the local manor house and country estate was purchased by a wealthy landowner in 1640 who joined the Parliamentarian cavalry at the outbreak of the Civil War. Randolph Knight became an officer in the Cromwellian army, distinguishing himself at the Battle of Horncastle and siege of Bolingbroke Castle." Amos stared dumbfounded.

"Apparently, he quickly became Oliver Cromwell's trusted confidant and right- hand man. Cromwell reputedly came here to stay with Knight at the village manor house, although no records of the meeting have ever been found, and no one has ever discovered why Cromwell would want to travel to such an out-of-the-way place, just as the war was gaining momentum – to this day it remains a mystery. The house fell into ruin, but the cellars are still thought to exist, marked by a solitary evergreen oak tree at the centre of a vast field. A grand residence in its time, the house stood in an elevated position overlooking sweeping grounds and an ornamental lake developed by the famous landscape designer Capability Brown. The stables are the only visible remnant of this historic estate and have now been transformed into posh homes. Their elaborate architecture and size indicates that the original manor house must have been a most impressive building. The grounds and lake are now a country park but were known in 1640 as Langhald Hall – 'Langhald' meaning

'Long Wood'; it's shown here on this local map."

Amos turned a ghostly shade of grey. "By my whiskers, can it be true! This 'country park', as you call it, is the place I call home. I am living next door to my enemy and I had no idea – I must warn the King! If what you say is truth not fable, perhaps there is reason rather than alchemy behind my journey through time after all."

"How can you be so sure this is your village?" the others asked in unison.

"I am named after my settlement, 'Longwood', what other proof is needed?"

The wind had dropped. Outside the dovecote, the night sky resembled deep blue velvet sprinkled with stars like sparkling diamonds. A lone owl kept a silent vigil. In the undergrowth something moved. The owl, ever watchful, trained a keen eye towards the disturbance. Cursing at the scratching holly spines, a bedraggled figure crawled backwards on hands and knees from the bushes on to the lawn, the soles of large leather boots sliding on the slippery wet grass as they fought to find grip. Sitting slumped in a heap rubbing his temple, Samson realised he was fully exposed in the moon's white glare. The angry summer storm clouds blown into the distance, just like his cover he thought tetchily. Not at all professional but there was no one about, so he had probably got away with it this time. Getting unsteadily to his feet, he swayed slightly as he rose to full height. Outmanoeuvred by those wily creatures and felled by a flying apple, not an impressive evening's work. He dusted the dirt off his breeches and turned for the farm – an evening with the chickens would be his penance.

Weaving towards the path, something caught his eye.

A glimmer of red was visible through the uneven cracks of the heavy dovecote door. He crept silently across the uneven sea of stubble surrounding the ancient building, trying to control his shaky legs in the over-domineering boots. Reaching the door he regained his composure and pressed his cheek against the rough wood, peering through the biggest crack. So this was the meeting point – and a very cosy one too, it would appear. He strained hard to listen but the thick timbers gave nothing away. An earnest discussion was in full flow led by the sleek intelligent creature who was obviously the brains of the motley crew. He leaned harder on the old door, willing the sound waves to transmit through the dense fibres; he could just make out scraps of conversation … he was sure he had heard his General's name. The ancient hinges gave an almost imperceptible creak, protesting at the pressure they bore. Like a flash, Pie wheeled round to face the door, homing in on the sound, eyes narrowed in concentration. Samson held his breath and cursed silently, trying valiantly to stay completely motionless. His heart hammered in his chest so loudly he was convinced it would give him away. Then it happened. For a fleeting moment, he and the creature made eye contact, an electric current running between them, Pie's analytical gaze appraising him through the tiny spy hole weighing up the situation, making a decision what to do next. He didn't hang around to find out. Turning from the door he fled in the direction of the farm as fast as his legs would take him, tripping and stumbling over the harvested field, eventually being swallowed by the inky blackness.

Inside the dovecote, with no explanation and for no

apparent reason, Pie dropped the map like a hot potato and darted towards the door. The others looked on bewildered. Spurred by some invisible force, she flew at the crack in the heavy wood, clinging on with her claws whilst she scanned the now empty field before her. Someone had been spying on them. Someone with a dark menacing stare, like nothing or no one she had seen before. Evil, piercing eyes had bored into hers like a laser as if burning a passage through time. What a ridiculous thought! – tingling fur and a sense of foreboding told her otherwise. She turned back to the startled group. "There was someone spying on our meeting through the door."

"Who in their right minds would come out in the middle of the night, stand in a prickly field and bother to nosy into a gathering in an old, ramshackle brick shack?" grumbled Bungy, frustrated at the unwelcome prolonging of the meeting which had already dragged on well past suppertime.

"Who indeed?" pondered Amos stroking his moustache thoughtfully. "Who would even think there might be a 'meeting' in such an unlikely venue?"

"Someone who is searching for something that we might lead them to ... someone who has been closely following our every move," deduced Pie. Bungy look round nervously at the dancing shadows in case the intruder was a phantom and had passed through the thick brick walls. Tal felt uneasy. He alone knew there were others like Amos at large in the nearby woods and decided this was information he would keep to himself for now; it would be his secret – anything for a quiet life.

"Well, whoever it was they must be wearing seven

league boots because they made a quick getaway," mused Pie. Bungy, only half listening, jumped to attention as a strong tang of leather stole up his nostrils, and a vision of a pair of hefty boots swam in front of his eyes.

8

Secrets and Lies

"How long does it take?!" Pie asked grumpily of no one in particular, as she jumped on to the kitchen windowsill for the umpteenth time to scan the path from the garden shed for signs of Bungy returning from his mission to find a suitable disguise for Amos. Despite the sinister spying eyes, they had all agreed that if they were to have a chance of helping Amos find his way home, a reconnaissance trip to survey the local woods and tracks for landmarks and clues was the only way forward – and run the risk of being followed. They would be obvious targets. Amos had not been seen in daylight since the day of the summer fayre and his 'unconventional' attire would most certainly attract attention so a disguise was essential – if bumbling Bungy ever appeared again. She had thought that sending Tal to assist would keep him focussed but they had been over half an hour already, what on earth were they doing in there?

The regimental ticking of the wall clock penetrated the comforting silence of the cosy kitchen, marking the relentless passage of time towards the agreed meeting hour. A welcome, soothing, sleep-inducing rhythm most of the time, but this morning every tick pushed Pie's frustration levels up a notch. At last! The shed door opened to reveal a most comical sight. A long, green gardening coat was snaking its way along the path like a Chinese dragon, propelled at the front by some means invisible to the eye concealed under layers of material dragging closely along the ground. The coat rose up exaggeratedly at the rear, like some off-beat pantomime horse where four skinny red legs, two paws at the back with a splash of white, could just be seen trotting underneath. The coat progressed haphazardly in a tipsy fashion towards the kitchen door like a drunk weaving his way home, ricocheting off the patio containers, tripping up the step and arriving in a heap at Pie's feet.

"Why don't you look where you're going?" blustered Tal.

"Why don't you go where you're looking!" countered Bungy, crawling out from under the collar, flopping his ample tummy on to the cool quarry tiles.

"Next time, you can go at the back and see how much you enjoy having a sensitive part of your anatomy pushed into unmentionable places!" barked Tal, reversing out abruptly, straight on to the Aga oven door fuelling his already overheated temper. Back and forth like verbal ping-pong, the angry exchanges escalated, threatening to overtake the whole morning and sabotage their plans to get out of the village. Desperate measures were needed. Jumping on to the window seat, Pie launched herself at the pantry door giving it a hefty swipe in mid-flight, before landing neatly in front of the squabbling duo. The door swung shut with a resounding bang, the latch connecting precisely into its keeper with a loud satisfying *clunk*, then … silence.

Only she had perfected the technique to unlatch the door, and the others knew it. The sound of the dropping

71

latch stopped the argument dead.

"All further meals are suspended until our research mission is concluded, so it's up to you – no action, no dinner. Simple."

An uneasy truce negotiated, the trio set off from the cottage towards the dovecote in an ungainly crocodile, supporting the heavy coat between them, the map stuffed into one of the pockets. They moved as quickly as possible over the rough stubble field hoping fervently that they were not too outlandish to attract attention and that the muddy splashes on the dark green coat would offer a degree of camouflage against the landscape. Arriving at the old wooden door, panting under the weight and stifling heat of the canvas, they were greeted by twinkling blue eyes peering around the jamb and an extravagant curly whisker, one half of Amos' majestic moustache, escaping around the opened crack in the woodwork.

"Aha! My friends, I see you have come up with an excellent disguise. Such ingenuity! You are to be congratulated." Bungy looked smugly at Tal who glared stonily back. Seeing another argument brewing Pie took control by extricating the map from the coat pocket to brief everyone on the route she had planned.

"To reach the Long Wood I suggest we head east out of the village down the lane, past the duck pond, and out towards Ivy Lodge Lane passing Swiss Cottage then on to the country park from there. To keep a low profile and avoid being spotted we can take a short cut through Fox's Folly Wood."

Alarm bells rang in Tal's head. He had not ventured in that direction since his strange, nightmarish experience in those woods a few days ago. "I'm sure I saw the farmer heading towards Fox's Folly this morning with the hedge flayer," blurted Tal. "Cutting the hedges is a very slow process and usually takes all day. If we go that way, we will surely be seen," he asserted, a slight note of desperation in his voice.

"Nonsense," retorted Bungy, still smarting from the morning's bickering and keen to score a point. "The tractor headed north down the valley to the next village – the rumbling woke me up early as he passed the cottage in the opposite direction."

"That's settled then. Fox's Folly will be an even better proposition," said Pie folding up the map. "We should have an easy passage."

Not if the phantoms in the wood have anything to do with it, thought Tal to himself, as he grimly followed the others out into the bright sunshine.

They made an unusual sight. A tall, slightly stooped, unkempt tramp shuffling along in a dirty overcoat following a short, motley procession of animals; one small, sleek and streamline, one fat, round and waddling and one tall, thoroughbred-looking, trotting in characteristic hunched Lurcher style, long silky ears flopping in time with his stride. It was the most idyllic morning. The lane out of the village twisted invitingly into the dazzling blue horizon; carving through the faded, yellow fields smouldering gently in the heat haze, it seemed to hover above the ground. It was a day to lose oneself in the beauty of everything, unless you were Tal and had seen a ghost. Amos blinked at the bright glare of the blazing sun which stung his eyes after days in the dark refuge. Preoccupied, he struggled to keep up with

73

the others – scanning the passing countryside he felt a faint twinge of familiarity, almost a déjà vu experience – he was growing more certain he had been here before. Fed up of bringing up the rear, Tal progressed to normal scouting speed overtaking a breathless Bungy and disgruntled Pie to take the lead. His nose was picking up something interesting round the next corner and he wanted to head off whatever was coming before the others got involved. The smell grew stronger arousing his senses, pulsing a warm electric current through nerve endings to the tips of his fur. He braced himself, checking the hedge for a convenient escape route. Expecting the gnarled old hunter from the woods, panic swelled in his chest making it difficult to breathe until he thought he would pop. Then, lolloping up the lane, honey-coloured ears flapping in slow motion, pink tongue lolling sideways, came Mollie, sweet, adorable Mollie who had more than a passing interest in Tal which she demonstrated at every available opportunity by flinging herself at him, smothering him with wet sloppy kisses – most embarrassing but quite pleasant, if there was no one else around. Not quite believing her luck, she locked Tal in her sights, colliding in a tangle of legs, ears and tails, spinning in joyous circles, pink tongue working overtime. The others caught up just in time to witness this romantic waltz, Tal protesting half-heartedly, "Gerroff, Mollie! Yes, I think you're wonderful too! That's enough now … I'm drenched for goodness' sake …" Pie, Bungy and Amos stared in amusement as the dance continued until Tal was eventually able to fend off her affections and keep her at a safe distance. Mollie stood panting breathlessly, ardour unquenched, preparing herself for a second overture. Tal had other ideas and shot through a gap in the hedge leaving the others and a flustered, love-struck Mollie standing bewildered in the middle of the lane. Sometimes it was hard being the village heart-throb.

The expedition wended its way slowly along the lane constantly alert, trying to keep a low profile and blend in with the countryside. The countryside on the other hand was broadcasting its beauty, amplified by dazzling sunlight and intensely blue, endless skies which framed the ragged bunch – it was hard to keep focussed, hard not to stop and wonder at the sweeping natural panorama all around them. Just ten minutes out of the village, however, Bungy was already huffing under his breath about the lack of sustenance. His legs, he'd decided, were not designed for trekking – they were short and too widely spaced to support the vital stores of energy concealed within his generous middle, which had, alarmingly, now started to scuff along the ground as overstretched muscles gave up their valiant fight. He sank down on the baking earth to take the stress off his paws and waited to see how long it would be before anyone noticed he was missing. With a bit of luck he could sneak back to the cottage and have the run of the kitchen; they'd never even notice he'd turned back. He watched as the intrepid trio disappeared round the bend and their backs receded into the distance. The heat of the sun toasted his fur, particularly the grey bits which were much hotter than the white ones. He was getting uncomfortably warm. The shade of the hedge beckoned whilst he considered his options. Perhaps a little snooze would help clear his head and revitalise his flagging muscles.

He sank gratefully into the long cool grass under the thick hedge bordering the lane. Bees buzzed busily in the aromatic wild honeysuckle twining itself through the spiky hawthorn over his head. Their gentle drone and the heady intoxicating sweetness cast a powerful spell, soothing his overheated, irritable body into a deep enchanted sleep. Some time later, seconds, minutes – he had no idea – he woke abruptly to escape an unpleasant dream where the pantry door remained firmly closed despite his frustrated efforts to release the latch which stubbornly refused to budge. A glimmer of realisation entered his half-awake brain; Pie swinging on the door handle, triumphantly suspending all access to meals until today's mission was completed. Drat. Now he was miles behind the others potentially jeopardising lunch, dinner and supper not to mention snacks … he scrambled out into the midday heat and was preoccupied with shaking off the sticky buds glued to his coat when a familiar pungent smell drifted up his nose.

Ducking back under the hedge he was just in time to see a large pair of boots pass quietly by; the person attached to the boots was at pains not to be noticed, surely an impossibility in such imposing footwear. Peering into the afternoon glare, Bungy stared open-mouthed at the retreating back of a large, burly individual with legs like small tree trunks that drove the boots in piston-fashion purposefully forward. Intent on his chosen path, the man strode relentlessly in the direction of Fox's Folly Wood. If he kept up this pace he would soon catch up with his friends … most peculiarly, the stranger wore the same kind of clothes as Amos, sort of old-fashioned, *historical* clothes …

As the boots ploughed on, something flashed in time with each step. Under the simple brown tunic it was just possible to see the tip of a long, shiny, fierce-looking implement which caught the sun's rays. An unwelcome tingle through his body announced to Bungy that it was looking highly probable that this rather solid, intense, *unfriendly*-looking individual was a second visitor from another time. Why these people couldn't stay where they belonged was beyond his tiny, under-nourished brain, unless ... this man was here *because* Amos was, and, what's more, had a reason to track Amos down – a mission ... *something to do with the Civil War*. The only people *that* serious who might need boots that big had to be soldiers – Amos and the rest of the party, including himself he realised with alarm, could be in danger. He had to find the others and warn them as quickly as his little legs would allow.

Crouching as low as possible he snaked out of sight along the hedge bottom parallel to the track, muttering and swearing under his breath as his fur snagged on the unforgiving hawthorn spikes. He was level with the boots now and could feel their steady rhythm drumming in his chest as the soles connected with the ground in a mechanical march. Drifts of a stale, sweaty odour wafted towards him as he crept quickly down his secret corridor, quietly overtaking them unseen. It was amazing how speedily he could make progress, like travelling in the fast lane of a wildlife motorway; quite good fun actually, he was starting to enjoy himself. Once past the boots he accelerated as much as the thicket would allow and headed through the cool, concealed undergrowth towards the wood, eyes scanning the track for signs of his friends. As he went along his mind replayed the events of the last few days. The marching boots, he was certain, were the same as the ones he'd discovered reclining in the hen house, and what's more, were most probably the 'seven league boots' that had transported the person spying at the dovecote door. He was, he decided, despite his sister's scorn, definitely cut out to be a secret agent. He was also mildly surprised to find he was now well ahead of the boots, mainly thanks to in-built four-wheel drive and short cuts taken by the hedge crossing fields whilst the track meandered and curved along their perimeter. In the distance he could faintly hear voices; Tal, Amos and Pie were deep in conversation on the path alongside the wood with someone not instantly recognisable, another of Tal's fan club probably – then it dawned on him it was someone he had not heard of for a very long time.

In a state of high alert, focussed on their safe passage, Bungy's absence had gone completely unnoticed by Amos and his companions. The encounter with Mollie, although harmless, had unnerved Tal. Already dreading what might lay waiting in the woods, he was finding it hard to be team scout. To add insult to injury, he was now being teased about his heart-throb status. A single cock pheasant disturbed in the long grass unexpectedly shot skyward. Wings drumming, shrieking a coarse, heart-stopping *'chock chock'* alarm call, the vivid blur urgently beat the air in frantic escape. Tal jumped a mile, his nerve ends frayed; for the millionth time he wished fervently that he'd never agreed to help. He'd decided he definitely wasn't a team player, more the solitary, wandering hobo type.

They had almost reached the 'rhino'. The nightmare memory of the last visit to this wood preyed remorselessly on Tal's mind despite all desperate attempts to block it out. Pie, as always, maintained an air of calm serenity and quiet determination, whilst Amos took in the landscape with an ever increasing air of growing anticipation. The track narrowed to an earth path as they approached the outskirts of the wood. Trodden over time by many pairs of feet, it cut a long, brown ribbon smoothly through the wild, ancient hedgerow of graceful yews, rampant brambles and woody blackthorn edged with ranks of towering stinging nettles which waved menacingly as they passed by.

Preoccupied with the jumbled thoughts crowding his mind, Tal was lagging behind. As he rounded the bend in the path towards the tree line marking the edge of the wood he heard jovial chatter, voices raised in greeting. There, in the middle of the path were Amos and Pie, their backs shielding the focus of attention. As Tal approached, Amos moved slightly to one side to reveal, large as life, none other than Bruce holding court – the last thing Tal wanted to see. Instinct told him to disappear into the undergrowth until Bruce had moved on but it was too late, he'd been spotted.

"Well, well, if it in't me auld friend the lonesome Lurcher, not so lonesome today tho' – brought 'is mates," chimed Bruce cheerily. Pie and Amos looked enquiringly at Tal. "Bumped into 'im down here few days ago, spent an 'appy hour together on one o' mi woodland tours din't we, lad?"

"Splendid!" interjected Amos. "You have arrived, young sire, at a most opportune moment." As he spoke Amos couldn't help noticing the uncanny likeness of this character to his own faithful hound.

Bruce looked amused. "Flowery talk there, squire – you not from these parts?"

"On the contrary, my friend – this is my land; these are my woods but er … just not my time …" Amos' voice trailed off. "We are surveying the landscape on our way to the ... 'country park' ... which is most likely to be my home." Bruce tilted his head quizzically. "It's a long story," said Pie.

This, Tal realised, was a perfect invitation for Bruce to wax lyrical about the wood – he needed a diversion.

Too late.

Bruce puffed out his chest importantly and got into his stride.

"I can guarantee yer the full, authentic, tour o't wood complete with real village life thrown in, can't I, lad? (looking at Tal proudly) – mekkin' swords, shoes for t'osses, bows an' them massive poles wi' spikes on't end ... an't best part—" Bruce was cut off in mid-flow by Amos almost choking, trying to get his words out.

"You describe the trades of my people, *my* trade! As woodsman to the King, I provide the timbers for the pikes and bows of which you speak. How is it you know so much of this?"

It was Bruce's turn to be momentarily speechless ... he looked completely stupefied and replied timidly, "Well ... ye sees I visit t'village regularly an' watch what goes on ..."

"Young sire, you must take us there! Take us there at once ... This could be my salvation!" exclaimed Amos.

"Weelll ... there's a good number of ye an' I prefers jus' te go meself. I took laddo Lurcher that day cos I thowt ee'd fit right in, an' ee did but ee upped an' ran off – got cold feet." Pie and Amos turned an astonished gaze in Tal's direction.

"You went to this 'village' in the wood?" asked Pie with an air of disbelief.

"You saw these 'villagers' but kept this a secret from all of us ... from Amos?" Tal stood rooted to the spot speechless – what could he say? He couldn't plead ignorance because Bruce had given the game away. How could he possibly explain his terrifying ordeal? They wouldn't understand or even believe what happened. Tal wasn't even sure himself that it might have been one of his less pleasant fireside dreams, and now it looked like he was about to return to the scene. He desperately needed that diversion.

Three pairs of eyes stared accusingly at him as he racked his brain for a suitable reply. Bruce was savouring the moment. Just when the only solution appeared to be a fast getaway over the neighbouring fields (they would never catch him) a tangled, scruffy, grey and white ball of twigs and burrs appeared at the top of the path trailing tendrils of ivy and bindweed in its wake. All eyes turned to focus on the strange vision as it loomed into view. As the bundle drew closer it was just possible to make out the line of a wide clownish grin beneath the scraps of foliage. Unable to speak, wheezing uncontrollably, Bungy collapsed at Tal's feet lolling on to his back to expose a wide expanse of pink skin and white fur dusted brown and speckled with sticky buds like a bad rash.

"*Heeeee Heeeee Heeee,*" rasped Bungy's breath in rapid whining gasps, his sides heaving. "Tried ... *heee* ... to ... *heeee* ... catch *heeee* ... you ... *heeee* ... up ...*heeee* ... boots ... *heeee* ... are ... *heeee* ... coming ... *heeee* ...' He sounded just like a squeaky toy Tal remembered having as a puppy.

"What are you talking about, and where on earth have you been to get in that state?" exclaimed Pie exasperatedly, momentarily turning her attention away from interrogating Tal.

Bungy took a huge deep breath … "The important leather boots, you know, the ones I told you about – they're coming this way attached to a tall, evil- looking man with very short hair carrying a long, shiny, fierce-looking, pointed stick and wearing funny old clothes, a bit like Amos' …" The words tumbled out in one long garbled stream. "Looks like someone else has got stuck here and is not very pleased about it." He went limp like a deflated balloon incapable of saying anything more.

"You have never mentioned any dratted boots before!" steamed Pie angrily. "Why am I the only member of this scouting party with any brain cells – it would have been extremely useful to know about them and this 'secret village' *before* we set off this morning!" She put on her most prim, indignant expression, owlish green eyes blazing.

Amos looked around gravely at the puzzled faces of his companions. "My friends, I fear we may be in great danger. If the little fellow's description is true, and I can scarcely dare believe it, we are being pursued by a cavalry officer from Cromwell's army. We have no choice but to head for this 'village' and hope we find kinship there. There is alchemy in the air and evil deeds at work here – we must seek the truth as it surely lies behind mine and the stranger's presence in your time." With that he stepped off the path and silently melted into the impenetrable darkness of the deep green wood.

9

The Way through the Wood

A gentle breeze lazily stirred the canvas flaps of tents arranged neatly in line while sunlight danced playfully over the lake adjoining the encampment. Serenity and industry came together as all around hummed a purposeful buzz of activity and familiar comforting rituals of everyday village life. Rows of rough trestle tables in front of each tent were laden with assorted kitchen paraphernalia – large misshapen stone flagons, woven baskets, wooden blocks and roughly hewn knives being vigorously employed in the preparation of a hearty lunch. A row of heavy cauldrons simmered gently nearby over glowing fires. Women in brightly coloured shawls and bodices, wide brimmed hats providing welcome shade, worked tirelessly in the hot summer sun, their long full skirts skimming the rough grass of the open field. A handful of children were trying in vain to concentrate on small tasks they had been given – making crumbs, peeling eggs and making butter, all the while distracted by the background *hiss* and *whoosh* of the blacksmith's bellows and bustle of the small band of musketeers cleaning their weapons.

To one side, a woman wearing a linen bonnet sat hunched over half an old oak barrel lost in the rhythmic scrubbing of recently carded wool which was slowly turning colour in the vivid dye deep within the barrels murky depths. A nose tingling, heady, yeasty aroma rose into the atmosphere to compete with whiffs of sour, milky curds as the brewer and cheese maker perfected another batch of beer and smooth roundels of fresh cheese to sustain the travellers. A small queue waited patiently in front of the laundress as she busily paddled washing, stopping occasionally to wipe the perspiration from her brow.

A thriving settlement, Elias Murro mused to himself, sitting cross-legged at the door of his tent puffing contentedly on a small clay pipe surveying the busy scene. He had chosen the location well for their temporary home. The linear wood along one boundary provided a good degree of shelter and concealment in addition to plentiful kindling, and the lake on the other boundary provided water. The spot also benefited from the sun's warming rays all day long. Standing majestically a short distance from the camp was a magnificent single evergreen oak tree some forty feet tall, its graceful boughs reaching far into the wide blue expanse of the midsummer sky. In folklore, the oak was the most widely revered of all trees. According to ancient druid mythology, the oak was associated with many powerful spells for protection, strength and success, healing and health, money and good luck. They were truly blessed, thought Elias, to have the good fortune to be protected by such a sacred guardian. The tree reputedly also held another quality. Mystics believed the oak offered a doorway to other dimensions where different realities and worlds could be perceived – a door through time. *Pah, utter nonsense!* Elias drew hard on his pipe blowing smoke high in the air, blowing away this ridiculous belief with disdain. The stuff of fable and legend ... of no consequence to their presence here – they had an earthly task to fulfil, very much of the here and now, not somewhere otherworldly. There was much to do he thought, tapping out his pipe on a nearby stone. Raising his towering frame from the warm grass, he collected his forked hazel stick and strode purposefully towards the band of young musketeers.

It had been easy to infiltrate this Royalist community. Travelling the byways with a band of tinkers, Elias had arrived at the small village close to the long wood masquerading as a hunter, selling his services and tooled leatherwork to the curious villagers. In a few short months, he had become a valued member of their community and taken into trust of circles close to the King. It was thus he had learned of their ambitious plot to ambush his leader General Cromwell whilst visiting one of his distinguished Parliamentarian officers, Sir Randolph Knight of Langhald Hall. Elias had to admit it was an audacious plan to undertake at the height of the Civil War. When his fellow Parliamentarian spies had suggested this treachery might be afoot, he had mocked the idea but had been quick to volunteer to go undercover and find out more. Now he found himself a protagonist in that very plot. Assumed a passionate Royalist, he had become one of the 'leaders' of the small, intrepid band of villagers putting the plan to kidnap Cromwell into action. He had to tread carefully concealing his true identity and Parliamentarian allegiance. Timing his intervention to sabotage their plan and save the General would be critical. There must be no disruptions or distractions to his mission if he was to pay back the outrageous treatment dealt him by the hand of his former allies, trusted comrades, his own Royalist army who had so unceremoniously dismissed him, branding him a traitor after years of faithful service as hunter gamekeeper to the King.

A long-legged tale based on the fertile imaginings of two young upstart Royalist soldiers eager to impress, jealous of Elias's status in the Royalist inner circle, had reached the ears of the King. Overheard in conversation by the soldiers in the local inn, Elias had been accused of sharing secrets with the enemy over a flagon of ale. Elias's companion on that fateful night, Will Strong, was, in truth, a man faithful to the Royalist cause. Will's twin brother Samson, however, had followed the puritan path and joined the Parliamentarians; word was Samson had become General Cromwell's favoured spy – the Strong family torn apart, divided by the conflict. Only the King's woodsman had defended Elias's honour but his protestations were dismissed by all as the ramblings of a simple old man who talks to trees. Come to think of it, the woodsman's faithful hound Bruce had appeared from nowhere, passing under the sweeping branches of the stately oak, and helped guide him towards this very location for their mission.

Mistaken identity, envy and youthful arrogance had cost Elias his beloved, respected position and standing in the Royalist community. Reputation shattered and life destroyed Elias, feeling the weight of his anger, had vowed bitterly to seek revenge. Retreating to his lonely cabin in the woods, he had waited for the right opportunity ... and here it was.

*

A strange, high-pitched squelching noise had begun to match his marching rhythm. Samson realised his feet were starting to complain, overheating in the heavy military boots. He was aware of an unpleasant trickling sensation between his toes as sweat started to gather in small pools inside the leather – the cause of the annoying squeak which now accompanied each soggy step. Disgusting, but all part of a soldier's life, particularly those on secret missions enduring the most extreme conditions – like … surviving in another century, probably the ultimate challenge a spy would ever have to face. Marvelling again at these bizarre circumstances he took comfort in imagining the lavish attention he would enjoy as he retold his story to the troops back home.

Back home. How would he ever get back home?

Despite the heat, a shivery chill ran through his bones, doubt creeping over his body like a black cloud blotting out the sun. He had a story to tell but no one to listen. Strange that he had been sent alone for such a dangerous mission; he'd assumed he must be considered the most elite of all the General's spies. On the other hand, had some strange sorcery been used to purposely remove him from the campaign, to banish him forever, trapping him in this unreal existence? He had to find the answer. He was certain it lay with the treasure and, unfortunately, probably with the old woodsman and his hairy friends. He must find them to secure his destiny. The travelling party was not far ahead, their voices becoming louder. He was catching them up.

Rounding the bend in the lane the path became a rough strip of brown earth disappearing into the distance bordered by wild and untamed hedgerows six feet high. Nettles as tall as him, delicate stinging fronds nodding in the breeze, formed an archway over his route. As he strode on to the narrowing path they brushed against the rough food sacks he'd found earlier in the hen house now hastily fashioned into a makeshift disguise to cover his orange scarf and dark tunic. Soon he spotted the small group ahead huddled together deep in conversation. They appeared to be listening attentively to another small four-legged character which seemed to be holding court – *Ye gods, another infuriating creature to contend with!* Then, something caused the group to turn as one and look straight in his direction. Samson dived sideways for cover, full length into the waiting nettles, stifling cries of pain as the stinging hairs struck home, prickling his face and arms like the stabbing of a thousand tiny, hot needles. Vicious white and pink patches bubbled instantly under his skin forming an irritating nettle rash to complement the raw holly scratches which already chequered his cheeks and forehead. *It would appear Mother Nature is on their side,* he thought grimly, gingerly sitting up and craning his neck to see if his ballet performance had been noticed.

The path was empty. There was no sign of life.

The group had completely disappeared, evaporated, dissolved by some enchanted invisibility powder. Drat!! How could that happen *again*? How could he be so incompetent losing four animals and one human in the blink of an eye? Struggling to his feet, skin and pride smarting in equal measure, he strode to the point on the path where the group had been talking. Scuff marks in the earth were all that remained, no tracks, nothing, just bare earth. The party hadn't carried on ahead; maybe they had slipped to yet another time dimension. Above his head a large, dark shadow flitted over the sun. A lonely, cat-like *'pee-oo'* cry echoed through the woodland on his right as a solitary buzzard flew silently past, coming to land in the upper branches of a neighbouring yew tree. Samson shielded his eyes to the sun searching the tree tops; the large bird watched him closely, unseen from his lofty perch amidst the dense, glossy, dark green leaves. Wizened ghostly faces conjured by the tree's red, peeling trunk seemed to mock and taunt him as he stood aimlessly on the path wondering what to do, which direction to take. Staring frustratedly at the tree, Samson suddenly noticed a small gap in the undergrowth beneath its twisted boughs. Here and there leaves were flattened and the faintest of tracks was barely visible winding into the distance through the rampant ivy which choked the forest floor. A small tuft of grey fur clung to a nearby holly bush confirming the way. The 'tree of death' in ancient fable had breathed new life into his quest. Performing an exaggerated bow in front of the tree he turned into the wood with a lighter spirit and a spring in his step.

*

Bruce's non-stop chatter was becoming very irritating thought Pie, as he launched into yet another far-fetched tale about a recent escapade. You would have thought they were all out for a Sunday afternoon stroll, a nature walk with running commentary, rather than a critical reconnaissance mission with life-changing implications. She needed to think and Bruce's incessant drivel was clogging up her brain, scrambling her thought waves. Important questions surfaced occasionally through the fog of relentless gossip. Who was following them and why? Echoes of their meeting in the dovecote swam in her head ... *someone with seven-league boots* ... she had casually remarked – now these boots were real and in close pursuit. Bruce chirped on and on and on ..., his scruffy tail ticking to and fro in front of her nose like a speeded-up metronome as he trotted gaily along the path.

"For goodness' sake! Don't you ever pause for breath? We are supposed to be on a secret mission and don't really want to announce our arrival." She hissed as loudly as she dared towards the disappearing rear end as Bruce weaved through yet another bank of dog mercury and wild garlic sending onion-scented currents swirling around their heads. Her nostrils smarted from the powerful fumes. *Not exactly a catnip experience,* she thought to herself, but at least the smell was helping to clear her mind.

"Don't ye worry, missy, I can guarantee we'll be as gud as invisible! Jus' stick wi' me. I'm an expert in subberfuge."

Subberfuge, does he mean 'subterfuge'? Pie bristled indignantly. *Not only does he talk a lot, he talks complete gibberish.* As for *missy,* well! She would treat that with the contempt it deserved and let it fly over her regal head. Hopefully, once they knew the location of the village, they could ditch Bruce altogether.

The cool stillness of the wood was helping Bungy regain his composure. The sticky buds gradually dropped off as his podgy tummy bumpily grazed along through the ivy. He was finding it hard to keep up; clambering over large, wandering roots of old ash trees was like doing a military assault course. It was obvious that their roots were designed to reach out with long, petrified fingers and grab unsuspecting passing creatures, like domestic cats, and yank them down deep into the earthy depths beneath their trunks to some terrible unknown fate. Having never strayed further than the cottage garden wall, Bungy was finding the outside world a challenging place. He was sure he had heard somewhere that witches were said to fly on broomsticks with handles that looked just like these roots. He scanned the sky quickly in case there were any overhead that might be looking to update their mode of transport. At that same moment a loud, mournful 'mee-ooo' cry pierced the silence. Bungy ducked trembling, paws covering his eyes, in case the witch also fancied a new travelling companion. There was a loud rustling noise right over his head. The witch had landed in the tree! He screwed his eyes up even tighter, trying to make himself invisible. He was sure witches preferred black cats; yes ... black was all the rage for witches. Perhaps he might be lucky; thankfully he was mostly white with scrappy bits of grey, a second rate choice for any discerning witch.

He held his breath.

The rustling carried on, amplified by the all-embracing silence. Suddenly something rapped him smartly on the back. Good grief! He'd been discovered and was destined to spend the rest of his life surrounded by dead toads, cauldrons, eyes of newts ... his imagination was working overtime.

"Is tha snoozin' agin? What a lightweight," mocked Bruce, snuffling in the undergrowth. Bungy, too traumatised to reply, gradually opened his eyes to be met by the cheery twinkle of the tawny terrier and the burning stare of a haughty buzzard perched high on the branch above him.

Phew! Not a witch in sight. He must really make an effort to keep up, and stay close to Amos who he was beginning to consider a friend, and, more importantly … seemed to understand the ways of the wood.

Bungy wasn't the only one scared out of his wits. Tal, bringing up the rear, followed at a distance in trepidation, constantly scanning the shadows behind every tree expecting one of them to turn into the giant tree-like man, trunk contorting, branches flailing like arms, slowly snaking their grasp towards him. They were nearing the stream with the dell beyond that hid the living nightmare.

Anytime soon they would all pass into the netherworld that existed in the meadow never to see home again.

Unless he turned back, now he was doomed to an unimaginable fate at the hands of the grizzled hunter. He couldn't see what useful purpose Pie and Bungy might serve in this strange parallel universe so they would most likely be spared and allowed home – if the 'time guardians', whoever *they* were, looked kindly on them. Bruce had reached the dry stream bed. The others followed him closely just as Tal had done on that dreadful day. One by one they cleared the stream bed picking their way through trailing branches and clinging ivy. Tal instinctively closed his eyes trying to keep the uneasy feeling in his tummy at bay as he stepped over the bed waiting for the air to shift and shimmer opaquely around him. He waited. Waited for the incredulity, for the cries of astonishment.

There were none.

There was nothing, just the pleasing sigh of a summer breeze and the gentle *swussssh* of waving grass. Tentatively, he opened one eye, then the other. No tents, no bellows, no Bruce. The meadow was completely empty. In solitary splendour on the slope running down towards the lake stood a lone, evergreen oak tree framed against the midsummer sky.

10

Friends and Enemies

A deafening, eerie silence enveloped the small scouting party as they came to an abrupt halt on the edge of the wood bumping clumsily into one another concertina fashion. Staring dumbfounded into the distance, they scanned the landscape for signs of Bruce's presence, but there were no clues anywhere – he had completely disappeared, evaporated into thin air like a genie dissolving back into its bottle. A vast field spread out before them parched and bare, jagged lines of stubble scratched geometrically towards the horizon, carved into the earth by the mechanical teeth of the combine harvester. Into the distance, beyond the lone oak, the only thing in sight was a sea of graceful, waving meadow grasses dotted with delicate blue harebells and pink spires of rosebay willow herb punctuated here and there with vibrant splashes of blood-red poppies and yellow toadflax. Not a scruffy terrier in sight.

They all stood motionless for what seemed like an age, blinking against the white hot glare of the sun from their shady refuge, under the hanging curtain of rampant ivy choking the trunks of the surrounding trees. Tal, rooted to the spot in disbelief, replayed the encounter with the 'villagers' and the tree man through his mind, checking and double-checking the route he and Bruce had taken that day. Yes, he was dead certain this was the exact spot where they had both passed into the clearing; the memory was indelibly imprinted into his very being. But ... how could a whole living village disappear without leaving a trace?

Pie was first to break the silence that held them frozen in the moment like some cursed enchantment. She didn't look best pleased; fur standing on end, she had the appearance of being electrified – it was a look Bungy knew well, which usually sent him running for the safety of his hiding place under the woodpile, until she had calmed down.

"I knew it! A wild goose chase! What else could we expect from a stupid ... *'street dog'* with a superiority complex?" Pie was boiling mad.

Bungy risked a knowing look towards Tal muttering under his breath, "Takes one to know one ... pots and kettles ... etc."

Pie spun round, eyes narrowed, glaring icily at her brother. "What did you say?"

"Oh ... nothing really just commenting on the dock leaves and nettles," replied Bungy nonchalantly, surprised at his own quick wittedness.

"If you've nothing useful to contribute, which is highly unlikely, kindly refrain from interrupting my train of thought; you're as bad as Bruce. Someone needs to assess the situation and make some decisions. You're unreliable and can't even remember to pass on vital information about threatening strangers and, what's more, Tal is obviously having delusions which have affected his mental faculties. *I'm* the only one with any brains around here!" Pie always used big words to assert her authority when she was exasperated, words which mostly lost their impact as Bungy hadn't a clue what she was talking about. The only thing he knew for certain was that it had been five hours, twenty minutes and ... several seconds since breakfast – a personal record, and, his brain had ceased functioning because his tummy was completely empty.

Amos meanwhile was looking and feeling lost and bewildered. His spirits, soaring at the prospect of being reunited with his kinfolk, reconnected with his life, were apparently now crushed, drowned in despair and foreboding. He sank slowly to the ground and leaned dazedly against a tree trunk staring blankly into space as Pie and Bungy continued to trade insults. Tal retreated to join Amos under the tree leaning his weight in friendly reassurance against Amos' legs. Amos, comforted, gently stroked Tal's smooth gleaming coat as they both mulled over the situation and what could possibly happen next. Now over the initial shock of the vanishing village, Tal secretly felt waves of relief flood over him and soon he too sank to the warm forest floor and began to doze, his handsome face resting on Amos' knee. Minutes passed, or was it an hour, it was hard to say; time seemed to have stood still. Tal was starting to enjoy himself, relaxing in the peace of the woodland grove, stresses of the day fading and, his doggy memory being notoriously short term, had moved on in his mind to something far more pleasurable – a gambol in the field with Mollie her soft, caramel-coloured ears teasingly flying in the wind.

The afternoon slumbered on in a dreamlike haze, the air thick with heat and silence. The sun arced gradually to the west, creating pools of dappled light through the trees, illuminating four lifeless bodies snoozing peacefully at the foot of a large ash tree. Events had caught up with everyone, including Pie, who, against her better judgement, also succumbed to a welcome afternoon nap, just a short one she told herself. Daily routines were important and old habits hard to break, so it was that the four companions gave in to the embrace of the ash roots and nodded off into a deep, untroubled sleep.

Amos woke with a crick in his neck and Tal's weight heavy on his legs which were now developing pins and needles. The summer breeze had become a warm, stirring wind agitating the branches of the tree above them. Its boughs creaked and moaned, sounding almost human as if it was trying to tell him something. In his work as the King's woodsman, Amos had many conversations with the trees in his care and was certain the trees were communicating with him, each one with its own distinctive voice. He felt more at ease with trees than people; there was mutual understanding and, just like his new friends, they understood one another. And now these trees were telling him something, something important that needed urgent attention. Amos scrambled to his feet, gently lowering Tal's head to the floor, straining his ears to the tree tops. A persistent murmuring kept coming and going on the breeze. There it was again ... a sort of confused, incoherent rambling, low-level muttering peppered with what appeared to be angry exclamations of rage. A heated conversation was disturbing the natural bond of peace and oneness with the ancient wood. He was wondering how best to respond to this garbled message from the agitated tree spirits when the sounds grew louder accompanied by the thrashing of heavy footsteps marching towards them.

★

The cool shade bathed Samson's overheated limbs as he strode deeper into the wood, faltering a little while his eyes grew accustomed to the iridescent silhouettes and shadows within its depths. Tracking had never been his strong point and the uncertainty of the path was frustrating him. He was a man of certainty, impatient to reach his goal and ultimately achieve recognition. Tracing the steps of a bunch of animals and an old man was not befitting a man of espionage; it was, frankly, verging on the ridiculous. He blundered on deeper and deeper into the wood, getting more and more bad-tempered, taking out his frustrations on the only available person – himself. "Incompetent … *pathetic!* A total failure in just about everything and getting nowhere fast! Call yourself a spy!" The angrier he got the louder his outbursts became as he stomped heavily along the path crashing through the undergrowth, trying to steer the large cavalry boots around twisted roots which seemed to deliberately be trying to trip him up. In his black mood, it never occurred to him that he was making a commotion, announcing his arrival to those he was trying to secretly pursue. Samson paused mid-rant and raised his eyes to the heavens as if looking for celestial guidance to ease his infuriation – at which moment his right foot connected with a particularly lumpy root sending him flying forwards head first towards the stream he had been following.

"Ye gods! These blessed boots are a liability," he yelled, his words ringing around the tree tops over his head. "Even my own possessions now seem to conspire against me." The fall shook him to his senses and he looked round sheepishly to check for any signs of life, but only the trees nodded an acknowledgement stirred by the wind. He was unscathed but caked in dust. Sitting on a nearby log he brushed down his tunic, thankful that against the odds he still seemed to have maintained a low profile, completely oblivious to the four pairs of eyes that watched his every move from behind a blackthorn bush three feet away.

"Who would have thought that an elite spy could be outsmarted so easily?" Samson muttered, "And just how difficult is it to find clues to the location of the treasure General Cromwell seems so eager to acquire? I *will not* fail in this mission; every challenge serves only to strengthen my resolve to the cause. I will take no quarter when I finally catch up with those stupid creatures. I will do whatever is necessary to obtain the treasure map and prove myself to be a hero!" His chest swelled with pride, eyes glittering with determination.

Behind the blackthorn bush Pie gasped in realisation. She recognised the steely flash of the stranger's eyes; she had felt their burning glare momentarily through the dovecote door several nights ago. So this was the person who had been following them – a spy, working for Cromwell. Things were getting more bizarre by the second. What's more, a bumbling spy with an attitude problem it seems – *we're living in a film,* she thought, *with character actors, soon someone will step out from behind a tree and shout "Okay, cut!"* Pie had watched a lot of films snug in her bed in front of the television. Not for the first time in the last few days did she question how they had all come to be embroiled in this strange, quite unbelievable situation – although it was giving her a major opportunity to take charge and organise everyone, something at which she excelled. She reapplied her mind to the mystery, preening her silky fur whilst she thought. What is the 'treasure' he's rambling about and how did he know that Amos was here at this exact moment? Something fishy going on, this couldn't be a coincidence, surely?

Satisfied with his appearance, Samson levered his solid frame from the log and stretched to his full height like a man renewed. Jaw set defiantly, eyes fixed on the path ahead, he lumbered past the band of companions, boots thumping the ground within a whiskers breadth of their hiding place. Bungy cowered as the heavy thuds reverberated through his body, leaving a clinging smell of sweaty leather in the air.

"The last time I saw those boots they were reclining gracefully in a chicken coup. Now it seems they have taken on a life of their own and become some kind of evil marching machine, trampling anything and everything that comes into their path, including defenceless cats … and dogs," he added, seeing Tal give him a hurtful look. "I vote we forget this whole thing and get back to the cottage in time for tea, before it gets dark – who knows what scary hobgoblins and will-o'-the-wisps will emerge at twilight." He looked up nervously through the blackthorn's crooked, thorny, angular branches and knobbly twigs which were closing in on him.

"Indeed I have heard blackthorn is known as the keeper of dark secrets – there is, I sense, magic in the air," said Amos quietly, with a sideways wink at Pie. Bungy shrank closer to the ground looking extremely worried. "But it is also a very protective tree, so as long as we're sheltered by it we should be safe," he added. "The wood is our friend, not our enemy. The spirit guardians of the trees, wood nymphs you might call them, are watching over us. They warned me of the stranger's approach and have now grown quiet as his unfriendly presence has withdrawn from their force fields."

For the first time since their meeting the animals gawped at Amos transfixed, fleetingly hypnotised, as if under some spell. Bungy was thinking he wouldn't recognise a wood nymph if it jumped up and bit his tail, but he was happy to accept that they were useful things to have around.

"The tree 'person' that I met at the vanishing village was distinctly *un*friendly," blurted Tal, instantly regretting opening his mouth as the others turned their stares from Amos towards him. "A man the size of a tree, with thick waving arms, tried to kidnap me for his stalking dog. His hair was matted like a thicket and he carried a long, gnarled stick forked at the top." The words rushed out before Tal had chance to stop them. "He had a funny name, Elias, I think it was, I didn't stay around to find out. When he strode towards me, his long bony fingers almost on my neck, I was off like a shot. I've never been so pleased to see Bruce go into one of his showing-off routines."

"Elias, you say?" whispered Amos. "Can it be true that he is also a fellow traveller in time? One of my Royalist friends, badly wronged and misjudged by many for a deed which was in truth fabricated in jealous young minds. What strange magic is at play here? Why are we three souls trapped in this future world? Could it be we are meant to rewrite the past?" His voice trailed off as he stared into some unseen distant place faraway in the deepest caverns of his mind, lost in a time unknown. Tal, Bungy and Pie, very much in the here and now, could only sit and watch as the old man drifted away from them to a life elsewhere, the trees around them quiet, as if watching and waiting for their kindred spirit to return.

"It must be nearly tea time," moaned Bungy, oblivious as usual to everything except his own stomach.

"You are right, my friend," agreed Amos, snapping out of his thoughts. "We can achieve nothing sitting here and night will soon fall. We must get back to our refuge and ponder on what we have discovered today. If we can find the village, Elias may be able to help us understand what is happening."

I doubt it, thought Tal who had decided he was not cut out for anything more adventurous than chasing hares and perhaps the odd deer.

"It seems there is only one way forward, find Bruce and we will find the village – he holds the key to its secret existence."

11

A Good Deed

After what seemed like an eternity, the companions arrived back in the village bedraggled and exhausted. The only thing that had kept them going was watching the sun descend gracefully towards the horizon; fields and trees on the hillside silhouetted a deep shade of purple against the giant, fiery ball. They stared in wonder at the beauty of the spectacle, walking towards the glowing orange light as if drawn by some invisible, magnetic force. All was quiet as they passed the duck pond; no one about as twilight crept over the village. Amos slipped away to the dovecote and the others headed to the cottage straight to the kitchen. Despite complaining all the way back about aching paws and being tired, Bungy miraculously found enough energy to be first at the pantry door waiting for Pie to perform her acrobatics and get the door open. "Come on, come on, will you, I'm wasting away here," he grumbled. Ignoring him Pie launched towards the door from the window seat. With a deft flick of the paw she freed the latch and the door swung welcomingly open at which point there was an ungainly stampede.

Seconds later, Bungy had demolished one bowl of food and started on Pie's before she managed to butt him out of the way. Not for the first time did Tal thank his lucky stars that his food was stationed at the opposite end of the kitchen so less inclined to be raided, although Bungy was now making a beeline in his direction and he'd only eaten half of his meal. Turning to face him, Tal planted his paws firmly on the quarry tiles in front of his dish and adopted the most aggressive-looking pose he could muster. Sensing a fight, Bungy nonchalantly changed direction, neatly swerving straight under Tal's body between his legs making instead for his bed, gently brushing his tail the length of Tal's tummy on the way. Before long, as darkness fell, the only sound that could be heard in the house was gentle breathing punctuated by the occasional musical snore.

Outside in the gloom of the dovecote, Amos wrapped his heavy cloak tighter around his shoulders and stared into the embers of a small fire, sparks feebly sputtering as the flames died away. Some berries picked along the way and the last few grains from his pockets had served as a simple meal. There was much to think about – eating was the least of his concerns. His thoughts kept returning to Bruce; another strange coincidence. The cocky, little chap they had met bore an uncanny resemblance to his own beloved hound; he even had the same name. Surely they were not one and the same, separated by four centuries, yet living in another time? His head reeled at the thought and all the boggling discoveries of the day, but the urge to sleep was too strong to fight. Curling into a ball cocooned in his cloak he closed his eyes and sank into a deep, dreamless sleep on a makeshift bed of twigs and leaves.

Tal unfortunately, did not sleep as peacefully – plagued by disturbing dreams, he was running to escape from Elias's bony fingers which stubbornly remained just an inch away from the scruff of his neck. No matter how fast Tal ran, the fingers were almost brushing his fur straining to capture him; so much so, by the time he woke he felt like he had run a marathon through the night. Dragging himself wearily out of bed he arrived in the kitchen in time to hear Pie announce that she would be withdrawing to her 'box' as she needed to 'think' about what they should do next following their day of revelations. She often disappeared for hours into the battered wicker box, which had once enjoyed a useful life as a picnic hamper, but in retirement had been commandeered by Pie as her own 'private' space. Now, furnished with an aging collection of small, tatty, knitted teddy bears she had carefully organised into comfy wall-to-wall cushioning, it was quite a luxurious bolthole. Best of all, there was no chance that Bungy, too stupid, or Tal, too big, would ever steal it away from her. She was the only one who had perfected the art of lifting the lid with her nose getting into the box head first, her tail the last thing to disappear silently into its depths, like a snake charmed slithering back into its basket. Bungy had tried on many occasions, but to his great annoyance couldn't for the life of him work out how to open the thing. Only Pie had the knack and knew exactly which corner of the lid to tilt. She was also lithe enough to manoeuvre her body elastically into a big cat stretch and step completely over the box side; Bungy would need a small hoist to attempt this.

So it was that she had disappeared one day, and though the others searched high and low she was nowhere to be found, until the lid of the box popped up unexpectedly sending Bungy running for cover into the shoe cupboard.

From that moment on the box had been claimed and had, apparently, now assumed the role of Pie's headquarters in this important mission. The last they both saw of her was the curling tip of an apricot and coffee tinted tail slowly disappearing as the lid gently closed with a quiet *whump*.

"Hmmmm – what do you think we should do today? Surely we don't always have to wait for Pie to make all the decisions," muttered Bungy, his mouth full of food.

Tal did his best to ignore him; he'd got his own ideas. The sun was shining and all he wanted to do was escape for a run across the fields.

"Poor Amos hasn't any food and it must be horrible living in all that pigeon poo – don't you think we should at least find him something to eat?" This sentence was accompanied by loud slurping and scraping noises as Bungy chased his dish clattering round the kitchen floor, making sure every last morsel of food had been devoured. Tal didn't reply, hoping Bungy would lose interest and waddle off for a doze on the patio. But still he persisted.

"You're highly qualified in scavenging – it's a Lurcher speciality ... perhaps you could steal something from the pantry. I'd try but I'm not built for it ... short fat legs and lots of wobbly bits that get in the way, whereas you, you're tall, athletic and can reach the higher shelves ... lots of interesting smells the higher up you get in the pantry. I once tried climbing up there but fell off the bread bin, anyway-"

"Okay, Okay, I'll have a look what's in there," Tal interrupted his flow knowing Bungy would drone on and on until he agreed to help. It would only take a few minutes and then he'd be out the door feeling the summer warmth on his back.

Once their eyes adjusted to the dim light in the pantry, necks straining upwards to peer at the shelves, they could see rows of bottles containing exotic-looking oils, cans wrapped in brightly coloured labels, dusty packets of flour and sugar, strange unidentifiable dry tubes and long, stringy shapes sitting alongside rice and tomato paste which they later came to know as pasta. *Very unappetising,* thought Bungy, *apparently nothing really ready to eat without cooking.* The jumble of smells overwhelmed Tal's super-sensitive nose. Somewhere, mingling with the burnt, slightly bitter aroma of roasted coffee beans, peppery spices and the earthy tang of root vegetables, was a tantalising sugary smell, a mouth-wateringly good one. Tal smacked his lips as his nose started to twitch. Pacing back and forth, nose lifted sniffing the air, he scanned each shelf in turn. His nose, usually very reliable, told him that the clinging sweetness was emanating from what looked like a small house brick sitting on a large plate on the middle shelf. "Bingo!" He said quietly. Bungy dragged himself away from inspecting the miniature gravy bones in Tal's treat box sensing a snack.

"Think I've found just the thing for Amos, with a bit left for us if we play our cards right." Gingerly Tal stepped on to the bottom rung of the vegetable rack to get more height and, before Bungy could blink, gave the edge of the plate a hefty downward swipe with a front paw. In slow motion, the brick carved a graceful arc up in the air then headed for the floor at alarming speed, following the plate which splintered into smithereens as it hit the unforgiving quarry tiles with a loud *smasssshhhh.* In one seamless movement, Tal darted under the flying object, opened his mouth, and deftly caught it before it hit the floor. "Mmmmm … sticky syrup cake, my favourite," he mumbled with his mouth full.

"Tea loaf if you don't mind," corrected Bungy, ever the food aficionado. "Well, put it down or there'll be none left for me … I mean Amos."

Ten minutes later, having nibbled two corners between them, Tal's conscience got the better of him.

"Right, no more, the rest is for Amos." Licking his lips, he pushed the cake out of Bungy's reach who had paused momentarily to unstick his whiskers and wash off a rather fetching, syrupy moustache.

Time was moving on. Shafts of sunlight bathed the rustic kitchen walls, illuminating knots and grooves in the twisted oak ceiling beams which could tell their own swashbuckling stories of a previous life in tall ships on the high seas. Outside, goldfinches squabbled noisily over the bird table and a peacock butterfly basked on the sunny windowsill, its kaleidoscopic wings spread wide to soak up the warmth. The new day had woken up and was calling Tal to escape while he had the chance.

"I'm off for a run. You can manage to deliver the loaf to Amos can't you …" Not giving Bungy a chance to reply, he shouted over his shoulder a quick. "Good – I'll see you later." *Much later*, he thought, trotting out of the gate feeling the spring of the lawn under his paws.

Bungy wrestled with his conscience for a while, deciding whether he could manage any more cake right now and whether he should hide it somewhere for later, but then he'd have to make up a story to explain why it never reached Amos. He wasn't sure he could carry the weight; perhaps he could legitimately trim a bit more off the edges to make it more manageable. A noisy, unexpected burp interrupted these deliberations signalling that there was probably no more available space, tempting though it was; sadly he had to concede, the rest of the cake was all Amos'. The next problem was how to transport it from the kitchen to the dovecote, not a small distance. He racked his brains. *Perhaps a lever and pulley system using the vacuum cleaner pipes or using a kitchen tray like a sledge?* Neither of these sounded convincing and involved the application of brainpower. *Too difficult,* he thought, yawning. Then, he remembered several mobile contraptions in the garden shed when he and Tal were looking for the disguise. About the size of someone's foot with a small wheel at each corner, he'd seen people whizzing up the street on these strange devices – one of them was just about the right size for a half-eaten tea loaf. Toddling off to the shed, he congratulated himself on his ingenuity, as ten minutes later he tied the battered cake remains to the rusty roller skate with some garden twine. Setting off in the direction of the dovecote, the twine through his teeth, he felt extremely proud and not a little frustrated that his snooty sister was not around to witness his inventiveness.

It soon became apparent that it was impossible for him to pull the skate forwards due to its weight and that a reversing approach was the only way he would make any useful progress. Clamping his teeth over the twine and crouching on his haunches he pulled the skate towards him, his own not inconsiderable size acting as a counterweight, giving the skate some momentum. Obligingly, the skate started to slowly trundle forwards. A wave of pride, tinged with a little incredulity, swept over him, another small triumph to mention to his sister. Feeling more confident, he gave another tug on the twine, this time with more gusto. The skate again obliged then accelerated towards him, enjoying a new-found freedom having been liberated from the dusty, dark shed. Bungy realised too late it wasn't going to stop. His creation had come alive and was making straight for him. Before he could jump out of the way, the cake skate walloped into him knocking him head over heels into a terracotta strawberry pot. Sitting up slightly dazed, he found he was pinned to the patio by the unruly vehicle, cake still safely on board. Hmmm, not quite such a big success, he would leave this bit out when he retold the story, but then cats were not renowned for their knowledge of physics. Back on his feet he started the process again, this time in a more stately fashion making steady progress inch by inch towards the dovecote, a journey which would take him over an hour.

Several sits down later, Bungy arrived in front of the old wooden door of the dovecote, puffed out and bruised from bumping into an assortment of objects that had sought to make his backwards trek as difficult as possible. The stretch from the garden wall across the stubble had been really hard work and constantly scanning the field for potential enemies had frayed his nerves. Relieved to see the door was slightly ajar, probably to dilute the acrid smell that assaulted his nostrils from within, he stuck his head and whiskers through the gap and called Amos' name in a loud stage whisper. No reply came. There were no signs of life. Bungy pushed harder at the door until his generous waistline halted further progress. Tutting loudly, abandoning any hope of remaining inconspicuous, he barged at the door and cannoned out the other side into the dark, smothering atmosphere like a cork popping from a bottle. Amos wasn't there. The charred remains of a small fire and some dried leaves and twigs were all he could make out in the enclosing gloom. *Phooooey! What a pong!* The stench seemed to invade his whole body clinging to his fur, making his eyes sting and coating his tongue with a metallic taste. *Only a desperate man would choose to live in this place,* he thought. As his eyes grew more accustomed to the dimness, he became aware of tiny, piercing, beady dots focussing on him from high in the rafters. Several startled pigeons stared indignantly down at him from nesting boxes arranged in neat rows tiered as far as his eyes could see into the ceiling. He made a mental note to rig up some kind of mask and do a bit of stalking in here sometime when his mission was completed. Remembering the cake sitting outside the door as a dead giveaway, he ran back to drag it inside and leave it as a surprise for Amos when he got back. *Got back from where?* Bungy wondered idly; surely it was dangerous for him to be roaming alone outside in the twenty-first century?

Ah, here is Amos now, the sound of footsteps approaching over the dry stubble, clicking and crunching as they trod on the stumps. Bungy went to the door anticipating a friendly greeting. A familiar stale, leathery smell drifted through the crack in the door, hitting his nostrils and ringing alarm bells. The cavalry boots were outside and about to convey a large, angry spy into the dovecote. He hardly had time to register the fact, his mind racing. The soldier must have been watching and waiting for Amos to go out, which means he probably saw me arrive with all the palaver I had getting in here. I'm either going to be trampled or captured, then tortured in the chicken run and pecked to the bone by hens seeking revenge, and no one will know where I am. He looked around frantically – nowhere to hide, just a big, empty, dark space in which his white patches would show up nicely and expose him. Large, hairy fingers curled around the door frame, the ancient hinges creaked and a leather toe cap took a tentative step on to the earthy floor. Bungy could feel the warmth of Samson's breath on the tips of his ears; any second now he would be discovered. Heart hammering like a piston in his chest he searched desperately around for the last time. The pigeons looked on with interest as Samson's tall menacing shadow blotted out the shaft of light cast by the open door as he stepped into the gloom.

12

Waymarks

It felt good to be alive thought Tal, trotting along the track to the small wood on the hill, a gently curving band of old trees growing wild, shaped only by the unpredictable forces of nature. It was his favourite wood. Every time he came he saw something different. All manner of trees grew here higgledy-piggledy, jostling for light, reaching to the sky. At this time of year, the canopy was a dense patchwork of mixed leaves, some like outstretched palms, others delicate teardrops; small, meandering paths crisscrossing through the undergrowth, cut cool, green tunnels of tranquillity in which Tal lost himself for hours. Ivy scrambled up every trunk in a race to the sunlight. It was like a lost world, something prehistoric. The silence and solitude was wonderfully soothing. Tal breathed deeply revelling in the moment, feeling the stresses of the last few days drifting away as he loped along. He noticed the edges of the leaves were starting to lose their youthful freshness, parched by a long dry summer. The relentless march of the seasons was ever present; autumn was waiting in the wings. He picked up a strong characteristic musky smell on the track heading into the deepest part of the wood, *Mr Fox has been a-hunting, I wonder what he caught, if anything …*

Allowing his mind to wander and daydream, reacting to the elements as he went along, it was a while until an alien *'Dum-di-dum-di-dum-dum'*, distinctly un-woody sound amongst the birdsong, managed to break the spell. *'Dum-dum-di-dooooo'* the sound continued, *'Doooo-dee-dooo-dee-dooooowaah'* it ended with a flourish. A humming sound ... a *familiar* humming sound. Out of nowhere, the overpowering musky smell was replaced by drifts of wood smoke and burnt leaves. Tal looked around alarmed to check for signs of a fire; the wood was tinder dry after all. Then *whooosh, clang, hiss*, the sound of air forced through leather bellows, metal on metal. He whipped around expecting to see some mechanical device heading towards him on the path. Instead, bold as brass, strutting in his direction was Bruce, seemingly oblivious to Tal's presence.

Tal stood his ground – he had a bone to pick with Bruce after the charade down at Fox's Folly Wood. Bruce had promised to escort them to the hidden village, but instead had upped and abandoned them, ruining Amos' chances of getting home. Bruce nonchalantly carried on his way, humming quietly, stopping occasionally to investigate interesting smells under the trees. "And just what do you think you were doing taking us all on a wild goose chase yesterday?" challenged Tal as Bruce trotted past. But Bruce kept going, no flicker of acknowledgement, it was as if Tal was invisible. "Hey, Bruce! I'm talking to you ... hey!" Tal bellowed after him as he rounded the next bend, stubby tail waving side to side in time with his steps. "Well! How rude can you get – typical street dog, no manners at all – I'm not putting up with that." Most unusual for Bruce not to stop for a chat – talking about himself was his favourite pastime. Tal ran after him.

He caught up with Bruce just as he passed beneath the spreading boughs of an imposing oak tree, the biggest and oldest tree in the wood. *This tree is probably the chief wood spirit, the guardian in charge of all trees,* thought Tal remembering Amos' speech. *What am I doing thinking about tree spirits? Something funny's happening to my brain.*

"Hey Bruce! Just you wait there, you scruffy, unreliable …"

"Weeell, if it ain't me ol' friend Lurcher laddo," chirped Bruce.

"You've just walked straight past me and blatantly ignored what I had to say … you take the biscuit you do … I've never met anyone as rude and ignorant as—"

"Don't you come along ere accusin' me o' tekkin' yer biscuits! I ain't bin nowhere near yer … I knows I'm a bit rough, but I'm no thief!" interrupted Bruce looking hurt.

"It's a figure of speech! It means … oh, never mind …" barked Tal, as Bruce turned abruptly away, having decided the conversation was over.

"Hang on, hang on," Tal realised he was on the verge of losing Bruce for a second time and he needed answers. "Look, when you ignored me back there I just thought it was rude and lost my temper."

"I'd be fibbin' if I said I'd seen ye," came the surly reply.

"But you brushed past me, I felt the air movement and heard you humming." "Nope, sorry mate, nobbdey about for miles this mornin'. Sure yer feelin' all right?" queried Bruce, peering quizzically at Tal's face.

"There can't possibly be two of you can there, a twin perhaps?" *Heaven forbid*, thought Tal.

"No, I's unique." Bruce puffed out his chest. "Tha

wain't find another one like me anywheres."

True enough, thought Tal and gave up. A trick of the light perhaps? Definitely not. Bruce had been as real as the nose on his face trotting jauntily by. Strange things happening lately, perhaps he had crossed into that lost world he'd created in his mind. It was all too much to think about and more importantly he needed to find out why Bruce had so conveniently disappeared. So, he forced his brain to focus on the pressing issue of the missing village imagining Pie's disdainful look if he didn't return with any useful information, and fell into step with Bruce as he continued on his way.

★

One more move and Bungy knew he would be flattened. Samson stood methodically surveying the inner walls of the dovecote, allowing his eyes time to adjust from the glare of the sunshine. He had not got as far as inspecting the floor. The large boots were inches from Bungy's nose, the reek of sweaty feet competing with the pigeon poo. The cocktail of smells was making his head swim and walking backwards had made him quite disorientated. His brain, small though it was, was working overtime to come up with a solution to the pickle he was in. Backwards, walking backwards – he'd been rather good at that; it made a change to find something he could do. That was it! There were hundreds of hiding places lining the walls – the nesting boxes. He just had to wriggle into one unnoticed and had to do it backwards so he could see what Samson was up to. In slow motion he quietly reversed towards the nearest wall, keeping his white belly close to the ground, which wasn't difficult as it naturally scraped on the floor. Lining up with the box was tricky but after a bit of adjustment and tight tail curling he squeezed his bottom between the rough bricks until just his nose and whiskers were visible. The pigeons craned their necks to get a better view. He must remember to keep his chin to the floor so the white and grey grin didn't give him away. Trembling uncontrollably, trying valiantly to stay calm, he knew he may be in for a long wait. *Think about something nice – that should help.* A conjured vision of a heaped dish of tuna appeared then quickly vanished as Samson drew nearer. *That's not going to work. I'll just have to be brave – earn some brownie points, if I ever get out of here to tell the tale.* He prayed fervently that Amos, wherever he was, stayed put until Samson had gone. In his frantic rush to hide, Bungy had completely forgotten the faithful skate with its precious cargo which remained stationary in the middle of the floor looking forlorn, if inanimate objects could do that – the roller skate was certainly doing a good impression. Bungy could murder a piece of cake right now and seeing it within reach was cruelty itself. If only he knew some magic incantation that would bewitch the skate and bring it to life to do his bidding – he could at least have a snack whilst he was trapped in this nightmare.

Samson, now used to the gloom, was knelt scouring the embers and scrabbling through Amos' makeshift bed on the floor, intensely focussed on his task. Every now and then he muttered under his breath. Bungy could tell he was getting frustrated and had seen how quickly he could erupt from yesterday's outburst in the wood. Keeping as still as possible, holding his breath, he watched the top of the matted head of cropped black hair bobbing up and down less than an inch from the end of his nose, the heavy-lidded, evil eyes scanning the dusty earth floor spattered with droppings. *How much longer will this torture last? It's way past lunchtime and any second now my tummy clock will go off.* Bungy tried to hold in his stomach to avert this happening, but these particular muscles refused to cooperate having been neglected for such a long time. A low rumbling, churning growl escaped right on cue. Samson stopped abruptly mid-search. Dark eyes glittering fiercely, he clambered awkwardly to his feet staring intently towards the door looking for the source of the noise, bracing himself for whatever was about to enter. Bungy could see the thought processes going through his mind as Samson instinctively started to move to a position behind the door out of sight. He turned his massive frame and lumbered silently forwards. It was then that the clumsy military boots met their match. Bored with waiting, the trusty skate all of a sudden found itself in the thick of the action. Bungy could hardly believe his luck. Rotating backwards almost in slow motion, one of the heavy boots stepped squarely on to the waiting skate. The skate gleefully shot forwards at a great rate of knots taking Samson's leg with it, completely upending the giant man as if he were light as a feather. It was quite an impressive somersault thought Bungy, as the soldier crashed heavily to the ground. A mini earthquake shook the floor reverberating right to the rafters making the nosy pigeons squawk grumpily, flustered by the tremors vibrating through their nests. Then, all was silent. No signs of movement. *Could a rusty, old roller skate have finished off an elite military spy?*

Bungy waited in disbelief. Seconds passed. He realised he was still holding his breath and the space was getting tighter. He let out a big gasp and could no longer feel the roughness of the bricks pressing on his fur. Samson moaned softly and stirred; sitting up slowly he gently cradled his head in his hands feeling extremely dizzy. The octagonal walls were spinning around him. He grabbed desperately at handfuls of earth, clinging to the floor until the spinning gradually stopped. Looking carefully around as if his head would topple from his shoulders, Samson spotted the roller skate sitting innocently in one of the corners, trying to look inconspicuous thought Bungy.

"What in heaven's name is this? Some kind of infernal device set deliberately as a trap! – coated in some fiendishly sticky substance, designed to leave its mark forever on the enemy. I must remove this foul mess immediately; it is already gluing my hairs together!" Getting groggily to his feet he staggered for the door giving the skate a wide berth, the *clump, clump, clump, clump* of the leather boots receding into the distance. "Phew!" Hardly daring to believe that he had escaped being discovered, Bungy stared at the roller skate – he was convinced it looked smug, having saved the day. Sadly, the syrup cake had taken the brunt of the operation and made the ultimate sacrifice – compressed by the cavalry boot, all that remained were sticky dribbles oozing over the skate wheels and the odd crumb here and there which the pigeons were now eyeing greedily.

★

Bruce's stumpy little legs worked overtime to keep pace with Tal's graceful jog as they bumbled along together following the winding path deeper into the inviting coolness, shaded by the dense, green, leafy umbrella. Fragments of sunshine flashed through gaps in the leaves playing tricks with the light, bouncing off Tal's gleaming red coat like the flickering images in an old slow motion film. They made an odd-looking couple.

"So what exactly happened yesterday when you up and left us all looking stupid after leading us miles off the beaten track to this non-existent village?" ventured Tal trying to control his exasperation.

"Tha's seen t'place for yerself, lad, tha knows it exists."

"I think that was some kind of illusion, some kind of hallucination brought on by sniffing too much wild garlic – it's known to cause strange dreams."

"Don't be daft, lad – how long 'as ye bin visitin' t'woods when t'garlic's in flower? Years I bet, an' ye've never had owt 'appen before. Village is there, ye just 'ave te look carefully an' ye'll see it."

"I'm not sure I want to see it after what happened to me – I'm still having nightmares about it."

"… An' that's nowt te do wi' wild garlic, is it mate? It's all in yer head, lad."

"I'm still not convinced – tell me how to find it then …"

"I stumbled on it by accident. Mindin' mi own business I was – off on one of mi moonlit walks, I loves explorin' when t'moon's full, meks everythin' shine wi' a silvery glow …" Momentarily Bruce stared unseeing into the far distance, lost far away in another moment in time.

"Ahem," Tal coughed theatrically.

"... Where was I, oh aye, so I's tootlin' around down at yon Fox's Folly soakin' up t'moonbeams, when I cocks mi ears te some liltin' music driftin' along on t'breeze – merry little tune it was, how did it go now, let me see erm ..." tilting his head on one side, Bruce racked his brain for a melody which apparently eluded him. Tal was losing patience again.

"Anyways, I wandered over te where t'music were comin' from, funny thing really, as if I were bein' sort of hypnotised, an't music were callin' me. As I gets to t'stream bed where tha follered me I smelled wood smoke an' saw a big ring of fire glowin' through t'trees, and round t'fire there's a group of folks in strange clothes dancin' an havin' a great time. Me, I'll allus mek one for a party, so off I trots to join in t'fun. Right 'ospitable they was too. Shared grub wi' me and let me sleep there wi' that big fella tha met who's built like a bloomin' tree." Tal shuddered involuntarily.

"Next mornin' they gives me more food an' t'big bloke teks me huntin' wi' him which were right good fun so ... I sort of hang around when I feel like it, come an' go as I please, in fact I kinda feel like I belong there ... which is a good feelin', I never really felt at home before – always been alone ... just wanderin' ..." Bruce's voice trailed off wistfully. Tal found he was actually starting to feel sorry for the scoundrel.

"You've still not told me why you ditched us and disappeared without a trace," probed Tal more gently.

"As I looked o'er mi shoulder I could see y'all waitin' under t'trees. When I got t'village passin' t'lonely oak I looked again, and there was nobbdey there – I assumed ye'd gone and got scared on me again, an' run off."

For a moment they looked at one another bemused.

"I stood under t'big tree for a whiles, strainin' mi eyes looking for yous, but got fed up."

"We were doing exactly the same, and cursing you – Pie was fuming. You don't want to get on the wrong side of little Miss Bossy Paws or your nose will be like a tea strainer – I have the scars to prove it. The strange thing is that I keep smelling wood smoke and hearing that infernal clanging of the blacksmith's anvil ringing in my ears when I least expect it, as if the village is haunting me."

"Well, I think it is a kind of magical place in its own way. Strikes me that ye has to be let in, only when t'village decides. Ye's certainly approved of cos tha's bin once afore, but other's ain't, and little Miss Snooty Britches obviously doesn't 'ave what it takes!" Bruce chuckled irreverently, scratching vigorously at the earth with his front paws spraying showers of dust backwards to emphasise his point.

"Hmmm, I don't think it's that simple. We both know the village exists but there's obviously a knack to getting into it."

"Waymarks."

"I beg your pardon," said Tal distracted.

"Tha 'as to use waymarks to find t'way."

"What do you mean?"

"Signs on trees dotted around – if tha knows where to look." Bruce winked conspiratorially. "Course, they're not allus there, best te look for 'em in t'moonlight, they shows up best in t'silvery light. Ancient carvin's, scary faces an' t'like. We've just missed full moon – best get yerself down Fox's Folly and look for 'em next time round." With that cheeky challenge, he dived sideways into the undergrowth and vanished.

Tal whipped round stunned. Yet again the wily terrier had given him the slip. He sniffed frantically at the mass of brambles but there was no lingering scent; it was as if he had been conversing with a ghost, one that had melted back into the spirit of the trees, perhaps from where it came?

Stepping from the path into a sunny glade Tal gathered his scattered wits. The conversation, and Bruce, had been very real. He at least had gleaned some information, far-fetched though it was, something in his bones told him it was still worth following up. Setting off back to the cottage he started to count the number of days to the next full moon.

The cottage door was wide open when he finally trotted up the path twenty minutes later, his brain smarting from all the mental arithmetic. He sauntered into the house having prepared his speech to the others; head high, feeling quietly elated that he had solved the riddle of the mysterious disappearing community in the woods. But there was no sign of life anywhere. Surely Pie wasn't still holed up in that smelly, hairy box of hers. He bravely nudged the corner of the lid open a fraction screwing up his nose, wincing in anticipation of a sudden swipe of the claw. The box was empty. Wandering into the kitchen he found the pantry door wide open – most unheard of. Even more extraordinary, there was no grey and white cat opportunistically perusing the shelves. Where was everyone – why did everybody keep vanishing around him today? Glancing through the patio door he spotted the end of a brown and cream tail sticking out from under the woodshed.

"Having fun under there?" he yelled into the gloom.

There was a loud thump followed by some unrepeatable muffled exclamation. Pie wriggled out backwards, her fur laced with dead spiders and dusty webs. "Can't see the attraction myself," she spat, seemingly flustered and most unlike her usual collected self. "Can't understand why my brother spends so much time under there, in fact I don't know how he manages to get under there!"

"So what are you doing spending time under there when you are supposed to be … *'thinking'?*"

"My aforesaid mentioned stupid brother appears to have completely disappeared. I've scoured all his favourite haunts leaving this dreadful place until last, but to no avail. He's now missed two meals so it must be serious!"

Not another one, I must be jinxed, thought Tal watching Pie carefully, as if she might suddenly become transparent in front of his eyes.

"I'm worried he might have been kidnapped by that angry spy who is looking for Amos. We have to find him."

Day turned to night and the pigeons folded their wings comfortably settling down to sleep. The darkness in the dovecote became impenetrable, thick and black. Nothing stirred. There was no sound, no light, except for the merest whisper of breath, the slightest glint of a sad eye and a pale, whitish glow tucked far away in a hidden corner.

13

A Tight Spot

Elias, a man of the shadows, was used to clandestine activities. He smiled inwardly, amused by the idea that this was just another stalking expedition but this time the stakes were much higher. He felt his way along instinctively, embracing the blackness of night which enveloped him, made him invisible. As the witching hour of midnight struck, he had left the camp silently to plan the route to Langhald Hall along which he would lead the unsuspecting Royalist troops into a trap. The troops, all young and passionate about the cause, looked up to him and respected his tracking prowess – they would follow him anywhere, innocent of what lay ahead. A delicious prospect, but something lurked in his conscience that soured the enjoyment. Mentally batting the nagging doubt away, he pushed on. Feeling the energies flow through his twisted hazel staff driving him along, his trunk-like legs covered the ground in giant strides.

Reaching the edge of the long wood he became aware of a pale luminous glow in the clearing. The waning moon radiated off the solid limestone walls of a magnificent house set high on a bank overlooking the lake – a ghostly presence in the all-consuming darkness. It had a sweeping flight of stone steps up to an elaborate, triangular portico entrance supported by huge columns which covered almost half the front of the house. On the three points of the triangle stood elegant statues facing different ways, each one looking out into the night, pointing into the distance, stone guardians scanning the horizon. Elias had never seen such an enormous building before and couldn't imagine why anyone would need so many rooms, each with full-length windows crowned with ornate, sculptured lintels. The house was really making a statement. He wondered what sort of people built something of these proportions and grandeur. There were six windows at the front on both floors and probably the same again at the back. Having lived in nothing other than his simple tent, he tried to picture himself wandering the corridors, walking through the endless rooms, a prospect that soon became suffocating and had him searching frantically for the imaginary door to escape back into the countryside he so loved. Just the thought made him feel claustrophobic – he took a deep breath of cool night air and surveyed the landscape.

Even in the dead of night he could make out the swooping undulations of the fields and textured shapes of the trees. A sense of calm washed over him; the countryside was home – no man-made walls would ever constrain him. Behind the house stood a row of rectangular stone buildings grouped around a central courtyard next to a walled garden. Through the entrance Elias could make out a pair of large, arched coach house doors big enough to accommodate a carriage drawn by four horses. This must be the stable yard which covered at least double the area of the house and was probably home to at least fifty horses.

The scale of the place was not what he'd been expecting, and, for the first time, Elias realised the enormity of the mission the Royalists were attempting – he was certain they had no idea what they were taking on. Worse than that, Elias had to somehow foil their plot and would have to now revise his ideas if he were to succeed in reaching Cromwell before they did. In his shovel-sized hand the gnarled hazel stick quivered in his grasp interrupting his deliberations. Not for the first time did he thank the ancient properties of hazel to bring the spirit to life. He felt its energies course again through his fingers, reinvigorating his whole being; with nature as his inspiration he would face no barriers in his task. A distant hue of pale pink in the sky hinted dawn was on its way; it was time to return to the camp before he was missed. Turning his huge tree-like frame away from the hall, he melded into the wood and disappeared.

★

Tiny pricks of light danced on his eyelids heralding a new morning and hopefully the chance of rescue. The pigeons had been inconsiderate bedfellows, flapping their wings at all hours of the night constantly shifting position. Bungy was sure they had done it on purpose to add to his misery. They glared down at him from on high in a kind of Mexican standoff not sure if it was safe to leave the nesting box with a predator so close at hand. Bungy was not inclined to let them feel any different – he was in a bad mood; they would have to stay put and wait for their meals like him. It was a bit worrying that Amos had not returned to his bed last night. What could possibly have happened to him?

During the long, dark, lonely hours of the night, his mind had wandered abstractly, he had let it roam freely hoping it might come up with a solution to his predicament. The only thing it had clearly recalled was a recent conversation with Pie who had been bossily nagging him about his weight, her favourite subject, warning him that one day his expanding tummy would get him into trouble, "Just like Winnie the Pooh," she had stated in a matter-of-fact way.

"Winnie the who?" he'd challenged her back.

"Winnie the Pooh – a bear that went to visit his friend Rabbit and got trapped in the entrance to his burrow, because of his generous waistline." She emphasised the word 'generous', disdainfully lowering her deep, green eyes on to the soft expanse of flesh that spread uncontrollably over his back paws like a deflated beachball, as he sat in front of her.

"How long was he stuck there?" he'd ventured.

"A week," came the reply.

"A week?!!" he'd exclaimed. '… And how on earth did he escape?" he'd enquired, already guessing the answer.

"By starving himself until his tummy was smaller than the space he was stuck in …" his sister had informed him gleefully. "Something you could never aspire to doing – it would take months in your case."

Even his own mind was against him, taking cruel pleasure in digging up that memory at this particular time. If anyone bothered to look for him, he knew he was looking at a Pooh-type scenario, whether he liked it or not. Suddenly the pigeons were not that appetising.

★

"There is nowhere else he could be," sighed Pie, chewing nervously at the end of her tail. Tal had never seen her this agitated. "He evidently didn't come back after delivering the cake; the pantry is untouched and the door wide open – it speaks for itself. Heavens knows what terrible things he has had to endure at the hands of that brute."

Tal felt empty inside, shuddering to think what might have happened. He could still feel the ground shaking as the colossal bulk of Samson the spy had catapulted out of the dovecote door a foot away from their hiding place behind the hay baler. He seemed demented, in a frenzy, alternately slapping his head and arms, he staggered blindly towards the farmyard as fast as his military boots would allow. As he flashed by Tal was sure he'd caught a clinging sickly whiff of treacle in the air. The spy was in such a rage that they had not dared to venture into the dovecote in case he returned. Dejectedly they'd headed back to the safety of the cottage, feeling thoroughly rotten for being such cowards.

The kitchen clock ticked loudly, intruding on their thoughts. Time marched on relentlessly as they dithered about what to do. After an hour of awkward silence they reached the same conclusion at the same moment.

"We have to brazen this out, get in there and search for Bungy. It's likely Samson will give the dovecote a wide berth in the next few hours, judging by his rapid departure – something exceptionally terrifying must have occurred. I just hope my idiotic brother managed to keep out of the way." Pie recovered her composure and put on her usual 'I'm in charge' expression. Tal tried hard to look confident but his stomach churned as a hundred giant butterflies beat a tattoo. Lurchers were not known for being bold; they were much better at long-range speed and agility, preferably running in the opposite direction from danger he thought nervously. Minutes later they were positioned strategically under the hay baler concealed behind a large dirty tyre, taking it in turns to peer out at the dovecote, scanning the immediate area for signs of life. Everything seemed disconcertingly normal. On the surface a quiet, calm day in the countryside.

The baler reeked of oil mixed with a dry, dusty aroma of hay which snatched at their throats. Tal also caught the unmistakable smell of burning leaves, a scent which had begun to haunt him. He looked around for a pall of smoke as he had done before but was slowly beginning to realise the source of the smell burned in another time, a time where he had a parallel life perhaps. No, Pie was still beside him – pulling faces actually, screwing up her nose. Her eyes had become slits as she fought to stifle the large sneeze that crept like a massive itch through her fur, building to an unstoppable tickling crescendo, threatening to give them away. Tal panicked trying to distract her with a gentle brush of the whiskers, shrinking away quickly, anticipating a prickly retaliatory swipe on the nose.

Too late.

"Aaaatishoooo!" A loud, noisy splutter rocketed into the silence as the giant sneeze escaped violently almost knocking Pie off her dainty paws. They flattened themselves against the tyre holding their breath, hoping desperately that no one had noticed. Tal sniffed the air. He peeked out carefully, nothing and no one as far as he could see. Trusting his Lurcher instincts he noiselessly gestured to Pie with a sideways nod that the coast was clear and they slunk

round the wheel into the welcome warmth of the sunshine.

Psssst! A sudden hissing sound punctured the silence. *Psssst!* There it was again, more insistent this time. Tal whipped round expecting to see the massive tyre starting to deflate. It was then that the tarpaulin covering the large machine started to ripple and rise slowly into the air like a hideous green monster coming out of hibernation. The sinister shape grew menacingly into a formless mound. *Psssst!!!* The noise apparently came from beneath the canvas. Transfixed, too frightened to move, Tal caught a glimpse of an extravagant moustache and scared blue eyes as the canvas rose higher to reveal a bedraggled Amos.

"By the Heavens, am I pleased to see you!" he stuttered. "What a night I have passed, what strange proceedings I have witnessed and what stories I have to tell," he garbled, struggling to counter the combined weight of the heavy canvas and his rough cloak as he clambered out of the trailer.

"We're in the middle of a rescue mission," replied Tal in a loud whisper, trying to maintain their cover. "Bungy has been missing all night after he came out to bring you a cake he and I liberated from the pantry. All we know is that Samson flew out of the dovecote yesterday as if being chased by a swarm of bees—"

"And my darling brother hasn't been seen since ..." interrupted Pie.

"We must find the poor fellow at once!" With no hesitation Amos, now safely on the ground, promptly flung his cloak over his shoulder, gathered his pike from the trailer and set off determinedly towards the dovecote with the others tagging along behind.

"So much for stealth," muttered Pie under her breath.

The solid wooden door was still ajar where Samson had shouldered it open as he ran, seemingly, for his life. Amos' few meagre possessions were scattered in disarray over the dusty floor, some coated in ash from the cold embers of his last fire – the heart of his temporary 'home'. Amid the disorder a peculiar sight greeted them. In the corner against the wall lurked an unfamiliar object. Leaning wonkily, having lost a wheel in the heat of battle, the intrepid skate sat nonchalantly as if it belonged there, at home yet at the same time out of place. Baffled, Amos approached the skate cautiously keeping at a discreet distance.

"By my whiskers, what strange contraption is this? And what is it doing in here?" Deciding the interesting object wasn't dangerous, Amos knelt down for a closer inspection. A thick, brown, glue-like substance coated the object and a not unpleasant sweetness worked on his taste buds.

"That strange contraption saved my life," came a disembodied reply from the gloom. Startled, the three friends strained their eyes towards the back wall where a faint white glow was just visible at floor level.

"Bungy, my dear friend – you are safe! What excellent news …" Amos rejoiced.

"What on earth are you doing down there?" Pie queried crossly whilst hiding her obvious relief.

"Bird spotting – what do you think?" Bungy shot back tetchily.

"I think a little praise is in order." Tal waded in to Bungy's defence. "After all he was unselfishly looking after Amos and almost got caught by that ruthless spy."

"Well, he could have made his way home and saved us all the bother of worrying, I mean, searching for him …"

Pie hurriedly corrected herself pretending to wash her paws as she tried to hide her concern.

"Believe me, I would have dearly loved to come home but I'm afraid it's not that simple," he sighed. "Just call me Winnie the Pooh."

"Winnie the *who* …?" asked Tal, bemused.

"You're not … don't tell me it's finally happened?" An *'I told you so'* expression crept slyly across Pie's face.

"What's happened?" said Tal, feeling he'd missed something.

"What type of being is a 'Pooh' when it's at home?" Amos asked in wonder.

"You're stuck down there, aren't you!" scoffed Pie knowingly, getting into her stride.

"I might be … just resting, but …" Bungy's voice trailed off. "Yes …" he sighed resignedly. "I am completely stuck."

"Aha! Well, perhaps you'll listen to me in the future … I—"

"I think we should help the little fellow escape," interjected Amos seeing a lecture developing. "After all, he was doing me a favour, and I think he's had enough of a lesson already at the hands of our 'friend' Samson. Now tell me about this 'Pooh' character and what befell him."

"Winnie the Pooh, a rather well-endowed bear, went visiting his friend Rabbit and got stuck in the entrance to his burrow, courtesy of his large round tummy. He was stuck for a week and had to starve the whole time to *slim down* enough to escape. His friends read to him to keep him company whilst he was stuck – so the story goes," replied Pie.

"Well, we'd better find an appropriate manuscript and get on with it. In my time cats have the opposite problem – very scrawny creatures, hunting day and night to survive," sighed Amos witheringly. "Who is going to take first turn?"

Tal was despatched to the cottage for some reading material. He wasn't a big reader so hadn't a clue what to look for. Fifteen minutes later they were all seated in a semicircle around Bungy flicking through the pages of *Favourite Fish Recipes* which Tal had found lying on the kitchen table. They settled on *'Tasty Tuna Melts'* and began with the list of ingredients. "Two prime tuna steaks ..." Pie started to read with a mischievous glint in her eye. "Butter, cheese and cream ..." Bungy's taste buds sprang to life. "Mix together in a bowl."

Starting to drool he begged them, "Stop, please! This is torture," but Pie was having her moment and proceeded to read the rest of the recipe licking her whiskers in pure pleasure.

"I can't stand thirty seconds of this let alone a week," he moaned.

"Next one." Pie turned over the page and scanned the recipe theatrically. "Cod in butter sauce – delicate flakes of lean cod slowly braised in a rich sauce ... hmmm ... sounds delicious." Out of the corner of her eye she saw her brother start to wriggle back and forth like a desperate chicken trying to part with an oversized egg. Backwards and forwards he rocked in a frantic rhythm, his eyes standing out with the effort. *"Phooooooooooooo,"* he eventually slumped on the floor like a balloon deflating.

The pigeons leaned forward nosily to watch the spectacle; one brave inquisitive soul even took a tentative fly past to assess the situation. Realising their unwelcome guest was no longer a threat, the pigeon turned for another pass, releasing a cheeky missile on the gathering below which just glanced the tip of Bungy's ear as it spattered to the floor joining the pile of smelly droppings that surrounded him. "Oi!" yelled Bungy glaring upwards. *Splaaaat!* He was being dive-bombed by the defiant pigeon that was now circling ready to swoop again. Bungy felt frustration welling inside him like a volcano until he thought he would explode with pent-up energy that just grew and grew. He'd show that cocky, feathered upstart, if only ... His whiskers started to twitch with an electrifying charge that rippled up his nose, down to his paws and along his spine. He was no longer in control of his actions – an imaginary force had taken over his being and was building and building ... The pigeon turned and stooped acrobatically in Bungy's direction showing off to his mates, sights locked on his target accelerating for maximum impact. *"Heeeeeyaaaawwww!"* an ear-splitting howl bounced around the walls as a grey and white flash flew into the air followed by a loud thud and a violent clapping sound. A tangle of fur and feathers lay at Tal's feet. The nesting box prison was empty. Jubilant and slightly dazed, Bungy turned to his friends who looked at him in amazement, "Pigeon pie anyone?" he enquired.

14

Food for Thought

Legs pumping like pistons, Samson hurtled towards the sanctuary of the hen house at breakneck speed, eyes stinging from the sticky substance clotted in his eyebrows that mingled with the perspiration running down his forehead. His mind whirled, trying to work out what was happening. *What dastardly evil potion is it that coats my skin, sticks my fingers and hairs together? I will probably be poisoned and die a slow, horrible, painful death alone trapped in this strange other world.* Hastily ducking to manoeuvre his large frame through the small wire door, he tripped stubbing the toe of one of the hefty boots which sent him flying horizontally towards the back of the coup past a row of startled hens. He landed with a loud *crrrump* face down in a pile of straw and feathers. Sitting up, eyes half closed against the cloud of dust, he dizzily watched the tiny white stars swirling around inside his head. Carefully he tried moving his limbs – much to his surprise nothing appeared to be broken. A wave of relief swept over his battered body. He had managed to escape safely, intact and could now hopefully get on with planning his next move.

As the dust settled and the tiny stars gradually subsided he looked down at his hands and arms. Something most odd had occurred – layers of feathers had appeared where his skin used to be. All the way up his arms, all over his hands, even between his fingers, sprouted a coat of speckled feathers interwoven with bits of straw. In total horror, he lifted a feathered hand towards his face. Where there was once rugged and weather-beaten skin grew a soft mask of straw and feathers. *I am a victim of fiendish black magic; the evil potion is slowly transforming me into a chicken!* Turning to a nearby water trough he leaned with apprehension to look into its murky depths. An extraordinary reflection, half man, half bird stared back at him – even his ears sprouted tufts like an owl. Rubbing frantically at his arms the feathers refused to budge, cemented to his skin by syrupy crumbs. In desperation he resorted to plucking them off one by one as if preparing a giant chicken for the roasting spit. The more he plucked the more the feathers attached themselves to his fingers; no amount of shaking got rid of them. *What kind of wicked torment is this … is a brave warrior destined to spend the rest of his days clucking, scratching and pecking? I must halt the spread of these bewitched feathers at all costs!* After a frustrated hour making no progress, he plunged his limbs one by one into the water trough scrubbing vigorously until his skin was raw and piles of sodden feathers littered the floor. Slumped in a corner, exhausted and itchy, he vowed to seek revenge. Never in history, before or since, has an innocent syrup cake and a rusty old roller skate caused such a commotion. It was, the hens agreed, the most amusing spectacle they had experienced in years, even more entertaining than watching the greedy, fat, grey and white cat with the silly grin being chased, belly wobbling, across the yard by the drooling farm dog the size of a small Shetland pony.

Adrenaline pumped through Bungy's veins, he had never before felt so alive and so ... *hungry*. Waddling over to the abandoned skate he inspected it carefully for any loose crumbs, resorting to licking off any morsels that were not completely glued on, his rough tongue rasping against the metal. The skate looked slightly indignant he thought; this was probably not the kind of treatment that befitted a hero. Feeling uncomfortable, Bungy sauntered back to the others who were busying themselves gathering together the remnants of Amos' belongings, and clearing a space to build a fire. Pie had called another of her 'meetings' and was occupied with a pre-meeting wash to ensure she looked her best. Tal was despatched to the kitchen again, this time for food – most disgruntled that he seemingly had been demoted to 'gofer' when only he knew the secret to finding the village and solving the mystery of getting Amos home. He returned with a box of small gravy bones, two cold sausages and some extremely sweaty cheese which announced its arrival before reaching the door. Amos delved into his pockets and turned out a handful of early blackberries for dessert. Pigeon pie was off the menu as the daring, dive-bombing pigeon had apparently only been stunned and managed to shuffle silently into the shadows whilst their backs were turned.

"A lot has happened in the last twenty-four hours." Pie adopted her 'very important' pose as she spoke. "I have been *thinking,* and got some ideas to share. I would have had a *plan* but my thinking time was rudely interrupted by having to rescue my stup ... my most courageous brother."

Glaring at Bungy she continued. "It seems Amos has news of an adventure overnight and Tal, er ... well, Tal ... went for one of his walks – nothing useful to report there." Tal's fur bristled in indignation. *Humph ... nothing useful ... little do you know,* he thought quietly, biding his time for the right moment to reveal what he had discovered. All eyes turned expectantly towards Amos.

"Well, fellow companions ... I decided I should seek the village alone. I do not wish to place my new friends in further danger. There are menacing strangers at large it seems, and perils from my own time that I believe I should face on my own, even though you are each most heroic and fearless. So, I followed the path to the edge of the wood yesterday evening hoping the village would appear. I am now convinced there are some mysterious forces at work, as the fields were once again empty." *I know why,* thought Tal.

"Frustrated, I turned back for the village and found myself in the midst of battle. Shots rang about my head and the sky rained pheasants. I was struck on the head by a partridge as it fell to the ground. Along the edge of the wood a line of men in rough clothes marched in my direction swishing large sticks, beating the undergrowth and shouting at the top of their voices. In front of them, helpless, panic-stricken birds hiding in the reeds leapt skywards, squawking in a frenzy of fear, only to plummet to the ground seconds later as a volley of gunfire echoed from the trees. Small excitable dogs ran hither and thither across the field, retrieving the poor birds which hung limply from their mouths. Several times I had to duck as gunshot whistled passed my ears. Then suddenly it fell quiet and, from the shadow of the trees, some twenty men in smart green attire bearing large shotguns stepped into the light, walking as one towards me. I spent the rest of the afternoon hiding in the bushes. It all happened so quickly. I was not paying much attention to the men themselves, but one of the beaters, at the end of the line nearest to me, caught my eye. He stood head and shoulders above the others and took one stride for every two taken by the rest of the men. He was dressed in what appeared to be scraps of sacking held together by large buckles, distinctly untidy compared to the others, but it was his large hat topped with a plume of feathers that looked out of place, yet strangely familiar.

"The 'tree man' known as Elias," interrupted Tal. "What's he doing involved in the local shoot?"

"Ah, this is your name for the battle I witnessed."

"It's called sport in our time. It's specially organised and people pay a lot of money to take part," added Tal.

"Hmm … you have strange customs in your world. We hunt for survival where I come from …" said Amos incredulous. "Anyway, in the end I made a den in the wood and spent the night there thinking I might find the village when there was no one around. Instead, I had the company of a rather annoying owl which took up residence in the tree above me and insisted on hooting each time I was drifting to sleep, as if trying to tell me something. I was also disturbed by the distant tolling of a bell, quite haunting I might say … though, I have now seen Elias with my own eyes. I must find a way to make contact with him and discover why and how he has travelled in time like me."

"I may have the ans— " Tal saw an opportunity but was cut off in mid- sentence.

"I have been working on a theory ... ahem," Pie butted in, placing herself in the middle of the floor to command attention as she prepared for her announcement, "I think it is time to explain what I—"

"Just a minute, just a minute ..." Tal could wait no longer and jumped to his feet standing in front of Pie.

"Can a fellow get a word in sideways here? I have some vital information." Pausing for maximum effect, relishing the moment, he took a deep breath.

"Oh for goodness' sake, what information could *you* possibly have? How to identify a hare at thirty paces," Pie scoffed disdainfully, walking underneath Tal to sit by his side looking bored.

"As a matter of fact, I had an extremely interesting conversation with Bruce yesterday."

"*Pah!* That scruffy, good-for-nothing mongrel! I wouldn't believe a word he said ... but then we all know that dogs are stupid," Pie snorted.

"Ah, well, that's just where you're wrong Little Miss Know It All—"

"Research confirms that cats are the more intelligent species, I have an article that proves it."

"Dogs are more sociable ... and—"

"Oh! For heaven's sake, can we hear what he has to say. I am four hundred years from home, any tidings are good ones," pleaded Amos.

Bungy rolled his eyes and quietly worked his way through both sausages, lining up the cheese for seconds.

"Well, like Amos, I also had a strange experience. I encountered Bruce in the top wood, so I yelled at him to stop and explain why he had abandoned us. But the

141

weird thing is it was as if he couldn't see me. He trotted right passed me as if I was invisible. So I followed him to a clearing under some oak trees where all of a sudden he saw me. We went through the wood together and he told me how he had first come across the village."

"Well, that's really helpful information. I must say," Pie countered sarcastically, inspecting her claws for something to do.

"... And how to find it ..." Amos, eyes gleaming, leaned closer to Tal.

"Pray tell us the secret," he whispered.

"You have to follow the waymarks."

"*Ffffmmmfff* ... what's a waymark?" asked Bungy, a mouth full of sweaty cheese sticking his teeth together.

"Ah, the ancient folklore of waymarks," nodded Amos knowingly. Pie pricked up her ears still pretending to be bored.

"Apparently waymarks, ancient signs carved on trees, can be seen most clearly in moonlight, especially around the time of the full moon. Bruce follows waymarks in Fox's Folly Wood and always finds the village. He also said it's a magical place and the village decides whether you can be let in or not." Tal glanced at Pie then looked swiftly away.

"That's all very well, but we still don't have anything useful to go on," retorted Pie. "We're still no wiser."

"Bruce's suggestion was to go to Fox's Folly Wood at the next full moon and look for the waymarks." Tal sat back on his hind legs and stared into the fire. "The next full moon is in exactly two and a half weeks from tonight. I worked it out."

"Cor ... nice one, matey," mumbled Bungy, sniffing

one of the gravy bones suspiciously. "We can perhaps have a bit of a break then from this spy malarkey, and get back to normal for a few days. I fancy a bit of hunting. Think I'll toddle down to the hen house for a bit of rustling."

"We absolutely can not have any 'time off'," spluttered Pie. "We have to find out as much as we can about the events of the Civil War to see if there are any clues that might shed light on the presence of Elias the hunter and Samson the spy. We need to know more about Langhald Hall ..."

"And we need to find out when General Cromwell made his visit to the village," Amos added. "My bones are telling me his visit, mine, the spy's and that of Elias are connected in some way."

"Didn't I mention when we last spoke about local history that I'd found the date of Cromwell's visit? Silly me ..." shrugged Pie with a kittenish look designed to disarm any negative remarks.

"It was the 5th of October 1643."

"Six and a half weeks from tonight," murmured Tal slowly into the hushed silence. "Another full moon."

15

A Spellbinding Performance

Light cascaded from the tiny windows of the village hall falling in neat squares on the green outside. Pie stepped daintily from square to square making her way to a position on the windowsill as if playing an imaginary game of hopscotch. Inside, the hum of animated chatter could be heard over the clatter and clink of teacups as the audience assembled for the local history group meeting. Tonight's speaker, Bertha Peasegood, was an expert on the English Civil War. A small, stout, formidable-looking woman with manly features, she was dressed in a long, green, hairy tweed skirt, orange sweater and red beret set at a jaunty angle, a pair of pince-nez glasses perched precariously on the bridge of her nose. An impudent thought scurried across Pie's mind then disappeared as quickly as it arrived, *That woman looks like a set of traffic lights,* Pie chuckled to herself, getting comfortable on the stone sill which was quite cool on her slim bottom. Autumn was definitely in the air. Once again she congratulated herself on her resourcefulness, on spotting the sign on the village notice board advertising the meeting. She couldn't believe her eyes when she saw the topic; it was as if fate had played a hand and was helping them in their quest.

Bertha twiddled impatiently with her pencil waiting for the hubbub to subdue. Gradually people began to take their seats. Outside Amos hovered nervously on the threshold, the tatty green gardening coat which had again been dragged from the shed, hung limply from his shoulders. He looked more like a tramp seeking a warming cup of tea than an amateur historian. Tal gently nudged the back of his knees encouraging him to take a tentative step through the doorway, the scraping of chairs signalling the meeting was about to begin. Tal gave Amos a heftier shove, the momentum of which catapulted them both into the stark, white fluorescent light of the hall. Many heads swivelled in unison craning their necks, curious as to the disturbance. Eagle- eyed Bertha was on her feet in a trice. "Sir! No animals are allowed in the hall. Please remove your dog this minute," she commanded, as if issuing military instructions to an army. More interested faces turned to look at Amos; not exactly the kind of entrance he had planned – low key was more what he was hoping for. Pie cringed and gave Tal a withering look as he made a quick exit.

"Can't you do anything right?" she hissed. Amos pretended not to hear Bertha's remark and shuffled to a seat on the back row. People in the adjoining chairs looked alarmed and hurriedly moved up to the next available seats, eyeing the unkempt stranger with wary suspicion across the wide gap which now thankfully yawned between them. Bertha tapped furiously with her pencil on the side of a glass making a loud ringing noise and everyone obediently faced the front as if once again at school.

A thin, mousy woman seated at the top table stood up to make the introductions but Bertha had been kept waiting long enough. As the woman opened her mouth to speak Bertha swept out of her chair round the front of the table, like a galleon under full sail, to take control of proceedings. The mousy woman seemed to collapse into a ball, disappearing behind Bertha's stocky frame and sinking quietly back to her chair.

"Tonight, Ladies and Gentleman ..." Bertha's foghorn voice rang round the hall, bouncing off the walls and light fittings. "Together, we will journey back four hundred years to the time of the English Civil War. We will learn about the important strategic role your twee, *ahem,* picture-postcard, village played in this bloody conflict and, in particular, hear about a most daring event that almost changed the course of the war, and history, *forever!*" The sentence ended with great emphasis on the word 'forever' and a sweeping upward flourish of the pencil like a conductor with a baton. She peered over her glasses keenly surveying the rows of chairs for reaction to her dramatic opening remarks. She liked to start with an impact. The audience, hardly daring to breathe, sat riveted to their seats. Then, in hushed tones, "And, we will also delve into legends of the mysterious spirit world, meeting the ghosts that reputedly still move silently through your village." She paused for effect, leaving the words hanging in the air. A palpable, electric current ran through the room, hairs prickled simultaneously on the back of forty necks. Bertha was a professional; the audience were in the palm of her hand, where she liked them to be; now she could begin her talk in earnest.

"In the summer of 1642, daily life changed irreversibly for one and all, with the advent of the English Civil War. The war, in many cases, pitched family member against family member and tore apart households on a massive scale. Nowhere was this terrible torment experienced more than in small settlements like this one, as countrymen were forced to pledge their allegiance to either the Royalist or Parliamentarian cause. The countryside became a vast battlefield, harvests were left to rot and properties plundered. Nearly a quarter of a million people lost their lives and the fighting continued for almost nine years. Even today, the war is sometimes still used by politicians in judging their contemporaries; 'Which side would he have liked his ancestors to fight on in the battle of Marston Moor?' is a question often raised in the heat of political debate." Bertha ploughed on. Amos felt the room start to spin. Struggling to focus on Bertha's voice, he was being pulled far away; she was speaking now as an echo from the end of an extremely long tunnel. His head reeled; a leaden, sickly feeling twisted his stomach inside out. *Nine years, a quarter of a million people,* the phrase ricocheted round and round in his head. He felt dizzy – tried to digest what he had heard. *What madness is this, do my ears deceive me?* A montage of images swam in front of his eyes; troops marching, pennants flying, his lathe turning a smooth ash pike, the King on horseback greeting villagers as he rode by. The heavy coat was pulling on his shoulders, a yoke round his neck making him hot, yet his skin felt clammy. A shiver rippled through his body despite the heat. Steadily he tried to steer his mind back to the present; it was vital to focus. "Focus, focus ..." he whispered to himself.

"The first battle, the Battle of Edgehill, took place on a dramatic escarpment on the 23rd October 1642. As the Cavaliers ploughed into the beleaguered Parliamentarians with their vicious fifteen-foot pikes, it looked as if fortune favoured the King, but in the end the battle ended as a draw with some fifteen hundred lives lost. Does anyone know what pikes were made of?" The question flung at the audience caused a flurry of uncomfortable wriggling, people pretended to look for a tissue or clean their glasses. "Ash." The words escaped Amos' lips without warning. As soon as they hit the air, Amos wished fervently he could wrestle them back in again. Bertha strode into the aisle to identify the mystery voice, scanning the room expectantly. Amos shrank down in his chair trying to be small and invisible. Bertha was not a woman to keep waiting. After a few seconds when it was obvious no one wanted to claim the statement, she bustled on answering her own question. "Well, someone in the room is well informed but unfortunately very shy – pikes were indeed made of ash. You have an abundance of ash trees in this area; this would have been a hive of industry at the time of the war." Amos pulled the collar of the coat above his ears disappearing into its folds, and vowed to stay silent from now on at all costs.

Bertha went on to describe a litany of horrific events in graphic detail, a most theatrical performance. The Local History Group was certainly getting value for their money. It was a relief when the interval arrived and the cheerful bubbling of the tea urn brought an element of normality back to the proceedings. Amos quietly slipped outside into the cool night air boggled by what he had heard. He couldn't decide whether to be thankful for what he'd learned or whether it would have been better to have remained ignorant. Either way, it was the strangest experience to be caught in a timeless limbo where future meets past, a past he had not yet lived. Pie shuffled along the windowsill until she was level with his right ear.

"What a performer!" she whispered.

Amos, still in shock, startled out of deep thinking, took a few moments to grasp his whereabouts. "My friend, I am speechless. It is overwhelming and I need time to digest everything. I fear I cannot return for more."

Pie's huge eyes fixed him with a kind but steely stare. "Oh, but you must go back Amos, the second half is about the village and its part in the conflict. There could be clues that will help us get you home again ..." She gave him her sweetest smile and rubbed her head affectionately against his cheek. Amos knew she was right. It was vital to find out as much as possible; this could be their only opportunity. Hearing the *trrrring* of Bertha's pencil calling everyone to order, he sidled back to his seat at the last minute.

The warmth of the tiny packed hall hit him like walking into the blacksmith's forge with the furnace fully stoked. Momentarily, the hot stifling air felt too thick to breathe, until his nose got used to the dryness. Modern heating was one invention he could highly recommend; his modest woodland shelter was draughty and damp at the best of times. The ornamental wall lights had been dimmed slightly for atmospheric effect and Bertha had swapped her red beret for a black velvet affair studded with tiny sequins which twinkled in the light as she moved her head. Around her shoulders was thrown a black shawl fringed with diamante and feathers. She reminded Amos of the travelling band of tinkers which would arrive in the village bringing with them women reputed to be clairvoyant and have healing powers. The women were often dressed in the most ornate

149

costumes and wore shawls decorated with beads; he was never sure whether they were, in truth, witches and always kept his distance. Bertha was weaving her own kind of spell now as she turned again to address the audience, small sparkles encircling her head. "We come now to what I call the 'folklore' surrounding the war and the remarkable events which, legend has it, took place right here in your village." Amos sat to attention, bewitched like the rest of the audience, by Bertha's enchantment.

"Many of you will be familiar with the story of Langhald Hall, said to be the most grand Palladian-style house for miles around. Sadly, only the cellars and the stable block remain today." A murmur ran round the room.

One brave soul ventured, "I'm afraid you may be mistaken, madam. To our knowledge nothing remains of the house – including the cellars."

Bertha rose on to her tiptoes to reinforce her point. "I can assure you, sir, my archaeological friends reliably inform me that the cellars are intact. Their exact location is marked by a single evergreen oak tree." She gave a false smile. "My friends are professionals; they are never wrong … now where was I …"

Amos sat up even straighter. "Not long after the start of the war, Langhald Hall was the scene of a quite unbelievable event, which almost altered the course of history itself. Originally a struggling yeoman farmer from the fenlands of East Anglia, one man rose swiftly through the ranks of the Roundhead army due to his skills in horsemanship and credentials as a cavalry commander. This man gained influential friends and allies, one of whom, Sir Randolph Knight owner of Langhald Hall, invited the commander to visit his manor house. Randolph Knight went on to become a distinguished Parliamentarian officer; his invited guest was Oliver Cromwell." Another hushed gasp travelled through the audience. "This occurrence is well documented, but what is less well known is that on the night of Cromwell's visit, a small band of renegade Royalist infantrymen hatched a daring plan to ambush and kidnap Cromwell then hold him for ransom."

"By my whiskers!" Amos smothered an exclamation with a fake spluttering cough. Realisation dawned with the force of a lightning bolt. A scramble of fragmented jigsaw pieces started to rearrange themselves in his mind, a picture was forming.

"We think the protagonists must have been disturbed, or Randolph Knight was forewarned, because the plan failed. It was discovered later that Cromwell had hidden in the cellars for several days until the coast was clear. You can imagine had they been successful, the outcome of the war may have been quite different, history re-written in fact!

"It is said a phantom horse can be heard galloping past the oak tree at the time of the full moon, supposedly carrying Cromwell to safety. And there is yet more intrigue. The stable block is also said to be haunted by the ghost of the 'Green Lady', the teenage daughter of a local Royalist family who fell in love with Sir Randolph. Legend has it that they would meet in secret in the Long Wood behind the stables. However, one night when the young Roundhead officer arrived to meet his lover, he found her brother waiting for him instead – sword in hand. When the girl came to keep her tryst, she found the body of her lover lying on the path. Overcome with grief, she threw herself into the lake. Her body was recovered the next day, wrapped like a shroud in weed and slimy green leaves. Some years later the bell on the stable clock tower started to toll, apparently of its own accord, usually between midnight and two in the morning, the time the young man met his demise. Sometimes at night the most chilling wailing noises have allegedly been heard echoing around the woods, a noise so strange – human, yet not human ..." The words hung suspended in the air. "It has been reported by ramblers that a figure cloaked in green weed, dripping in stagnant water, has appeared walking from the shadows then vanished into the trees. The Green Lady, still searching for her lost love."

Amos realised his mouth was gaping open, like a hungry goldfish, as he gawped in realisation at these fascinating events, which actually made some sense to him – he knew he was the only member of the audience who could knit together all the information and make a complete, living picture ... Hmmm ... there was still one piece of the jigsaw missing; he wondered whether he dare ask a question, though Bertha's *pièce de résistance*, the sensational revelation about the doomed love affair, had taken him completely by surprise. He ventured a look round and noticed stunned expressions on many faces. It had been quite an evening; Bertha would be a hard act to follow.

Adjusting her spangly shawl Bertha relished the moment. Peering over her spectacles at a small pocket watch she noted with military precision she was exactly on schedule – time was almost up.

"Well, Ladies and Gentlemen, I hope you have had an enjoyable evening and found it informative. Before I leave you, are there any questions?" Silence. Shuffling bottoms, glances at watches, gathering of coats and bags – a low hum of expectation and liberation.

"Er, I would be interested to know if tales of 'treasure' being found on the field behind this hall had anything to do with the war." A thin, reedy voice piped up from the back row, directly across the aisle from Amos. The voice belonged to a little man dressed in blue and yellow farm overalls. An unlit pipe stuck to his lip waggled up and down as he spoke, a pork pie shaped hat perched neatly on his head. "Us at farm are always coming across bits of metal – gets stuck in't plough blades."

Bertha's eyes gleamed. "How interesting. It would be wonderful to see these 'treasures' sometime. In terms of the war, things like silver plate, owned by generations of the same family, became highly sought after. Spies were used by both sides to hunt down and collect as much silver as possible to fund their respective campaigns. Any village gossip about treasure would undoubtedly attract spies, many of whom were little better than henchmen, very undesirable individuals." Bingo! The missing piece of the puzzle – the angry spy Samson, he is on some misguided mission searching for treasure that no longer exists. Amos felt like he could hug the little man. The man looked over at Amos and nodded companionably, it was almost as if he had read Amos' mind. There was definitely a connection there, Amos felt it.

In danger of exceeding her time, Bertha removed the beret and shawl to indicate she was now just plain old Miss Peasegood and the learned historian Bertha had left the building.

The timid, mousy woman behind the top table started a round of applause, to which Bertha replied with a flamboyant bow. The evening had been a resounding success, for some it had been a lifeline.

16

Hidden Talent

Deep in the woods a meeting of a different kind was taking place. Elias and the band of Royalist troopers sat huddled round a fire in the middle of a small clearing away from the encampment. It was long past midnight. The fire crackled and spat sending flickering tongues of flame leaping towards the stars. Reflected in the crimson glow, expectant faces of the gathered young infantrymen became ghoulish masks as they listened intently to their leader. Curls of blue smoke rose into the night leaving a bitter, musky haze hanging in the air. A persistent wind moaned through branches of the surrounding trees which creaked and groaned as if awakening, stretching after a long deep sleep. Unnoticed on a swaying bough high in the canopy perched a tawny owl – watching the shadows, surveying the woods, listening attentively. The troopers, full of adrenaline, were eager for their mission. Elias picked up his twisted hazel stick and scratched out a rough sketch in the earth just visible in the firelight, marking out a plan of the position of the house and the stable block, the proximity of the lake, the woods and the evergreen oak tree, which would be their muster point if the mission had to be aborted. Only Elias knew this would not be needed.

"Friends, I have thought long about our mission and believe it is cunning and trickery rather than force that will win the day." Faces dropped around the fire. "The task is greater than first thought; the size of the challenge dwarfs our resources so ... we must use ingenuity." He paused surveying the group noting crestfallen expressions. "I know many of you signed up on the assumption that you may at last get an opportunity to wage war personally on our sworn enemy, but I must impress on you that we need brains not pikes if we are to succeed in this ambush. Once Cromwell has entered the house we are lost. We must apprehend his entourage as it arrives in the parkland, most likely as he and his men deposit their horses at the stable yard. My proposal is that we masquerade as a band of travelling tinkers and farriers which happen to appear at the stable block just ahead of the Parliamentarian visitors. We should be able to track their progress using the long wood as cover, and it doesn't even matter if we are seen as we will be suitably dressed for the charade we enact. This is a comradeship rather than military visit so the General will be travelling light in terms of guards – we may even outnumber them. At any rate, my plan is that we overpower the group unexpectedly having first befriended Sir Randolph's grooms and then strap Cromwell to his horse, whisking him back to our secret camp keeping close to the lone oak ..." *So as to benefit from its powers,* he thought to himself. "Before anyone has time to realise what is happening. The element of surprise will be all important. If we are not swift, it is possible some combat may ensue." A spark of enthusiasm gleamed amongst the young men. "But we should avoid this at all costs." The spark fizzled then died. Several of the men, two in particular, looked sullenly at Elias.

"You get us here, tracker, on false pretences," protested one.

"We are here to fight and will not be denied the sweet smell of rebel blood," raged another, his words ricocheting off the trees, trailing away into the blackness.

"This is an *ambush*, young sir, not a battle. Is there anything between your ears or is your brain stuffed with hay like that nag you call a horse! Think for a moment. We will hold *the* greatest prize if we pull this off – General Cromwell himself will be our prisoner. We can demand a mighty ransom for him – dictate the course of the war even, if we secure his capture. You think only for yourself, young sire, and are blinkered to the potential victory that is close at hand. We act for God and the King!" snapped Elias frustrated, glowering in turn at the men who by now looked quite sheepish. "Who is with me for the cause in this daring endeavour and who is here for personal glory?" He looked again around the group waving his hazel stick angrily in their direction, his temper simmering just below the surface. The men looked at one another; the two surly renegades lowered their heads muttering under their breath. One by one the troopers stated their commitment to the plan. Begrudgingly the renegades fell in line with the others, although their shifty eyes told a different story. Elias stamped his stick on the ground sending a tremor through the earth, the group sprang to attention. "We are agreed then, the plan is in train, a kidnap in broad daylight from under the noses of the Parliamentarian guard – revenge is sweet ..."

"Revenge, sir? Is this not a plan to give the Royalists the upper hand? How can this be revenge?" A very young infantryman sitting at Elias's feet looked up at him enquiringly. Puzzled glances flashed around the circle in the dancing firelight. Elias realised at once he had revealed his innermost thoughts and true intentions. Hastily he replied that it would be an act of revenge against the Parliamentarians for challenging the sovereignty of the King. It was his turn to avoid the gaze of the troops. He could not look them in the eye. He could not look them in the eye because the whole plan was a lie –a complete fabrication. It would never see the light of day and the troopers would see no action – they would be overcome by one of his powerful potions and be fast asleep in the forest.

*

Leaning against the cold stone wall of the village hall catching snippets of information relayed by Pie from her perch on the windowsill, Tal was frozen stiff. He couldn't remember how he'd ended up with this job, after all Bungy was more Amos' chum, so how come he was fast asleep against the Aga in the warm kitchen and Tal was here outside, bored and cold. Pie, sensing his frustration peered imperiously down at him; her luminous, owlish eyes, glowing supernaturally in the dark, sent a warning. How did she know what he was thinking thought Tal irritated, how was she able to read his mind, which she did on a regular basis? – he was convinced she was some kind of charmed cat with special powers. Pie darted another look his way, as if Tal was thinking out loud, but this time she looked genuinely shaken.

"What is it?" he whispered up at her.

"The Hall; it's haunted, apparently, by a ghostly green

lady covered in weed and slime. A disembodied, wailing noise is heard in the woods, and the bell on the stable clock rings in the middle of the night all by itself! The ghost was the lover of Sir Randolph Knight who owned the hall but she was from a Royalist family. Her brother bumped off Sir Randolph, so she threw herself in the lake and drowned. Remember ... at our meeting in the dovecote, I told you about the legend of the infamous Green Lady – well it seems it's true!" Pie, waving her paws in agitation, nearly fell off the window ledge as the words tumbled out in a mad rush.

Tal started to shiver, but not from the cold. Good job Bungy wasn't within earshot, as he would have conveniently disappeared at this news, not even appearing at mealtimes until someone else had been volunteered to get involved.

"That's great. Just great. We're trying to send a lost woodsman back in time four hundred years, everything's pointing to the Hall being the place where he needs to be ..." Tal paused for breath. "And now you're telling me there's a mad, frustrated, smelly, green ghost running amok in the grounds ... well, the tree man with the long, bony fingers was enough for me so count me out from here on ..." This last sentence arrived in one long, gabbled string of words at great speed – without waiting for a reply he bolted through the nearby garden gate for the sanctuary of the cottage.

Even though it was against house rules he scrambled frantically on to the old, camel-back tapestry settee where he felt secure, protected by the high padded arms. The remnants of some walnut logs smouldered in the grate, filling the air with rich aromatic sweetness. Gradually, the warmth thawed his frozen limbs and the heady smell gently soothed his troubled mind, coaxing him into a deep sleep.

His subconscious, however, was still processing the things he had learned that night and soon Tal the dreamer was being pursued through the woods in a terrifying nightmare by a writhing, tortured spirit smeared in green weed. No matter how fast he ran the apparition gained on him, screeching and wailing as it flew through the air. A dank, pungent smell invaded his nostrils as the long, green, choking tendrils dripped and whipped cold, clammy water all over his fur. His lungs were bursting with the effort; his heart pounding as he tried to accelerate away, but instead found he was running on the spot. Glancing over his shoulder, he saw slimy, green fingers reaching for his throat and felt the prickle of their touch on his fur like tiny electric shocks. It was no good. He was doomed. The weight hit him like a brick, winding him into wakefulness. Tal thrashed around on the sofa trying to wrestle off the ghoul which clung to him like an octopus.

"*Hey,* can't anyone get a wink of sleep around here in peace! There's room for two on this sofa you know," yelled Bungy, clinging in desperation to the upholstered cushions, claws ripping at the thread as he tried valiantly to avoid being dragged to the floor by the weight of his rapidly descending stomach. Unbeknown to Tal, Bungy had wandered sleepily into the room settling on top of the sofa arm for a snooze in front of the dying fire. Dozing off with his limp, flabby undercarriage spreading slowly over the arm, gravity had taken over. Fast asleep, Bungy started to slide gracefully off the arm, paws first to circle Tal's neck, with the rest of his hefty bulk following and landing with a heavy smack right on to Tal's unsuspecting tummy.

"You great *lump!*" cried Tal, secretly relieved to find

that the electric shocks were only Bungy's claws desperately scrabbling for grip to stop him flying off the sofa.

"What on *earth* is your problem? Anyone would think you were locked in a tussle with the *Creature from the Black Lagoon*," – one of Bungy's favourite old films which he watched nervously from behind a cushion.

Not quite, thought Tal, *but closer than you could imagine*. "Just a bad dream which your acrobatics saved me from. Serves you right for trying to pinch my spot. What's wrong with your own bed?"

"The tapping is keeping me awake."

"What tapping?"

Tap … tap, t, tap, t, tap, tap, tap, t, tap … An annoying, intermittent clicking sound drifted through from the kitchen. *Tap, tap, tap … tap … tap, t, tap …*

"That tapping …"

Now fully awake, Tal realised the sound had been masked by the screeching ghost in his dream. He had to admit the sound was quite irritating, like someone practising Morse code on his eardrums.

"Well, what's causing it – go and find out?"

"It's Pie typing."

"Doing what …?"

"Typing."

"I didn't know she could type."

"Neither did I. She's not terribly good at it – keeps hitting two keys at once. She's getting all hot under the collar, so I wouldn't say anything if I were you unless you want the pincushion treatment."

Peering quietly round the kitchen door they observed a most unusual sight. Standing on her hind legs on a chair,

Pie was staring intently at the keys of an ancient typewriter perched precariously on the edge of the kitchen table. Muttering quietly under her breath, completely engrossed in scanning the typewriter keys, she was unaware of being watched. Creeping round the back of the chair Tal could make out a line of letters on the page which read ...

b z b j j j k l d m m d l h s n n z

I wonder which language that is, he thought, knowing that Pie knew a lot of things he didn't. Perhaps it was a code. Bungy jumped on to the window seat and leaned over to get a closer look.

"What does *beezedbeejayjayjaykayledeemmmmmmmdeelayhsssnnnnnzed* mean?"

"I'm just practising, okay? Getting back into the rhythm and used to the keyboard again ..."

"You mean you've done typing *before?*" Tal looked on in wonder. Pie never ceased to surprise him.

"When I was a kitten I used to pounce on the keys fascinated to see them dance as words were printed on the page. If only I'd paid more attention to spelling, I wouldn't be finding this so infuriating – the typewriter keeps misbehaving, printing letters I've not typed."

"Hmmm – operator error if you ask me," mumbled Bungy to himself.

"No one's asking you, actually – and if you think you can do any better, be my *guest*." Pie flounced off the chair in a huff.

"I was only having fun ... fun ... you remember that, surely?" Bungy looked sheepish. "Why on earth are you doing this typing thing at an unearthly hour when all sensible cats are fast asleep somewhere warm and cosy ... like just here come to think of it ..." He yawned theatrically turning in circles to get comfy on the window seat cushions.

"Because ... *I'm* the one with any brains around here, and *I'm* trying to type some clues to go with a fake treasure map that we will use to throw Samson the spy off the scent."

"But surely, finding the village and getting Amos home is our priority?" Tal looked baffled.

"Exactly! But, there is every chance Samson will try to follow us and we'll lead him straight to the village, which could ruin the whole plan. So, we give him what he came here for. He's looking for treasure to fund the Parliamentarian campaign – treasure that doesn't exist now – four hundred years after the war, but he doesn't know that ... yet."

"Er ... how do we know for certain he's looking for 'treasure'," murmured Bungy drifting in and out of sleep, trying to feign attentiveness.

"Because Bertha says so ..."

"Who's Bertha?" a tantalising dream of crowded bird tables beckoned.

"Bertha the historian who gave the talk tonight at the village hall." Pie glared at her brother, overexaggerating each word. "Keep up *will* you ... where was I ... oh, right at the end, someone asked a question about finding silver plate in the field behind our cottage."

"Any type of plate suits me as long as there's food on it ..." sleep was taking him over like a big cosy blanket; it was pointless trying to fight it any longer.

"Wait a minute ..." barked Tal.

Bungy, startled out of his dreamlike state, misjudged the windowsill and, for the second time that night, scrabbled desperately at the cushions for grip. This time gravity won, sending him crashing on to the unforgiving stone quarry tiles with a painful thump.

"Wait a minute ... wait a minute, you conveniently didn't mention spies looking for treasure when you told me about the green, wailing ghost." Tal fixed Pie with a glaring, accusatory look.

"What *green, wailing ghost?*" Bungy had never been more awake.

"We've all seen how scarily determined this 'spy' is ... he's on a mission." Tal was getting agitated.

"Correct ... perhaps dogs aren't so stupid after all!" Pie gave him her best superior smile.

Bungy, sprawled in a heap on the floor, was trying hard to recover his composure, and keep up with the 'ping-pong' conversation. It was like watching tennis on the television – he'd only done it once, and it had made him dizzy. So far he didn't like what he was hearing. He had a bad feeling about what was to come. For what seemed like the millionth time, he wished he could wind the clock back to that moonlit evening when he would most definitely have stayed in his warm bed leaving the bank voles to get on with it.

"There's a ghost? Where? What's that got to do with us and Amos?" he spluttered, heaving himself upright.

"The ghost is at the Hall, the Hall is at the village, the village is where Amos needs to be to get home, the village is where we're going at the next full moon, er, rather ... where you're going. I'm retiring from this adventure lark forthwith and going back to tracking hares for a living." With that, Tal climbed into his bed, circled three times and slumped on to his favourite cushion, his nose up to the Aga – bum facing the others as a sign of protest, making his intentions crystal clear, so he thought.

The penny suddenly dropped. "A ghost ... at the Hall! You know I don't do ghosts, or witches for that matter. Why didn't you tell me about this earlier?" Bungy, whiskers quivering directed his question to the end of Tal's tail. Loud snores rumbled from the depths of Tal's bed although one wary eyelid was open.

"It's no good pretending to be asleep; we know you're hearing every word." Pie realising another mutiny was brewing had to act quickly. *Come on, be reassuring,* she thought to herself, when what she really wanted to do was biff them both on the end of the nose with a sharp claw.

"Look. If we make a decent job of this map, I'm sure Samson will fall for it and follow the clues intently. We've seen how focussed he can be, so let's give him something to focus on instead of us. I've got this 'Doorstep Walk' pamphlet from the local council which shows all the paths, woodland, etc and has bits of history thrown in. With a bit of imagination it could be transformed into a *'treasure map'*. We know Samson is desperately looking for something because he ransacked Amos' possessions and was spying on our meeting in the dovecote. My guess is he's actually quite stupid and believes that someone from the Royalist side has plotted the exact whereabouts of the collection point for silver taken from local households on its way to the mint to be melted into coins to pay for the King's campaign. Such a hiding place would naturally be kept secret, but Samson is not the brightest spy in General Cromwell's army – although I get the impression he thinks very highly of himself. We can send him on a wild goose chase whilst we head off in the opposite direction. All we have to do, once it's ready, is plant the map where he'll easily find it and we're free to get Amos on his way." She hoped she had done enough to convince them. There were other parts of her plan that she had carefully omitted to mention; they would have to be handled delicately when the moment was right.

Despite being a pain at times, Bungy was proud of his sister. He knew she could be counted on to keep them out of trouble – it all sounded straightforward to his simple brain. Tal, refusing to engage with the conversation, kept his back resolutely turned listening surreptitiously with one ear. The plan sounded relatively easy he had to admit, but she had not mentioned getting to the village. Sooner or later they would all have to go to that awful place; there was no getting away from it; that place where he had escaped kidnap by the skin of his teeth. He decided from here on he would take a back seat and encourage Bungy to be the hero; after all he'd got them into this mess in the first place.

"So, we need to get on with the map. Put your thinking caps on and help me with the clues while I get back to the typewriter. By the time you have the clues worked out I should have mastered the typing." Ignoring their lack of response, she climbed back on to the chair. *Tap, tap, tapp, t, tappp, tap* clicked the keys as letters popped up on the page. Bungy, exasperated, squeezed himself between the end of Tal's nose and the oven door which radiated welcome heat on to his back.

"Look, mate. She's got it all worked out. And we can't give up on Amos," he whispered into Tal's ear which twitched with the bristle of Bungy's whiskers. Tal turned his nose away. Bungy persisted, waddling round to squat in front of Tal, crouching low until they were nose to nose.

He looked Tal straight in the eye. "We need a top-notch tracker with a good nose for the trail – do you know anyone? Perhaps we should ask Bruce to step in if you're not up to the job." With that he turned to walk away appearing disinterested, only to be catapulted abruptly backwards by Tal's heavy paw trapping the end of his tail. *"Oi!"* Bungy retaliated by trying to swat the end of Tal's nose, but it was just out of reach.

"You, my friend, are looking at the number one tracker in this neighbourhood, so *don't* you forget it. I can track squirrels from forty paces in the densest undergrowth … and catch the little blighters. Please refrain from batting my nose as it is a highly tuned, precision instrument and our primary secret weapon in this endeavour."

Bungy wriggled out of Tal's grasp with a mock grimace, all the time smiling inwardly to himself – Tal was back in the game.

"Oh, before I forget," interrupted Pie. "I suggest we plant the map near Samson's hideout. If I remember rightly you spotted his big leather boots reclining in the hen house, didn't you brother?" Not waiting for a reply she continued. "Seeing as how you know the exact location, it would be best if you could make the drop." *Make the drop! My sister watches far too many movies*, Bungy decided. Then another large penny dropped in his mind with a resounding clang. "Hang on … hang on … *me* 'make the drop' … good grief!" He shot a look at Tal who whispered smugly, "Who's smiling now … mate …?"

17

Warnings

After a marathon evening of mental effort Bungy's brain had turned to mush; he was incapable of thinking about anything, even whether he was hungry or not, which was slightly worrying. The infernal *tap, tapping* of the typewriter keys had infiltrated his brain as if an angry woodpecker was knocking on the inside of his head trying to escape – it was all too much. The tortuous map modification had taken virtually all night. Pie was a hard task master. She had rejected first time around every single clue he and Tal had come up with, saying they were far too obvious, stating that someone hiding treasure would make it really difficult to find. There had been more irritable arguments and disagreements; how exactly did you phrase four-hundred-year-old clues? Shouldn't they be written with a quill and ink rather than a typewriter? – something Pie had seen on a television documentary. How many clues were enough? What if Samson couldn't read? Should they draw pictures instead? … the possibilities were endless. Eventually they managed to agree on six clues typed in a strange old-fashioned font Pie had discovered on the typewriter after trying virtually every permutation of lettering, much to the others' frustration. "It's got to look right, or he will smell a rat," she had reasoned as she selected the next style. *Tap, tap, tap.* "Hmmm ... No, that's not flouncy enough."

"What kind of look is *'flouncy'*, for heaven's sake?" Bungy rolled his eyes which he struggled to keep open; they felt like sandpaper grating on his eyelids. He glanced at the kitchen clock yet again; the ticking was keeping time with Pie's tapping, driving him to distraction. It was just approaching four thirty in the morning; outside birds were starting to chirp cheerfully announcing the new day.

"Old English writing was very decorative; we don't want it to look too modern or the game will be up."

"This spy is pretty stupid. We've already deduced that. I don't think it will matter what it looks like – he'll be so excited to find the map he'll just want to get on with finding the treasure ... so just, *TYPE THE CLUES!!!*"

"There's no need to shout."

"THERE'S EVERY NEED TO SHOUT! I CAN'T REMEMBER WHEN I LAST WENT TO SLEEP!!" Bungy yowled hysterically.

Tal, slumped on the quarry tiles, let out a long, noisy sigh covering his eyes with his front paws; he was exhausted. He had surprised the others with his extensive vocabulary; he knew over thirty-five really useful words and had been the originator of most of the clues. His most impressive clue was based on one of his discoveries when roaming the village. They had decided it could

be the first clue, starting Samson off in the wrong direction. It went ...

Face the dawn in holy space
Peace and grace be to this place

The first line referred to the sun rising in the east over

the rooftop of the Old Vicarage. The second line was the inscription Tal had discovered on the Old Vicarage doorstep. So Samson would set off heading east, whilst they took the path due south towards the lake at the country park – ingenious. Not bad for a 'poacher's dog' as Bruce liked to call him.

At last the 'Doorstep Walk' map, after some shredding and clawing round the edges to give it an aged appearance, was transformed and, they all agreed, would pass, to a bumbling spy, as an ancient document. They would get Amos to give it a final look before Bungy was despatched on his mission to deliver it to the hen house. As a watery sun cast its early rays over the cottage garden, three weary souls staggered to their beds and fell into a deep, deep sleep.

One detail Pie had conveniently 'forgotten' to remind everyone about was that in the next few days there would be a full moon, and they needed to try and follow Bruce's 'waymarks' to find the hidden village. It was no good setting off on the night of Cromwell's visit not knowing where they were going. There was a small lunar 'window' when the village would be visible. They had to be certain they could use it to their advantage and send Amos back in time. From Tal's harrowing experience in the village, it was clear they would need their wits about them and be well prepared for the unexpected; a trial run to the village was a must. Was her accident prone brother going to be up to all this she speculated, frowning to herself? If he could pull off setting the trap for Samson that night, the others would have one less problem to think about – so far Bungy had just scraped through. There was no one else. She sighed – he was all they had …

There was something fishy, it occurred to her, about the appearance of the secret village, its location and the arrival of Amos all at the same time. And, the village had an accomplished tracker, the 'tree man' Elias, who had wanted Tal as his hunting hound. Could it be that there was more to these developments than a lucky coincidence? Was there some organised parallel universe-type intervention going on, or was this really what had happened all those years ago being replayed in some kind of 'timeslip' reality, a reality in which they apparently now all existed? Maybe the tracker chose the site for the Royalist encampment for its proximity to the Hall? Why would he do that, unless there was a reason to be in that precise location at an exact moment in history? Were these, perhaps, the renegade Royalists preparing an ambush? A sudden thought came to her like a lightning bolt … *could Elias be the chief protagonist in the plot to kidnap Cromwell?*

The more Pie let her needlesharp mind explore these questions, the more she could hear Bertha the historian recounting the events of that fateful night. *But according to Bertha the ambush was thwarted. What had really happened? Pie wondered … Was Amos anything to do with sabotaging this daring plan, could he too be a spy …?* Having a nimble, inquisitive brain, she concluded, was sometimes more a curse than a benefit; a melee of jumbled thoughts fought for her attention. Whatever her suspicions she must keep them to herself for now. The only way to find answers to all these questions was to keep quiet, press on with the plan, and wait for more clues to be revealed. She glanced at the calendar on the kitchen wall. Tomorrow evening the moon would be almost full. They had to prepare, and she needed to check with Tal exactly what that scoundrel Bruce had told him about these 'tree carvings' they had to find. She ran swiftly across the worktop past the kettle and out through the open kitchen window into the heat of the midday sun – she knew exactly where her team would be at this time of day, and headed for the old apple tree, branches almost grazing the lawn under the weight of hundreds of plump, Bramley apples, turning a glorious shade of rose pink in the sunshine. The tree created a natural umbrella against the sun's fiercest rays and was always a favourite spot for an after-lunch snooze, only today the inviting shady patch of lawn was completely devoid of horizontal bodies. At that moment, a squawking, squabbling mob of baby starlings dived towards the bird table like feathered kamikaze pilots, jostling for the greatest share of peanuts. Several pairs touched down momentarily then took off again in close combat screeching aggressively, wings fluttering furiously on the attack, swiping each other out of the way. The din startled Pie who swung round to see her dimwit brother sat underneath the bird table, head spinning round and round like the sails of a windmill, desperately trying to track any one of the swooping birds as a potential snack – instead he was just getting dizzier and dizzier, eventually toppling sideways into a heap. "Oh, give me *strength,*" exclaimed Pie under her breath, as she ran across the lawn to nudge him to his feet. "Good clown impression brother! Have you seen Tal? I need to talk to him urgently."

Bungy swayed violently staring at her cross-eyed. "Ooooh, you're all swimmy." He burped unceremoniously. "I must say, I feel rather sick ..."

Pie tried to control her temper. "Don't bother, I'll find

him – he can't be far away; don't know why I don't just do everything myself," she called over her shoulder, bounding athletically across the lawn. *I bet he's with Amos.*

But Tal was far away. He too had consulted the calendar and realised what Pie would have in mind. Well, she had the brains but he had the speed. Without a second thought, he had stolen out of the garden gate, trotted down the lane keeping in the shade of the avenue of beech trees, then switched to overdrive as he pelted out into the countryside, putting as much distance between Pie and her 'plans' as any Lurcher worth his salt could achieve.

The unpredictable summer weather, sunshine one minute, inches of rain the next, had turned the track out of the village into a long, hairy, six feet high tunnel of wild grasses, rampant weeds and white, nodding spires of cow parsley. The hedgerow too had thickened, mushrooming in size to conveniently provide cover for a small but expanding army of rabbits; Tal made a mental note to come back at nightfall, for a spot of bunny hunting.

He didn't stop running until he reached the safety and stillness of the copse on the ridge. Cool depths enveloped him; the air thick, heavy with silence save the occasional fly buzzing past his ear – paradise, complete paradise. Tal never ceased to be amazed how quickly his troubles dissolved under the stately branches of the trees. He gazed solemnly for a moment up into the canopy, marvelling at the vivid tapestry of fresh colours radiating over him, feeling calm descend around him in green running waterfalls.

Slowly he lowered his gaze feeling refreshed, revived, back in control of things. To his complete astonishment he found the end of his nose millimetres away from the tip of a bedraggled ear the colour of copper wire.

"'Avin' a bit of a Zen moment are we, ol' son? Made a bootiful picture that would ..." Bruce cocked his head sideways and gave Tal a knowing wink.

"How long have you been standing there?" grunted Tal, embarrassed.

"As long as it took ..."

"As long as what took ..."

"Until ye's realised I wos 'ere."

"I didn't realise you wos ... ahum, were there," said Tal, baffled.

"Let's jus' say I's been expectin' ye ..."

"Expecting me? But I've come out to esc ... I mean, for a run that's all ... Why would I be looking for a ragamuffin such as you, when what I'm really looking for is some peace AND QUIET ...?" Tal raised his voice, hoping this commanding tone would send Bruce on his way. But Bruce stood his ground.

"Ye's really are dumber than I's gid ye credit for, lad ... ye's got the nose for it but can't use it, so's it seems ..."

"What are you prattling on about?" Tal's hackles started to rise, calmness evaporating by the second.

"Is thee a Lurcher or in't thee? Tha's a tracker, mi friend, an' if tha's gunna find t'village tha'd better pay attention, lad. Now, follow me ..." With that Bruce spun round and with a cheeky hind leg skip, trotted purposefully into the gloom. For two pins, as the saying goes, Tal would have cheerfully gone in the opposite direction leaving Bruce to his own devices but something was nagging him, telling him he had to find out what Bruce was up to. He tried momentarily to distract himself, think of something, anything else, but an invisible hand it seemed, was grabbing him by the scruff of the neck pulling him along in Bruce's wake.

Against his better judgement he loped after Bruce, hoping he had not pulled off another of his vanishing tricks. For a dog of small stature Bruce kept up a brisk pace, his short legs covering the ground with a surprising turn of speed. Tal followed obediently along a path he knew well, twisting between gnarled trunks and over fallen logs. Mentally he was ticking off familiar landmarks on the route; the next junction was framed by two tall yew trees, their graceful fronds forming a dark tunnel leading to a small glade where a large beech tree had toppled in high winds. Here the path took an abrupt diversion round the forlorn, rotting remains of this once magnificent specimen; Tal had zigzagged past it many times. But, there was no fallen tree, just the path winding endlessly into the distance. Tal blinked, confused. The same thing happened on the next section, and the next, still the path wound on relentlessly; perhaps they were stuck in some hidden labyrinth, heading nowhere. Through gaps in the trees he caught glimpses of the neighbouring field and saw barley swaying gently, ripening in the sun. Swallows skimmed and darted through the crop, feasting on the abundance of tiny flies. Strange, everything looked normal, was normal out there, but here, deep in the woodland, the paths were playing tricks on him.

Tal's tracking instincts were giving him warning signals. Completely disorientated, he was about to insist that Bruce stop and explain what on earth was happening, when rounding the bend Tal found him lying flat on his back in the cool undergrowth of a small clearing, exposing a smooth pink tummy, small, stout legs pointing skyward.

"Aaaah …" he sighed. "As me granddad used to say … 'just airin' mi knowledge' … can't beat a bit of a freshen up after a good walk. Pleased te see ye kept up wi' me, Lurcher boy."

Tal ignored Bruce's nonchalant attitude. He was in no mood for social chit-chat – he wanted facts, and quickly.

"Just where is it that you have brought me and what has happened to the usual path through these woods? A straight answer for once would be appreciated," barked Tal, any essence of earlier good spirits non-existent.

"Steady, lad, steady. Keep ye foxy red fur on … if ye did but realise I'm tryin' to help ye, give ye a clue …"

"A clue? What kind of a clue … what about?"

"Do ye want to find this village or don't ye …? I'm tryin' to give ye a head start, get ye on the right path …"

"How can we be on the right path when everything about it is *wrong?*"

"Well spotted, laddo! There is something between those floppy ears after all then. This path only appears on t'eve of t'full moon and disappears when t'moon starts to wane. Tha's only got two nights, tonight's t'first one by the way, then t'path will start to fade. I'll tell thee na, lad, tha dun't really want to be out 'ere ont' second night cos when t'path starts to disappear, tha'll get *really* lost, hee hee – ye might be all right for a whiles, but ye'll 'ave to 'urry. I'd choose tonight if it were mesen …"

Tal sat open-mouthed, dumbfounded.

"Shut thi mouth, lad, an' pay attention. Now, tha sees this 'ere triangle shape…" Bruce trotted to the side of the path and raised a scruffy paw to point at a strange, crooked lattice of three interlocking branches woven into an upside-down pyramid. Tal had never noticed this odd formation before. It looked like a rustic wooden window which had come adrift from a ramshackle hut. It was quite large, and one arm bent outwards creating an archway over the edge of the track.

"When tha gets to 'ere, tha's gettin' close to t'village. Ye *must* stick t'path like glue from 'ere on. Look carefully at the biggest trees linin' t'route an' tha should be able to mek out some signs carved int' trunks after this point."

"What kind of signs?" Tal butted in.

"Owt that dun't look like it belongs on a tree, stupid ... when t'moon lights 'em up, tha'll see 'em well enough. Some's quite amusin', some's a bit, well ... meks yer 'air stand up some do ... but keep goin', dun't be put off whatever tha sees. Main thing is whatever ye do, dun't look back, just keep goin', don't stop until tha' can see t'village through t'trees ... and dun't think tha can tek any short cuts cos, I'm warnin' thee, if tha strays off t'path ye might never see that cosy cottage o' thine again. Unless ye've got a long ball o' string tha can bring wi' thee!" Highly amused at his own joke, Bruce dissolved into giggles which turned into a volley of spluttering coughs.

"Oh, an' another thing afore I forget. In t'moonlight, do not in any circumstances pass under t'boughs o' yon mighty evergreen oak tha saw next to t'campsite. Ye's been warned!" Bruce planted himself right in front of Tal and looked him straight in the eye. Tal could see for once that Bruce was deadly serious.

"Wha ... what would happen if I did ... just out of interest ...?" asked Tal in a small voice looking coy, somehow he dreaded the answer.

Bruce stood up on his hind legs, front paws in the air inches from Tal's nose. Tal could smell his foul breath as he stared intently into Tal's frightened eyes. In a low whisper, prodding the end of Tal's nose in time with each word, Bruce replied, "Do ye fancy life in 1642, lad? ... cos that's where ye'll be ... *with no way back* ..." These last four words accompanied by extra hard prods for added impact. Tal gulped; his throat dry – he must remember to warn the others. Stunned, all he could imagine was being trapped at the bidding of the 'tree man' with no escape, a truly terrifying thought, beyond all comprehension.

For a few moments he was speechless, eyes closed in horror. He stood for a while in the safe familiar tranquillity of the wood digesting Bruce's words, firmly cementing in his brain the need to tell everyone not to go anywhere near the oak tree.

Opening his eyes Tal was puzzled. "Why are you going to all this trouble to help us?"

A wistful look flitted fleetingly across Bruce's grizzled, hairy face. "Let's just say I have a vested interest, lad. I've lost summat precious. You an' yer little gang are t'only chance I's got to find it agin ..." Bruce's head drooped, as if a large weight were pressing it down. Were they tears Tal could see pricking at the corner of his eyes? An awkward silence hung between them on the breeze. Then, as if someone flicked a switch, Bruce puffed out his chest and adopted his usual cocky stance. "I's countin' on ye, Lurcher boy ... SO DUN'T MESS IT UP!!" he bellowed.

Just at this moment Tal became aware of a peculiar sensation travelling through his body like a wave of electric current, a growing realisation spreading through his nerve endings arrived in a rush at his brain. It was then a large penny dropped from a great height into a slot in his befuddled mind. He had the answer! He knew how to get Amos home! He must rush back at once to report to the others. He could save the day – only *he* had the key to unlock the riddle that had been baffling them all the last few weeks. Jubilant he turned to find Bruce – give him his due he had come good in the end; it was only right to thank the scoundrel. Looking around, the clearing was empty. Tal was completely alone, the only sound a distant merry tune, notes floating on the air, and a faint smell of wood smoke on the breeze. Bemused, Tal studied the path ... he had the answer, but which was the way home ...?

18

Harvest Moon

Standing alone in the clearing, Tal paused to drink in the changing twilight landscape. Already the sun was dropping low in the sky and an impressive moon was on the rise, glowing pink in the last reflected rays. Was this a harvest moon thought Tal? He had often wondered what this meant. The large, pale, disc blushed then smouldered as the pink deepened to burnt crimson eventually fading gradually to burnished silver, a clear, white light in the darkening sky. Tal stood spellbound watching the magical transformation, the green woods now monochrome with silvered leaves. The path ahead lit by a ribbon of light beckoned him in the direction of the village; bark on the trees jumped into sharp relief, strange unseen script appeared on their trunks or was it just a trick of the moonlight. Tal had no idea how long he lingered bewitched in that space. Tempting as it was to follow the silver path he must head back to the cottage now or he may never escape this enchantment – the wood was watching, waiting. Some force, otherworldly, an energy, flowed around him. Behind him, the track out of the woods looked just as it had in the daylight. He turned sharply setting off at a jog glancing once over his shoulder, feeling the cool earth striking through his pads. Soon he picked up the lane back into the village. Accelerating into an effortless run he pounded along the cinder track, oblivious to a dark shape sweeping silently high above the tip of his tail. Making a beeline for the dovecote, guessing everyone would be gathered there, he failed to see the large tawny owl alight on the weathervane in the centre of its roof, keeping him in its sights.

There was no one there. The door stood wide open, he stared into the dark, gaping, empty space which stared blankly back at him. Where was everyone? Was it a trap? Samson could turn up any minute. Not waiting to find out he shot over the field and across the garden, arriving at the kitchen door in a lather.

The door was slightly open.

The rumble of low voices came from inside. Quietly, Tal put his long snout up to the edge of the door and sniffed. Familiar scents drifted towards his nose, the unmistakable, reassuring odour of his housemates and a whiff of slightly mouldy, damp earth, an Amos smell. Pushing the door gently with an outstretched paw it swung into the room with a tired groan. The talking ceased abruptly. Tal stepped on to the red quarry tiles, claws clicking on the stone announcing his arrival. "Phew, it's only you ... hey, that rhymes, I made up a poem ..." Bungy, in his own world always slightly out of the loop, waddled over to headbutt Tal on the nose in welcome greeting. Pie was not so complimentary.

"And just where do you think you've been without us? Deserting the team ... disappearing without a trace. Gallivanting around the countryside with that floozie Mollie, no doubt ..."

"I don't think that I've been anywhere, I mean, I know

where I've been … er … at least I think I know where I've been," Tal stammered trying to evade Pie's intense, piercing gaze.

"I just went for a run to one of my usual haunts which got a bit involved and turned out to be different from usual because of the moon but Bruce kept me straight and showed me the way … and—

"I should've known that good-for-nothing vagabond would be in the picture somewhere …" interrupted Pie sharply, fur starting to bristle, whiskers quivering.

"He's a good sort really when you get to know him and what's more he's on our side. I trust him."

"How can we trust someone that breaks promises and dumps people in the middle of nowhere," sulked Bungy, ganging up with Pie.

"He's helping us so we can help him find something he's lost …"

Amos, prowling warily around the room inspecting the kitchen appliances from a safe distance as if they were instruments of torture, stopped dead in his tracks listening keenly, thoughtfully twirling the ends of his moustache, brilliant blue eyes locked on Tal's face.

"Go on my friend," he whispered.

"Well, Bruce reckons he has lost something – 'precious' was the word he used. He didn't say what, but he went all misty eyed on me – not what I expected from a street dog."

Amos slumped down in the nearest chair staring into space. "By the stars above us, he spoke thus … you are sure he spoke thus, my friend? Could it be …" He mumbled. "Could it really be …"

"Could it be what?" Pie was getting exasperated.

"Could it be that I, my good self, am that something ..."

"Are you telling me that *Bruce* is your *companion?*" Pie's eyes were like saucers.

"Hah! That's a good one, Amos ..." Bungy guffawed, completely misreading the mood and entire conversation.

"It's no joke, young fellow." Amos gently patted the top of Bungy's head, "When I first saw this ... this ... 'street dog' as you so call him, t'was such as I had looked into a crystal ball, a magic lantern showing me images of my home life, too painful for me to bear ... my fireside, my faithful hound Bruce at my feet ... there is no other like Bruce ...'

"You can say that again," muttered Pie under her breath.

"I cannot be mistaken; time has thrown us yet another piece of the jigsaw, but how can this be, how can this be ...?" Shaking his head sorrowfully, his voice fell to a strangled whisper, barely audible in the awkward silence.

Bungy looked at the floor wishing a hole would appear big enough to swallow him up.

For the second time that day Tal was dumbstruck. Too many loose threads swirled round in his mind making one big tangled knot. The knot became a large coin which dropped into the same slot as it had earlier in the day, slowly unravelling the mystery. Bruce and Amos ... it made sense if you thought about it. That would explain Bruce's strange way of talking, a kind of four-hundred-year-old modern slang.

"So, as I was saying, Bruce gave me, us, a big clue about where to pick up the path to the secret village ... which is only visible, by the way, around the time of the full moon. *I've seen it!* It's incredible! I felt this overwhelming urge to follow the path as soon as the moon started to shine, the path materialised right in front of my eyes glowing silver in the dark – it was pulling me, drawing me in, like the shadows behind me were pushing me forwards ..." Tal gabbled on filling in the stilted gap, trying desperately to remember everything that had happened. "Anyway, I know how to get there, to the village, I have the answer ... erm ..." He paused, breathless. There was something else he needed to mention, but in the heat of the moment he couldn't quite remember what it was – it would come back to him.

*

It was an unusual, exotic taste for a discerning palate, but it grew on you – anything new was worth a try the hens concluded, having spent a happy few minutes pecking at what loosely resembled slightly burnt sausages sticking out from behind one of the straw bales. Being of an inquisitive nature they were always on the lookout for an alternative menu, and today their luck was in. As news spread through the coup, a small queue formed to taste this unexpected delicacy. One by one, the hens took their turn to nibble on the podgy, pink things, helpfully there were ten of them to go at, and, although some were bigger than others, there was plenty to go round. Occasionally one of the objects would twitch which added a small frisson of excitement to the hens' experience; it was, they all agreed, like finding super worms.

Distressed and exhausted after his ordeal, Samson had fallen into a heavy sleep and was deep in the middle of a really strange dream where bit by bit his body was turning into a giant chicken, until all that was left were his toes. He had tried to put on his beloved military boots, but the thick ruffling feathers up his legs got in the way. It wouldn't be long before his toes turned into claws, he could feel them tingling already, he must hurry, find a way to save his feet so he could at least still walk about, find a way out of this dreadful place. There it was again that stinging sensation. His toes were prickling, time was running out. He lashed out in his dream fighting off some invisible foe, some wizard that cast the spell over him. One foot had already grown three claws, now four, then five. He must do something before he permanently became a chicken. His other foot started itching. One toe curled under and grew a spiny nail; the next began to go ... then ... *CRASHHH!!!!!*

His fist collided with a solid, wooden nesting box smashing the timber to smithereens, bits of wood and splinters rained down on his forehead. *"Aaaaaargh!"* The dream evaporated. In a flash, Samson sat up amid a blizzard of startled chickens, wings flapping in his face, piercing screeches tearing his eardrums, his toes smarting, red and angry. But he smiled; he was deliriously happy.

"I am not a chicken, I am still a spy, I still have skin not feathers! 'Tis but my toes, my toes are aflame." He looked accusingly at the hens who recovered their composure with alarming speed realising the tasty morsels were joined to a large, furious human who would soon be on the warpath if they were not careful. They stared innocently back at him and scratched busily at the floor with calculated nonchalance, as if nothing was amiss.

My training for the army has not prepared me for the extraordinary challenges I have had to face, but I am a better spy for it – I can face anything, well, just about anything. The blurred image of the half man, half bird floated into his

185

mind. He groaned. *I can face all terrors but that one … If I leave this dratted hen house I may again meet a sticky end, yet if I stay, I am condemned to a house of feathers … The devil plays with me, what choice do I have but to stay in my stinking refuge for now whilst I gather strength, and think of a way to protect myself against the evil that awaits outside.* Rubbing his toes Samson reached for his faithful boots which looked rather pleased to see him. "One step at a time my beauties." He felt the reassuringly strong, supple leather in his fingers as he yanked the boots on to his feet. Wincing as they pinched his tortured toes he declared, "I must endure the pain to become a better spy. I am determined to find and follow those confounded creatures once and for all. They will unsuspectingly lead me to the treasure and the way home from this hellish existence at the same time. I must make ready for the most dangerous and important mission of my military career. I will bide my time and prepare." He got to his feet, wobbling as the boots took control of his legs. Stooping under the eaves of the coup he ventured cautiously into the run outside and took a deep breath. He would wait a while, then he would strike.

Waiting is exactly what the intrepid friends did not want Samson to do. Their plan relied upon him leaving the chicken shed so that Bungy could plant the fake treasure map without him noticing. And so began a frustrating period for the one member of the band with the shortest attention span. Bungy was given orders by Pie. Go to the hen house, watch for Samson leaving, nip inside and leave the map, somewhere not too obvious, and leave quickly without being seen. She had repeated and emphasised the last three words several times. *Without being seen.* Whichever way you looked at it there were some major logistical challenges for a chubby, grey and white cat not designed for speed. He was a pretty good hunter that was true, but his colouring would be a dead giveaway in a small, confined space occupied by the most vicious and merciless of adversaries, the hens – he grimaced, remembering the way his tail had throbbed for days following some previously well-aimed pecks from those bossy, feathered beasties.

'Nipping in', as Pie so quaintly put it, would not be quite the piece of cake she had inferred it would be. If only it was that easy. Running the gauntlet of the hens was almost as bad as being chased by a pair of heavyweight boots attached to an angry spy. Hmmmmm … he couldn't quite understand why he had been selected for this task. In the end, Pie had convinced him that he would be the hero of the hour and reminded him, that out of the three of them he had the highest body fat to skin ratio, so would have more protection against any well-aimed nibbles along the way. Somehow this didn't quite add up, but he couldn't work out how. At least the surveillance operation got him away from the tension that was building at the house in preparation for tonight's safari through the wood, following Bruce's funny tree faces. Muttering to himself, he waddled off in the direction of the farm. "Pah!" Bruce was really taking them for a ride this time … and to think he might have some connection to Amos was ridiculous.

Strange things happened in the moonlight, he should know, that's how this whole crackpot scheme had come about … why on earth they needed a 'dry run', as Pie called it, was beyond him, seemed a bit daft; why not wait until the big night? One expedition to the woods was quite enough; look what happened last time ... they were almost in the clutches of a witch and were chased by a buzzard. *Too much excitement for me; perhaps I can stay at home this time on the grounds that I'm needed to watch the hens, er, the hen house ... a lot depends on this spy fellow ... oh dear ... far too much to think about ... I'm not qualified for this detective lark.* Hot and bothered, having worked himself into a state, he found a shady corner in the farmyard behind one of the barns with a good view of the chicken run. He settled his weighty undercarriage on the cool concrete with a soft *'flummmmpp'* noise, his grey body invisible in the shadows. He'd worn himself out churning over all the happenings in his mind. A heat haze shimmering over the vast, white concrete yard in front of him was slightly hypnotic. He watched mesmerised as swallows swooped and dived at breakneck speed in and out of the barn door catching flies, and soon their to and fro rhythm was rocking him to sleep. It occurred to him briefly that the only challenge right now was how to stay awake, as he slowly, helplessly, descended into an inviting, all-enveloping blackness.

Back at 'base', as Pie liked to call it, there had been an air of anticipation and high alert all day. Pie had decided it was safer for Amos to sleep in the wood store for the time being, to avoid the possibility of being targeted again by Samson, who was obviously desperate to find Amos at all costs, assuming he would lead the bumbling spy to the treasure. In the daylight, Amos, nervous in such unfamiliar surroundings, had spent the day slinking around the cottage, peering suspiciously at the twenty-first-century devices and modern paraphernalia with frightened eyes. Terrified at the prospect that by flicking a switch (whatever one of those was) it was possible to conjure up light and sound out of nowhere, he trod gingerly about trying not to make any sudden movements. Jumping at the slightest noise, he had added considerably to the palpable tension in the room. Pie, not having Bungy around to complain at, had spent most of her time hissing orders at Tal who was now thoroughly fed up of the whole business. Staring wistfully out of the window, ignoring her as much as possible, he noticed that the sun was starting to set and the moon was already on the rise. Just as it had in the wood yesterday, the moon appeared much bigger than normal and sat low in the sky, extremely close the horizon. A light, early autumn mist cloaked the giant orb in a swirling veil giving it a yellow tinge. "I'm sure it's a harvest moon," Tal muttered under his breath to no one in particular.

"That is correct. The September moon is known as a harvest moon as it's often a burnt yellow colour and larger than usual, providing much needed extra illumination for farmers busy harvesting their crop," Pie interrupted his train of thought like a clockwork, furry encyclopaedia. "It's good for us, as we will have more light to see where we are going … if we ever manage to get out of here tonight! We can't wait much longer for my stupid brother. I can't start to imagine what kind of scrape he's got into this time … If we don't leave soon, I think Mr Nervous over there," nodding surreptitiously towards Amos, "will be too frightened to do anything …"

"We don't have much time." Tal paced up and down the kitchen fretting, Bruce's words ringing in his ears. "We have to go very soon; the path will disappear at sunrise and we will end up lost forever in the wood."

"That settles it – we will leave my brainless brother a note and set off at once." Pie leapt nimbly off the window seat a whisker's breadth from Amos' nose and disappeared round the kitchen door. Amos jumped to his feet striding after her, wrapping his thick cloak around his shoulders on his way out of the door. Tal, caught by surprise, scrabbled to get a grip on the tiles as he shot after them both down the garden path in the twilight.

The long, polished blade flashed and danced in the moonlight as Elias inspected his handiwork. Satisfied with the result, he sheathed the sharpened hunting knife and picked up his satchel. Everything was going perfectly to plan, even the stars and heavens were with him, sending a glorious harvest moon to light the way to the clearing where he would forage for the particular herbs and mushrooms he needed for the sleeping potion. The ingredients needed to dry and mature to increase their potency, so he must make the most of the intense moonlight and gather them tonight. With Cromwell's visit just over a month away, this was the last full moon, and it was slowly on the rise over the encampment scattering glittering darts of yellow over the surface of the lake. Putting on his dusty, felt hat he reached for the gnarled hazel stick, feeling the handle's smooth contours under his thumb. The stick felt alive in his grasp, almost humming as it struck the ground, keeping time with his strong, quiet strides over the field. For his size, he moved silently like a wild animal towards the darkening woods, the rest of the village fast asleep. The shadows quickly swallowed him up. Elias knew the exact spot to head for; even the trees had given him a sign, an upside down pyramid of branches locked together, a triangle right at the side of the path.

19

The Guardian

Swoooooooosh! Bungy's brain registered the sudden draught of air as it swept from the top of his ears to the tip of his tail. *Crikey … the wind's getting up. Swoooooooosh!* Another big gust strayed along his body from tail to ears this time, riffling his fur in the wrong direction. *Mmmm, not unpleasant actually,* he thought. Turning over, exposing his pink and white patched belly, he waited for the next gentle waft to caress his hot, ample tummy. *'Tu-whit, TU-WHO-HOO-HOOOOOO!'* A mighty current of air blasted less than two inches above him, accompanied by a foghorn like screech; the shock sent him reeling in somersault back on his haunches. Perched on the farm gate, directly above his head, a large tawny owl fixed him with an accusatory glare as if to say, *'Wake up, you layabout!!'* At that moment, Bungy would go as far as to say the owl looked annoyed, very annoyed – if owls ever lost their temper, he wasn't sure, but this one definitely looked extremely cross. It was dusk. *Where did the afternoon go, where am I, what was I doing, why is this owl pestering me?*

Bungy's sleepy brain struggled to keep up with the random, muddled thoughts his half-awake consciousness was throwing at it. The owl continued to stare at him without blinking. Behind the gate, sounds of contented clucking as the hens settled down for the night, were a lightning rod to his memory. Hens! I remember now, it's all coming back to me! *Watch the hen house ... but nothing much was happening, and I must have nodded off.* What on earth was he doing – trying to justify his actions to an owl of all things, how ridiculous. Bungy sat up and studiously cleaned his paws, feeling the pressure of the creature's unrelenting stare bearing down on him. He would sit it out – ignore the stupid owl, it would give in long before he did. Didn't it know that cats hunted birds, agreed it was a bit on the big side, but he liked a challenge. The owl gave him a disdainful look, as if it had read Bungy's mind, and took off with a flourish of heavy wing beats landing in the top of the nearby walnut tree. It glowered at Bungy, vigorously flapping its wings, shaking the branches so hard that a few under ripe walnuts, in their bright green armoured casings, rained down in his direction. *'Tu-whit, tu-who-hooo'.* "Trees! ... That's it!" Bungy spluttered, dodging the smooth, green missiles. "The mission to find the village, follow the tree signs ... in the moonlight. It is moonlight already. Oh crumbs!" Realising he was in the wrong place and probably in a lot of trouble, Bungy ran through the farmyard back to the cottage with as much speed as he could muster, undercarriage swinging wildly from side to side. He reached the garden just in time to see the tip of Tal's tail and two white hind paws disappearing down the lane into the gloom.

"Do keep up; you're supposed to be our tracker, why are you lagging behind all the time?" Pie was getting impatient with Tal who was preoccupied, racking his brains trying desperately to recall all the instructions Bruce had given him. There were some really important things they had to do, and more importantly not do, but he'd gone blank, for the life of him he couldn't remember any of them. Hoping it would all come back to him when they got nearer to the path, he speeded up alongside Pie, putting on his most confident expression. "Still no sign of my dimwit brother – he's probably been accosted by a hen." *He's henpecked enough as it is*, thought Tal, giving Pie an accusing look.

"Let's just hope he doesn't appear out of nowhere and mess things up – if he can ever find us that is …" She added sarcastically, "Just where does this magic path begin then …?" Pie, green eyes glinting in the moonlight, stopped to wait for Amos who was being hampered by the weight of his cloak, the blade of his pike flashing silver as he strode towards them. The chilly night air caught at the back of their throats mingling with the dank, musty smell of fallen leaves and dampening earth; nights were drawing in now as the long dry summer made way for fresh, crisp autumn. They made a strange spectacle silhouetted against the hovering moon at the end of the lane where the rough track to the wood began, small spirals of breath the only sign of their living presence. At that moment, the familiar route to Fox's Folly Wood appeared quite unearthly, shimmering eerily, levitating above the ground, a burning finger of light stretching away into the distance, disappearing around the bend. Tal took a deep breath, stepped on to the shining track and into the unknown.

Getting into rhythm with his best speed-waddle, Bungy found he was keeping them in sight; he could just make out Tal's two white hind paws if he strained his eyes. The moon gleamed with an intense brilliance, and a disquieting, brooding stillness hung silently over the countryside. The hedge threw dense, forbidding shadows all around – deep, black shapes, outlined in a dazzling, supernatural white glow. "Thank goodness, I'm not out here completely on my own – it's a perfect night for witches, goblins and all manner of spooky goings-on, there's something strange in the air ..." *Mutter, mutter ...* "The things I get dragged into ... completely out of my comfort zone." Grumbling under his breath, talking to himself for moral support, Bungy pressed on, trying not to look too closely into the menacing depths of the hedgerow. Instead, he fixed his eyes on Tal's ghostly paws as they bobbed ethereally along, floating in the air, seemingly unattached from any living being. As he reached the start of the path he could just make out the others disappearing into the gloom, rounding the bend towards the towering blackness of the wood. The cold night air stung his nose as he puffed and blew, hurrying to catch up. Once they entered the wood he knew he stood little chance of finding them, and would be facing the terrors that lurked within completely on his own. Shuddering, he realised his options were limited. Carry on, and hope he caught up without being abducted by some mischievous sprite or an evil witch who might force him to perch on the back of a broomstick. Turn back now, and risk bumping into a pair of large military boots attached to a frustrated spy, or end up being dive-bombed by an angry owl. None of the options were in any way appealing, and making speedy decisions had never been a personal strong point, especially on an empty stomach. Even with the roasting he expected to receive from his overbearing sister, the need to be with his friends outweighed a desire to go back alone – he wasn't that brave. So, with trepidation and an anxious glance at the sky, he trotted on to the moonlit path bracing himself for what lay ahead. High in the branches of a nearby tree, a large owl watched silently as the small grey and white shape melted into the shadows.

Tal's heart was going like a train, every beat thudding against his ribcage, almost knocking him sideways, as he stepped out of the clear light into the penetrating darkness of the wood. The others followed him, Pie stealthily padding close to his hind legs, Amos behind them; the slight rustling of his cloak over fallen leaves the only sound breaking the enveloping silence. Tal had no idea what he was looking for, and how he could possibly see anything in this total blackness. Thank goodness he knew the path because he was quite literally following his nose at this stage, praying that Bruce's assurances would hold true, that somehow the trees would guide them to where they needed to be. They walked for a while going deeper into the heart of the wood in suffocating darkness, no one saying a word, unspoken anticipation hanging between them, as if they were collectively holding their breath. Predictably Pie was the first to speak. "What exactly are we looking for?" her voice quivering slightly, lacking the usual bravado.

"Markings on the trees," Tal whispered quietly.

"What kind of markings?"

"Anything that doesn't look like it should be on a tree apparently ..." Tal tried to sound upbeat, but every step along the track, as black trees engulfed them, he questioned his judgement in taking Bruce at his word.

"Can we honestly trust that scruffy mongrel ...?" Pie regained a little composure, then remembered Bruce and

Amos were companions. "Er … I'm sure Bruce has our best interests at heart, never judge a book by its cover that's what I say …" she added quickly.

Amos, deep in thought, seemingly oblivious to this exchange, let out a small cry. "My friends, do you see what I see … this has to be a sign?" Their eyes, grown accustomed to the gloom, followed the line of Amos' pike as he pointed towards the trunk of a tree a few yards away. Halfway up the trunk they saw what looked like a giant paw print etched into the bark.

"I wouldn't like to meet the owner of that footprint …" Pie joked half-heartedly, trying to relieve the tension.

"I believe this must be our first waymark," said Amos, rummaging in the pocket of his breeches for something. He drew out a small square of roughly hewn wood and a compact, vicious-looking knife with a curled blade which sat neatly in the palm of his hand. Tal and Pie watched as Amos made several small angled cuts in the top corner of the wood.

"What are you doing?" asked Tal intrigued.

"If we have any hope of returning from this venture, we need to retrace our steps. I am inscribing our route using an ancient, primitive tree alphabet – it is often used in my time to communicate with trees and as a secret code to convey messages, but mainly it is reserved for inscriptions to the dead." Tal and Pie exchanged an anxious glance, sharing a common thought. *I think I'd prefer not to know this*, thought Tal, as a shiver ran up his spine. "If we follow my inscriptions in reverse, we should regain our route, retrace our steps; it is also a precaution to …" He paused, choosing his words carefully. "To counter any tree spirits which may not, shall we say, be in our favour." Sometimes the others wished Amos would leave the past where it belonged, in the past.

Forking on to the path alongside the marked tree they crept on, Tal becoming more aware by the second of the passing of time and the waning moon which threatened to disorientate and imprison them if they didn't speed up. He quickened his pace, extending his long legs into a graceful trot, peering into the darkness for the next clue. It was becoming more difficult to make out the path; the trees had become denser, crowding in on them, their branches interlacing in thick twisted knots, labyrinthine and sinister. The earth struck cold through Tal's paws as he wove between the boughs negotiating clumps of tangled roots, a smell of rotting leaves and decay lingering in his nostrils. Summer was dying but the trees were alive, watching, sensing, waiting. He was beginning to wonder if Bruce had led them astray and that the waymarks were another fictitious invention conjured up by an overactive imagination, yet Tal had seen another side of Bruce and wanted to believe him. Processing these passing thoughts, momentarily distracted, Tal was brought abruptly to a halt confronted by a stomach-churning sight ahead. The path took a sharp right-angled turn in front of the most colossal tree Tal had ever seen. It straddled the path like some monstrous, evil giant. What could only be described as a monstrous, contorted 'face' glowered down at him from halfway up the trunk; two enormous, empty, black, sunken 'eyes' struck deep into his soul, rooting him to the spot. Several inches above the eye-like holes ran a series of smaller, ugly gashes in a straight line, giving the appearance of some kind of crown. Beneath the eyes was a much bigger, gaping hole, a 'mouth', hideously twisted into an anguished, silent scream.

Tal felt sick. He started to tremble violently, unable to move.

"Whatever is the mat ..." Pie grumbled bumping into Tal's leg then faltered mid-sentence as her eyes were drawn like a magnet to the empty, woeful gaze of the tree. Unable to escape and resist the pull of the woodland giant, the more they were overcome by feelings of despair and overwhelming sadness, they felt drained and hopeless, as if all their energy and life force were being sucked into the very sap of the tree. They both sank to the ground at the foot of the tree unable to move, paralysed by fear, bound by some powerful enchantment.

*

Some kind of sixth sense was guiding Bungy along. He'd got no idea why, but his instinct was telling him that he was on the right path. He also seemed to have developed an innate fearlessness and was feeling quite adventurous all of a sudden, even starting to enjoy himself. He had got used to the dim light, his excellent night vision steering him between the trees and over the knotty roots which kept trying to trip him up. At this pace he should catch up very soon. *Hmmm, don't know what all the fuss is about, this tracking lark, it's easy peasy, the feline species is designed for it ... hang on, what was that..?* A strange, green glow briefly skittered through the branches ahead of him, casting fleeting, luminous shadows across the path. He paused looking around but it was completely dark, nothing there. He continued slightly less confident. There it was again, like a green ribbon weaving in and out of the trees then disappearing as suddenly as it had arrived – very odd. Focussing straight ahead blaming the moonbeams, he carried on, pretending all was as it should be, although his quickening heartbeat told him different. *Wooooo ooooo ooooaaaahhhhaaaoooo* ... The sound, like nothing he had heard before, made his blood run cold. A disembodied, tormented wailing noise echoed through the wood bouncing off the trees, penetrating deeply into his head, filling him with dread and horror. An icy blast of dank air circled his body; vile-smelling drips of cold water splattered his fur. Through the trees the green glow was getting closer; a shapeless entity, it barrelled along branches turning the bark green as it approached. With a sickening thump he felt his heart turn over and his stomach turn to lead; it wasn't a green glow after all, but slimy, green tendrils of weed whipping and choking boughs as they passed through the air. As the flaying, searching tentacles grew nearer, the stench of rotting flesh, long dead, attacked his nose and made his eyes water. *Woooooooo ooooooooooaaahhhh* ... it was coming his way. *The Green Lady!* He dived cowering behind a stump as the icy air swirled the dead leaves into frantic spirals. Not three feet above the ground weaving through the trees travelled the troubled spectre of the Green Lady, transparent, yet with enough substance to make out the anguished, plaintive expression on the once youthful face – the deep hollowed eyes, full of pain, searching fruitlessly for a lost love. Bungy hardly dare breathe. The phantom hovered directly above his ears, listening as if alert to his presence. Foul-smelling droplets showered down on him as he lay trembling in the undergrowth. Far in the distance a muted bell tolled a mournful note as the ghost hung tentatively, its head turning this way and that searching, ever searching. The bell tolled again. Bungy shook with every chime. Then, as quickly as it had arrived, the spectre rose up towards the tree tops, turned and flew away in the direction of the old hall. For several minutes Bungy couldn't move. His petrified body had frozen, muscles turned to stone by spasms of fear, his fur wet and rank like an icy glove. As the smell and dampness receded, he carefully elongated his neck like a telescope and peered towards the canopy. The boughs had returned to normal, the clinging, smelly weed had vanished. Shaking his fur until he resembled a wire bottle brush, he jumped over the stump and ran faster than he had ever run before until he reached the next clearing.

*

Amos, slowed by his great cloak getting snagged on broken branches and tugged by brambles, arrived at the foot of the enormous tree to find his friends apparently resting.

"This is no time for repose, my friends. Come, we must hasten whilst the harvest moon is abroad." He bent to gently stroke Tal's silky ears. Tal tried to lift his head, but it weighed too much. Amos felt Pie's slender frame quiver under his touch but already her fur was feeling cold and lifeless. Then, he looked up at the tree. In an instant he knew they had been bewitched by the evil, tormented spirit of this forbidding ancient tree. He should have warned them not to pause for any length of time or look directly into the sunken hollows in the trunk – it was almost too late. He knew such a tree existed solely to protect something extremely important, its powers designed to repel anything which attempted to pass it by. Amos averted his gaze as he felt a weight like a stone start to pull him down towards the earth. He had no choice. Kneeling close to the hound's handsome head, keeping his eyes glued to the floor, Amos shook Tal roughly whispering urgently,

"Rise my friend, rise, do not give in ..." Tal stirred then slumped again. Amos shook him harder until eventually Tal sat up swaying groggily, looking slightly drunk. "Wake up, my friend, you must wake up ..."

He turned to Pie gently folding both his leathery, old hands round her middle to pick her up, she felt like delicate china in his grasp. He shook her gently at first trying to get her blood pumping, stir some adrenaline. When there was no flicker of response Amos reluctantly shook her harder fearing the worst.

"I say, Amos, steady on ... I know she can be a pain at times ..." Tal watched in disbelief – what was Amos doing? Amos continued shaking, Pie's legs swinging lifelessly in the air like a ragdoll.

"I would never, ever advocate this treatment to animals but she is under a spell – we must somehow get her to wake up, and quickly ..."

At that precise moment one green eye opened then the other.

"Do you mind ...!" hissed Pie, hanging limply in the air.

"You're awake. By my stars!! That was close, my friend ..." He looked at the tiny bundle in his large, rough hand and almost wept.

"Not a moment too soon. I stumbled on you both trapped in the aura of this guardian tree. We must be on the right path as a tree like this usually guards something of great import."

"Oh well, that's all right then ..." huffed Tal, keeping his back turned against the hollow stare burning into his back. "I suppose that makes sense of something Bruce said to me about not being put off and not looking back." Amos stared at Tal.

"Bruce said this? Then it is true. This is my faithful hound. Only he would know the ancient ways of the wood. You must heed his warning; he has much wisdom to impart. It would serve you well to note all he has to say ..."

Tal squirmed uncomfortably. There were other things Bruce had warned him about – er, what were they, if only he could remember?

"Come, we must make speed. Hark! Is that not a bell tolling the passing hour?"

Pie glanced at Tal who was evidently thinking about the same thing ... the ghost of the Green Lady.

Stooping his giant frame to clear low branches, Elias moved quietly and swiftly through the shadows with cat-like agility. Like the woodsman Amos who had once been his friend, he felt most at home, most alive, when surrounded by the timeless spirits of trees. He was at one with them, felt their magic course through his veins, sensed their atmospheres and subtle feelings, their reflection of the peaceful energies of the wood around him. Growing up in the King's forest he sometimes visited a sheltered glade far away from any human sight or sounds. If he stood perfectly still in this place he experienced strange sensations, as if his feet were being dragged down into the soil and his arms were being pulled up and outwards to reach for the sun. He would lose feeling in his limbs which became immobile and his breathing would slow almost to a complete stop, yet his body felt airy, light and full of oxygen. A rushing feeling coursed from his toes right to the top of his head like sap rising, and his mind, quiet, stilled and open, was bombarded by friendly, whispering voices imparting secrets and telling stories of events long past. He had spent many hours in this dreamlike state, his skin warmed by the sun, no discomfort or aching in his arms, feeling only peace and tranquillity. He had often wondered about these magical moments and their influence on his being but had long since accepted without question his heightened awareness and intuitive ways of understanding the natural world. Perhaps if he had stood there for long enough he may literally have taken root and had quite a different existence.

The path was growing clearer now, highlighted in the pale yellow glow of the harvest moon. Just as he'd expected, Nature was leading the way, there was no need to look for waymarks. In the distance he could just make out a strange angular shape on the path like an arrowhead pointing into the gloom, could this be a reflection of the pyramid marking his destination? He strode purposefully on in the direction of the shape, eager now to maximise the clarity of the light in aiding his mission to locate the herbs he required. Time was of the essence.

Slowly Tal and Pie came to their senses. Tal felt like he'd drunk a whole bowl of slops at the village pub, as he sometimes did on the quiet. Usually it had the opposite effect, making him hyperactive, bestowing on him supreme powers of strength and speed. A leap across an enormous dyke had most definitely been fuelled by a generous helping of ale he seemed to recall. This time, however, he was moving in slow motion, things blurring around him, it took all his effort to put one paw in front of another. Pie was staggering drunkenly, weaving around behind, hanging on to Tal's tail so she didn't wobble off the path into the brambles. Amos, wrestling with the uncooperative cloak puffed profusely under the strain of doubling his speed, making sure he kept them both in his sights. It seemed like they were going round in circles; the path wasn't actually going anywhere. Sometimes they reached a complete dead end and had to reverse; more worryingly they also ended up at the place they had left only five minutes earlier – the wood was playing tricks on them as it had with Tal and Bruce. Tal was getting frustrated; he'd anticipated this might happen but it was making it very difficult to maintain some degree of authority with the others. In truth, he was questioning how on earth he and Bruce had managed to arrive at the triangle in the clearing. And time was running out. Bruce's word's resounded in his head … "This path only appears on t'eve of t'full moon and disappears when t'moon starts to wane … t'path will start to fade … *when t'path starts to disappear tha'll get really lost.*" He had decided not to mention this little detail to the others; he didn't think it would have gone down well. He knew it was down to him alone to find the path, *and fast!*

Nose to the ground Bungy was gaining on them, having picked up a most distinctive smell of woodsmoke which could only be emanating from Amos' cloak; the scent left a clear trail through the wood so he ploughed determinedly on, blissfully unaware of the menacing presence of the gigantic tree guardian. The scent was extremely strong, he noticed, at the base of one particular tree; the roots of this tree were the biggest he had encountered on the journey so far. Without looking up, after zigzagging wildly in and out of the roots for a while, he scampered on to the right-hand path completely unaware of his narrow escape from the influence of the tormented tree. His fur was drying but there was the most terrible pong all around him – he couldn't shake it off no matter how fast he ran; it was there clinging all the time. Fortunately his nose had tuned in to the smoky mustiness so it was now on autopilot. The others were leading him quite a dance, up and down the same track several times, round in circles; even with limited navigational experience it was obvious that the tracker (Tal) didn't have a clue where he was going. Typical dog, all talk and no sense of direction, just wait till he caught up with them …

Elias forded a small stream; the triangular shaped shadow was but a few yards in front of him. Drawing his knife from the satchel in readiness he quickened his pace towards a pool of light filtering through the naked branches which were slowly turning monochrome in the radiance.

A fleeting shaft of light glanced off Tal's paws then was extinguished. Another flicker, then another, then clearly, only feet away, a glimmering oasis of light swam in front of them. The trees parted to reveal a clearing bathed in moonlight. Tal scanned the trees around its perimeter and spotted the crooked branches plaited into an upside-down triangle.

"This is it! … This is the place. We're really close to the village now. This is where Bruce brought me. He said the moonlight would show us the way from here, point out the path … there it is, look …!"

Across the small clearing a dazzling thread of light wound through the wood in the direction of the lake. Despite the bright full moon, no other path was illuminated, only this one.

"Well done, my friend, we are indeed very close; I can feel it within me." Amos gently patted Tal's head.

The scent is really strong now; they must be very nearby. Stopping to take a breath and get his bearings, Bungy was transfixed by a blaze of light ahead in the trees. "Oh no," he groaned. "Not again … I've just got dry …" He slunk on his tummy towards the light, swivelling his head skywards on the lookout for anything green flying his way.

"Come, my friends, we must hasten, let us take the path and find what we came here for …" Amos stepped towards the shimmering light. At that moment there was a muffled crack across the clearing, a twig snapping. Amos hesitated instinctively, nerve endings tingling. His eyes strained. In the glare it was hard to make out anything in the shadows, but something or someone was lurking there. He waited, heart pounding. In the half-light it looked like one of the trees was coming to life, bending and stretching its boughs as it awoke. Then, out of the blackness, a large, rangy figure in a tattered, black felt hat slowly emerged into the moonlight.

"Elias!" gasped Amos under his breath. The weather-beaten man was parting the undergrowth with a long, gnarled stick, looking intently at the forest floor. He had his back to them. Tal sensing something amiss walked to the edge of the clearing and froze in his tracks. In front of him, near enough to see the dirt encrusted wrinkles on the backs of his hands and catch the pungent aroma escaping from the battered leather satchel, stood the tree man – the worst

possible scenario unfolded in front of his eyes. He dived nervously behind Amos and stood trembling uncontrollably, tail between his legs.

"What's going on?" whispered Pie, unable to see ahead. Being petite sometimes had its disadvantages.

"Th-th-the t-t-t-tree m-m-m-man." Tal tried to speak but his teeth chattered wildly. Pie peeped around Amos' ankles her eyes wide in disbelief at the sight in front of her. Together the three of them stood riveted to the spot praying their presence would not be discovered. Tal's ears twitched, he was picking up another sound, this time from behind them. Whatever next! They were being surrounded on all sides. Elias continued to comb the ground, apparently oblivious. Out of nowhere a voice broke the silence like shattering glass.

"There you are! Well … you wouldn't believe what I've been through to find you lot … I survived an encounter with the Green Lady, let me tell you …" Bungy gabbled on as the others faced him with alarm, speechless and terrified. "You could at least look pleased to … what are you all staring at?" Turning to follow their gaze he stopped abruptly mid-sentence as a towering shape, floodlit in the clearing, rose into the air and slowly turned its massive bulk towards them.

20

A Mystical Message

Temporarily blinded, dazzled by the intense, white light, Elias was unable to make out whether shapes in the distance were substance or shadow. Keen hunting senses told him he was being watched, as a predator watches its prey. He had heard something, but *what* exactly he was unsure – it was time to find out. The small group of friends meanwhile had carefully taken a step back further into the gloom hoping to blend with the trees. But it was to no avail. There was one thing Amos knew for certain; Elias was one of the best hunters of his time and that his instincts would lead him straight to their hiding place. The huge harvest moon hung low behind the trees, a searchlight probing every inch of the long wood. Four trembling, frightened souls watched helplessly immobile, petrified with fear, as the immense man lumbered across the clearing – long limbs swaying like branches in the wind, one shovel-like hand gripping a sturdy, gnarled stick, the other holding a vicious-looking knife. Despite his size, it was taking the man an eternity to travel the short distance, his towering, suffocating shadow swallowing them slowly one by one. It seemed almost like Elias was moving through a dream in slow motion, prolonging the agony until the final moment. The big adventure would soon be over.

Tal felt sick. Flashbacks of bony, blackened fingers, feeling, searching, grasping, assailed him from every direction – he was powerless to stop their assault … where was Bruce when you needed a distraction he thought desperately. A voice he knew well was screaming in his head … *Run! What are you waiting for …?* Seconds passed like hours as the giant shape filled the small clearing, gradually eclipsing the moon's brilliance as it moved relentlessly in their direction.

Driven by adrenaline, no coherent rational thought and an unbidden force he did not recognise, Tal turned suddenly to the others and whispered urgently over his shoulder.

"Listen … whatever I do next just ignore it and run, escape! You *must run* …!" The words were still hanging in the air as he took a mighty, athletic leap out of the trees and sprang lithely straight into Elias's path. A fiery, red flash smouldering in the moon's rays was all the others saw as Tal boldly stood his ground two paces from the advancing tracker. The gigantic man stopped abruptly in complete surprise mentally assessing the situation, cogs of his brain churning mechanically. His fearsome gaze burned down on Tal, brows knitted together in perplexity as Elias sifted his memory. Then a knowing look of certainty and sudden realisation spread across the craggy features releasing the furrowed brows, it was accompanied by a low, growling sound rumbling from the belly of the earth.

"Of course, the enchanted hound – a first-class working dog which magically disappears in the blink of an eye." *Now's the time for a repeat performance,* thought Tal. "Methinks you will not escape me a second time," growled Elias, stooping towards Tal.

"Methinks I will …" barked Tal defiantly, turning

swiftly on his heels and racing away into the waiting empty blackness. From an overhanging branch high in a nearby ash tree a lone owl took off silently, swooping into the night in Tal's wake.

★

Life as a chicken was pretty boring concluded Samson having spent a few uneventful days getting his strength back and his mind focussed. The gentle rhythm of the days, however, had been restorative, there was something to be said for the simple life that's for sure, he may well keep some chickens when he got home as a form of therapy. *Nay! … How could I, a warrior through and through, even contemplate such an idea. The dratted chickens have infiltrated my very being! By the stars, I am undone!* – longing for home tore again at his being. It was hard to be professional and objective when emotions were dragging him down. The dry, dusty atmosphere and bitter stinking aroma of droppings were also getting to him now. The tall, handsome regimental boots stood half-heartedly to attention in the corner of the run. Forlorn yet always ready for action, they exuded a mixture of anticipation and frustration. Samson could imagine them hopping frustratingly from one foot to the other when his back was turned, desperate to get moving, complaining to each other of his inertia, his inactivity. Addressing them formally, as if on parade, Samson declared his intentions.

"You will be pleased to know that I have formulated a plan. Tomorrow we take our first steps towards victory. I am content I now have the measure of the ways of this strange world. Our enemy is a creature of habit; they eat and sleep at the same times every day, like our feathered 'friends'" – he waved a thick hairy arm theatrically around the coup. "They have favourite haunts which I know well … it is just a matter of time before their secrets are revealed to us. Be assured they are no match for our military cunning and guile – we will be victorious!" With this rousing cry he made an exaggerated salute to the boots which responded, he was sure, by standing bolt upright bristling with pride. "I am talking now to my own boots; it is definitely time to get out of here!" Little did Samson realise, events were about to take an unexpected turn in his favour, without him lifting a finger.

*

Running like the wind, Tal sped nimbly through the trees away from where his friends were sheltering. They could find their own way home using Amos' tree carvings; he preferred to rely on the power of his legs, his internal compass and superior night vision to navigate the twisting paths to freedom. It felt good to unleash all the pent-up energy simmering inside. Catapulted into the night by some enormous, invisible elastic band which had reached its limit, Tal ran far, far away from the grasp of the desperate tracker, surviving capture a second time. He might not be so lucky in future. Racing out of the trees into the open, his eyes welcomed the shadowy outline of a gently undulating patchwork of purple fields curving long and open towards the horizon in the receding night sky, a stark contrast to the choking murkiness of the wood. On he pounded, taking in great gulps of the cool fresh air, paws satisfyingly drumming the beaten earth, each stride nearer to home. Breathing heavily, slowing to a trot on the outskirts of the village his heart leapt as the silhouette of the old dovecote came into view. Passing the village pond the resident ducks, huddled together on their deck, eyed him drowsily from the depths of dreamless sleep, peeking curiously from beneath tightly folded wings. *It must be nice to be completely oblivious to all the nocturnal happenings in the countryside, out beyond the trees,* thought Tal, envying their peaceful innocence. *What I'd give for a quiet life* – things, he realised, would never be quite the same again, that was for sure. Breathless and relieved he walked quietly into the silent, serene cottage garden; the sky bruised a deep violet blue as dawn approached. It had been a long night and Tal was shattered yet adrenaline still fizzed in his veins. Finding a dark corner in the woodshed he circled two or three times and flopped on to a piece of old matting, waiting for his breathing and heartbeat to settle down. Soon the familiar earthy vapours of sap and freshly sawn wood gently soothed his nerves and it wasn't long before he drifted into a fitful sleep. A strange half-light bathed the garden when Tal woke later, disturbed by faint crunching noises on the gravel drive. A weary, dishevelled trio rounded the corner pausing under the old apple tree whilst Pie identified a suitable window she could open to get into the house. Amos stood twirling his long moustache deep in thought mulling over the evening's events. Bungy tottered from side to side finally collapsing spread-eagled like a starfish at the foot of the tree, his wobbly belly flopping on to the dew-soaked lawn between outstretched legs. *"Hmmph hmmmppphh mph pff,"* he uttered trying to speak with his nose buried in the wet grass. *"Hmmp hmmp pfffff!!"*

"We can't understand a word of what you're saying, dear brother of mine," sighed Pie, too tired to chastise him. Bungy swung his head from side to side rubbing his nose on the grass in the process.

"I think our friend is expressing the view that he doesn't wish to repeat last night's experience," offered Amos wisely. "And, may I say, neither do I." The dancing, blue eyes had lost their twinkle. "It seems going home comes at a cost too high to pay; I must resign myself to a life in your time. I am a fool. Elias may have the solution I seek yet confronted by him tonight my instincts warned me against him – I know not why …" his voice trailed off. Dropping his eyes as if to inspect his battered leather boots, Amos pulled a dirty piece of sacking from his pocket and blew his nose noisily. Pie gave Amos a curious look, might her suspicions about him be false after all. There was something that didn't add up; a good spy would have worked it out by now – she must be losing her touch.

"*Aaaaaaatishooooooo!*'" The sneeze blew Bungy on to his feet backwards into the base of the solid tree trunk, snapping Pie out of detective mode back to reality.

"*Owwch!*" Bungy shivered despite the warmth of the sun's early rays. "I tink I'de caught a code in by dose. It's probably all dat 'orrible greed slime drippid all ober me."

We're never going to hear the last of the Green Lady encounter, thought Pie, *I can see it coming. Give me strength …* She looked at the sky as if to seek some divine intervention then shook herself briskly from head to toe, brushing off the stress of the last few hours.

"Right!" she pronounced decisively. "The bedroom window is ajar. You lot wait here whilst I climb in and go downstairs to open the conservatory door." With that she shinned acrobatically up the apple tree, trotted out along one of the longest branches and jumped on to the adjacent tiled roof. Balancing carefully she tiptoed daintily along the guttering, on to the glass roof outside the bedroom window and squeezed through the tiny opening, disappearing from view. Amos and Bungy waited quietly, a dejected looking pair, both far away, lost in their own thoughts.

Whilst all this had been going on, Tal had wandered from the woodshed and ambled up behind the party. Amos and Bungy motionless, waited in silence for Pie to appear at the door.

"You made it home then, the tree map obviously worked," Tal enquired, looking up into Amos' wrinkled face. Startled, Bungy and Amos, jumped at the sound of Tal's voice.

"Don't ebber do dat again …!" cried Bungy abruptly, his nose pinker than usual.

"Thank you for saving our skins might be a good place to start," grunted Tal, turning to walk away.

"Wait, wait, my friend, you are our hero!" cried Amos. "He's just exhausted, as are we all. Who knows what fate would have befallen us if you had not acted so gallantly …"

Bungy turned sheepishly to Tal, eyes red-rimmed and puffy. "I'b sorry, batey. Do hard feeligz …" Bungy waddled up to nuzzle his head apologetically against Tal's.

"Hey, keep your germs to yourself!" Tal took a big step back.

"Dese are bost likely enchanted gerbs I'll have you know, I'm probably udder a spell cast by de Green Lady … did you dow I bet de Green Lady in de wood?" Sensing an audience

Bungy rambled on, wheezing with every breath. Just then Pie's slim frame appeared dangling from the conservatory door handle. Leaving Bungy in mid-sentence talking to himself, Amos and Tal made a beeline for the cottage.

*

The bright green liquid bubbled vigorously in the cast-iron pot suspended over the fire. Elias stirred the mixture abstractedly with a sturdy twig keeping down wind of the foul-smelling fumes spiralling into the air. One whiff of the reeking cloud had the potential to knock him out for some considerable time. He had prepared this brew many times always respecting the potency of the foraged herbs. But this time he was stirring whilst preoccupied with the evening's developments and was starting to feel drowsy. A loud musket volley brought him sharply to his senses, black clouds of smoke wreathed towards him on the breeze. The young troopers, keen to get to work, had insisted on practising musket and pike drill every day despite Elias's repeated warnings that the ambush would involve no combat. He was growing tired of their brooding aggression and selfish, uncontrollable desire for personal glory. His herbal potion would quench their bloodlust. To make absolutely certain, he slipped in an extra few stems of the most powerful ingredient, his lips curving into a cruel, satisfied smile. After simmering for over an hour, the vivid liquid was ready for decanting into a small leather bottle which Elias kept hung round his neck on a piece of nettle rope. A few weeks' fermentation would render the potion quite deadly depending on the amount administered. He was tempted to use large amounts to teach the renegade troopers a last fatal lesson should they show no sign of cooperation. He would wait and see. The next full moon was not long away and his ambitious plan would then be in play. He had plenty to think about before then; the reappearance of the red hound in the wood had been tormenting him. What in the name of the stars was happening?

Withdrawing into his dirty tent he sat cross-legged on the floor tightly clutching the long hazel stick in front of his knees, feeling the smooth, twisted bark between his fingers. A surge of energy powered through his hand and up his arm. Closing his eyes tightly, letting his mind slip into a trance, he waited for the hazel's magical presence to inspire and awaken his intuition. The energy surged in waves travelling through his whole body until his being was as one with the ancient rod. His senses sharpened, electrified. Smells of damp canvas and freshly disturbed soil intensified wafting pungently into his nostrils as the rod, making involuntary swinging motions, scratched a perfect circle in the earth in front of him. Elias kept his eyes shut, his body rocking back and forth following its fluid motions, allowing the rod to move freely, channelling his instincts through its woody tissue. The rod paused momentarily, moved forwards slightly then continued to carve patterns in the dry earth. Elias sat quietly, feeling the magical powers of the hazel unleashed in his hand. Eventually the rod became still. After several minutes Elias, drained and exhausted, opened his eyes.

In front of where he sat was a large circle sculpted in the earth. Within the circle was inscribed a drawing of a tree with many radiating branches, elaborately drawn despite the heftiness of the solid, old stick. To the side of the tree were two symbols, one an oak leaf, the other representing the full moon. Elias knew the oak was associated with success and fortune; surely this was a good sign. Suddenly the rod began to quiver uncontrollably. It took all his strength to keep it pointed at the ground. He wrestled with the flailing rod trying to wedge it into the earth but it overpowered his grasp. Dragging his arm violently it lashed wildly at the drawing, scoring a deep, diagonal gash across the centre of the etching. As Elias watched in horror, his faithful rod tore his body sideways, flinging itself towards the opposite edge of the drawing. The frenzied stick scored a second deep gash across the middle of the circle, leaving a large, angry cross totally obliterating the carefully drawn tree and symbols. Elias shivered; his hazel rod had never let him down, but this time it had fought him to destroy the very image it had created. This had to be an omen. Something untoward he had not planned for, something dreadful was going to happen on the night of the ambush, something involving the evergreen oak. He must be prepared, or his plans would be as the dust at his feet.

21

Mother Nature Intervenes

Another raindrop began its haphazard journey down the long conservatory window. Bungy watched in fascination as the slow trickle gathered momentum, collided with other droplets, then rushed towards the bottom. Was that one thousand and four or one thousand and five? He'd lost count, but it was more fun than watching snooker on the television. He could never understand what happened to the balls when they dropped out of sight. He'd looked under the television screen every time but they were nowhere to be seen. Raindrops, on the other hand, grew in size on the way down landing with a big, satisfying *splosh* on the windowsill, then the whole process started again – very entertaining. He couldn't remember how long he had been sitting staring at the window; it had been raining for days. The long, dry, lazy summer had given way to changeable autumn weather. Strong gusts of cold wind had bowled away any remnants of gentle, hazy clouds bringing with them random passages of blustery, heavy showers which threw themselves at the cottage with all the energy of stroppy teenagers barging around their bedrooms. It was good to have a change from the ceaseless monotony of heat, dust and harvest mites thought Bungy, particularly the mites which drove him to distraction nibbling at his sensitive skin. His delicate white fur and pink undercarriage smarted in the sun's rays; the dust from the combine harvester made him sneeze and the heat made him feel like a lump of lead – all in all a pretty miserable time for a handsome, country moggy. So, *Hello autumn, you are welcome here … er, one thousand and six or was that seven?*

The incessant rain had brought proceedings to a resounding halt. Tal, making the most of the opportunity to catch up on some long overdue sofa time, was sprawled upside down on the antique, camel-back settee (normally out of bounds), legs wide open, paws pointing to the ceiling, slim tummy and manly accoutrements unceremoniously exposed in full view. He had not moved for hours, days even, thought Bungy.

Not everyone was enjoying the unexpected leisure time. The longer the rain fell, the more bad-tempered Pie had become. It was not in the plan. She had a plan and wanted to stick to it – she needed to be in control and she wasn't. Mother Nature was dictating events, and there was nothing anyone could do about it – not even Pie. After several hours on the windowsill muttering grumpily, willing the rain to stop, she had stomped off to her 'thinking box' and not appeared since. The lid of the tatty box was resolutely shut and a 'leave me alone' air exuded from inside. *She really needs a 'Quiet Please' sign or something similar,* thought Bungy, feeling helpfully creative, and jumped off the sill to hunt for paper and drawing implements.

Amos had retreated to the woodshed. Nothing had been seen of him except a fleeting glance one morning when the door opened to reveal a white face crowned with thickly matted, wild hair pointing in all directions. A small pile of spent ashes were scuffed on to the path, then the door closed with a snap as the gusting wind tried to snatch it from Amos' grasp. *He must be hungry,* thought Bungy. A flashback to the last food delivery incident was enough to banish this thought from his mind. Amos was used to living frugally, he would be fine, he was, after all, a woodsman, so what better place for him to sit out the weather but in the woodshed. Quite pleased with this logical thinking, Bungy continued the search for materials for his project. In the back of his mind an overwhelming feeling of relief swept over him, a feeling he had not expressed to his friends, but one that kept him calm – the longer it rained, the longer he could put off having to deliver that stupid 'map' ...

*

Peering through the chicken mesh was making Samson cross-eyed. The rain belted down the farmyard forming rivulets of brown slurry which collected into a large, muddy swamp in the gully outside the hen house. On all fours he had been watching with growing alarm as the water level rose. At this rate, he and the chickens would soon be sloshing around in this disgusting mess as the small tidal wave grew with each new torrent than ran across the yard. Curses! This was not what he needed at this stage in his mission. No one would believe that an elite spy could be thwarted by a natural disaster such as a flooded chicken house! He would have to keep quiet about this or risk being the laughing stock of his peers. Why had Nature chosen this moment to intervene when he was ready for action – a cruel twist of fate indeed! The chickens, previously unperturbed, now sensed danger – in some kind of crazy dance they hopped erratically from one foot to the other trying to keep dry, all the time screeching with fear. It was enough to drive even the most elite spy to madness. "This is a test; I must see this as a test of my prowess," muttered Samson grimly as the sludge crept upwards towards his knees. Distracted by the catastrophe developing outside, he failed to notice his beloved military boots slowly sinking into the stinking mud. It was almost possible to hear a strangled gargle as they filled with the foul mixture then disappeared under the surface of the smelly puddle of filthy water with a sticky *sluuuuurrrrppp*. An hour later, Samson, bent double under the rickety plastic roof, crouched precariously on the last dry straw bale surrounded by the terrified chickens. They made a comical sight – a furry island amongst a sea of sludge. The rain had abated and the river slowed to a trickle. Samson thanked his lucky stars that he had been spared an untimely and embarrassing demise. The chickens were doing the same. He surveyed the damage. It was not a pretty sight. "Wait a minute, where are my boots, my precious, loyal boots?! We have been through such a lot together." He jumped down into the squelching slush which came above his calves, shivering as the cold sliminess crept over his skin. He waded with difficulty to the corner where his boots had leant so regally before the flood. Stooping towards the sludge a powerful smell attacked his nostrils. Samson recoiled, then, taking a deep breath and holding his nose, plunged his arm into the soggy mush. Feeling around he came across the unfortunate boots, completely submerged and heavy with mud. A loud sucking noise heralded their freedom. Cradling them to his chest Samson climbed back to the summit of 'hen island' and flopped down dejected. The boots had a pathetic air about them, all signs of bristling military prowess left at the bottom of the squelching depths.

The weather had dampened spirits in the camp and fuelled frustration. Wet canvas lay heavily on creaking frames rocked by the gusting wind. The site, normally buzzing with activity, was deserted as villagers sheltered from the onslaught. Black abandoned campfires littered the ground. Hides and leather shields thrown hastily over muskets and pike blades darkened by the rain, dripped monotonously, droplets splattering to the ground in a random rhythm. Elias pushed the flap of his tent aside and peered outdoors. The rain had just about stopped – the site was sodden. One of the hunting dogs trotted by with a swish swash as it pattered through the puddles on the ground. From a tent over by the lake the sounds of an acrimonious argument grew in volume, voices familiar to him – the renegade troopers, full of their own importance – laying down the law to some unfortunate who found himself sharing their accommodation. With every day that went by these young men became more unpredictable – the awful weather only serving to fuel their bad temperedness. Elias knew they were dangerous – it was not long to the full moon; he had to hope he could manage their egos until then. He may have to draw on his potion early in small doses if they continued in this way – perhaps they were the saboteurs of his plan?

Weak rays of lukewarm sunlight filtered through the weave of Pie's wicker box gently teasing her fur. She blinked sleepily, stretched, then quietly propped up the lid with her nose to survey the scene. The lid would only go so far, strange ... it seemed to be held down by something. She pushed harder until it flew open with a twang. Leaping out over the side, the source of the problem soon became evident as a long piece of sticky tape stubbornly attached itself to the back of her neck. Worse still, it appeared the tape was joined to a large square of paper which flapped wildly and, very annoyingly, insisted on following her around. No amount of shaking and rubbing against the table leg seemed to bother the offending piece of paper; in fact the paper seemed to be enjoying the ride. Getting increasingly irritated she hurtled through the cottage into the snug, launched herself on to the high arm of the camel-back settee and shook herself furiously from head to toe until, overbalancing dizzily, she fell like a stone right into the middle of Tal's soft exposed belly. There was a loud *'ppphhhhooooaaahhh'* sound like the sudden deflation of a large balloon. Tal winded and taken by surprise, shocked out of deep slumber, shot to his feet yelping and barking in self-defence while Pie scrabbled desperately to regain a foothold on the edge of the cushion. In the ensuing brief but noisy commotion, fur flying in all directions accompanied by much hissing, spitting and yowling, the offending paper became dislodged and serenely drifted to the floor revealing a scrawled message ...

DUNOTTDISSTERB

It was late in the afternoon before some kind of uneasy peace descended on the household. Bungy couldn't understand what all the fuss was about; he had been considerate, making sure his sister was left alone to relax, but she seemed more uptight than ever – so did Tal come to think of it ... most odd. *Peculiar housemates,* he thought, as he mooched towards the kitchen anticipating a spot of afternoon tea. Afternoon tea was not, however, on the menu. Ambling into the kitchen, bathed in late afternoon sunshine for once, he paused to sit in a pool of rays enjoying the gentle heat from the warm quarry tiles on his bottom. His antennae detected there was a bit of an atmosphere. What was it? … He wasn't quite sure. Looking up his gaze was met sternly by the others who had evidently been waiting for him to arrive. An ominous, chilly shiver trickled through his fur despite the sunshine on his back.

"It's time …" said Pie.

"Certainly is … time for afternoon tea. A splendid idea … *hmmm* … I fancy …"

"It's time for action."

"What kind of action …? Eating … that's my kinda action … why is everyone looking so serious?"

"The rain has stopped – we have to act quickly and get back to surveillance at the hen house …"

Bungy instantly lost his appetite.

"But … but … it's still really damp out there and … and I've only just recovered from a code in by nodze …" he sniffled for added effect.

"Don't be a baby … you know perfectly well we have a plan. We have to act or poor Amos will see out the rest of his days in the woodshed instead of the King's wood!"

It was a moment Bungy had been dreading. Head drooping, he made for the door.

"Wait! You need the map," shouted Pie. "You know what to do … watch for Samson leaving the hen house then place the map in the coup, somewhere not too obvious or he will smell a rat."

"Smell a rat! ... The only thing you can smell in there is the stinking chickens."

"It's a turn of phrase ... oh, for heaven's sake ..."

Bungy batted the tatty piece of paper off the dresser and picked it up carefully in his teeth. He slunk towards the door a dejected figure.

"Hang on, hang on ..." Tal trotted after him. "I'll ride shotgun ... keep you company. You never know, those chickens could be a handful, you're hen pecked enough already ..." he chuckled, turning to glance at Pie who narrowed her eyes into a piercing, sarcastic glare and turned, nose in the air, to place her back firmly between them.

Pie watched the unlikely pair head off across the garden, round the edge of the field. Passing the dovecote they disappeared out of sight behind the large hedge which shielded the chicken run. They made an odd couple but she was glad Tal had gone along as chaperone; he would at least make sure her brother stayed awake. It was time to do some proper detective work and question Amos about the mystery man Elias.

The door to the woodshed was ajar. Sitting cross-legged on the floor Amos' face, illuminated by light from a small fire set in a ring of stones, showed the strain of the last few days. "Ah, my friend, it is good to have your company. I have made some decisions that I wish to share with you. I am a man of peace – I want nothing but to live a simple life. I am not cut out for a life of adventure ... so, I have decided to make my life here, and give up all prospects of returning to my former existence. I have become fond of your wood store and feel quite at home. Though on a much smaller scale than my own simple abode in the forest it will serve admirably as a residence in your time. I have all that I need. I hope you will accept me into your family."

Pie felt her keen interrogation mode dissolve as she looked into the once twinkly, clear blue eyes now dulled and lacklustre. "Of course you are part of our family and we would love to have you living here in the woodshed – there is much you could do to help, but ... but, well, you see ... er ... I still think there is a way back for you ... and, more importantly, I think you, we... we have no choice ... Fate is playing its hand. We have to see this through to the end because if we don't, if I'm right ... well, if we don't, things ... events ... history ... will be changed forever. If we don't go to the village on the evening of Cromwell's visit by the next full moon, something will occur which will rewrite history ... and I think we are the only living beings that can keep history on track. If we don't keep to our plan, then the Royalist plot to kidnap Cromwell will succeed, Cromwell will be held to ransom, the Parliamentarian army will surrender, the King will be saved from execution and who knows what will happen after that ...!" She paused breathless realising she was gabbling at full speed. Amos stared at her in astonishment.

"My dear, learned friend ... you have indeed done much thinking in your wondrous 'thinking box', I must try it sometime ... yet, I fear it is rather too small to accommodate me ..." He smiled warmly.

"I think you aren't taking me seriously; you're making fun of my conclusions ... I'M DEADLY SERIOUS, sorry ... I've worked it out ... er, I think ... that's why I'm here to fill in the gaps, to find out if my assumptions are correct. You and Elias are the keys that unlock this puzzle and what we do next will shape life as we know it ... perhaps even our own existence! ... Good grief! I hadn't thought of that before ... *aaaahphhhhh* ..." she groaned and slumped on to the dusty floor exhausted staring unseeing into the fire. Amos gently stroked her silken fur and wondered again at how he had come to find himself in this strange halfway world. Whatever happened he knew he had made some amazing, incredible friends that he would sorely miss if all Pie was saying was true.

"Speak, my friend, ask your questions ... I am listening. I will, however, say but one thing. Both you and I know from Bertha's splendid presentation that the plot was *foiled* ..."

Despite knowing this fact, Pie could tell from the tone of his voice that Amos had already reached the same conclusions as her – that the appearance of Amos, Elias, Samson and even Bruce all at the same moment in time could not be purely coincidence. That there was some inexplicable reason why they had all been drawn together, and that everything that had happened so far was leading them to the secret village on the night of the next full moon, which just happened to be the date of Cromwell's visit – another coincidence? ... highly unlikely. There were other unknowns like, why choose to camp close to the site of Langhald Hall, why not camp elsewhere? There were many questions and coincidences but only one answer. Amos, Pie and the others were *meant* to be there.

"You said Elias had been wronged, misjudged. What happened to him?"

Amos sighed heavily. "Elias was, like me, a respected, loyal and faithful servant of the King. As royal hunter and gamekeeper Elias was much in the King's favour but he is a simple man and underestimated the ambition of some young, jealous arrogant troopers determined to undermine his place in the royal household. An innocent evening drinking with his close friend Will Strong, a Royalist to the bone, changed his life forever. Overheard by the upstart troopers Elias was accused of passing secrets to the enemy."

"But how could that be so ... you said Will Strong was a devout Royalist the same as Elias?"

"Unfortunately the troopers were unaware, or maybe they chose conveniently to overlook ... that Will was a twin. His brother Samson is a staunch Parliamentarian ... and General Cromwell's most favoured spy ..."

"You ... you mean that ... you mean that Samson ... the spy Samson is ...?" Pie flabbergasted, struggled to spit the words out.

Amos nodded gravely. "I'm afraid so. Samson is, or rather was, unknowingly Elias's downfall – a case of genuine mistaken identity or calculated sabotage – you decide ..."

"And what happened to Elias ...?"

"Banished by the King and dismissed forthwith from any ties with the Royalist army."

"But ... but ... why then does it seem that Elias is helping the Royalists with their plot ... to redeem himself ...?" Pie paused, then, with a puzzled expression, said slowly as if talking to herself, "But the Royalist plan failed ..."

"Quite so ...."

"Does that mean *Elias* is the one who *sabotages* it ...?" said Pie incredulously, eyes the size of saucers.

"I have wrestled with this conundrum ... whichever way it is examined ... the same conclusion is reached ... It would seem my old, dear friend Elias is seeking revenge and is now in league with the Roundhead rabble."

"You ... you mean he has become a ... *Parliamentarian spy ...?*"

"As much as I wish to disbelieve myself I can only conclude this is the sorry fate that has befallen him ... he has swapped allegiances and now masquerades as a Royalist supporter to wreak vengeance and defeat upon the King's cause to settle his own personal score."

"Can the course of history lie in one man's hands?"

"When the moon is next full ... we shall find out."

22

All at Sea

Tiptoeing around the puddles Bungy grumbled all the way to the farmyard, his pads were clogged thick with damp earth and he had grown several inches in height courtesy of the clinging mud. The wet soil clung between his toes until his paws felt like lumps of wood, every step was a mammoth effort for an overweight cat used more to home comforts. Tal, used to rugged conditions, took it all in his stride.

"Stop whingeing will you ..." He muttered for the umpteenth time. Bungy gave him a withering look and ploughed on alongside the hedge.

"I'm not built for this terrain. I'm more of a carpet cat. Give me a nice deep shagpile any day."

"Try being a bit more 'Zen' will you. Imagine something pleasant, imagine this is a gently undulating green pasture leading to a special place, I don't know ... a pond full of unsuspecting goldfish swimming temptingly near the surface, a pantry door wide open ... or, try and imagine yourself floating an inch over the earth. You need a different mindset my friend ..."

"And you need to stop eating those herbal dog munchies ...! What a load of old baloney, how come you're so chipper this afternoon? Ah, I see ... a run in the country, anything to escape 'she who must be obeyed'. *Ooww!* These pesky field stones are a flippin' nuisance. Who's this Zen bloke then? ... Oooh ... see what I did there, made up another rhyme. I'm quite good at poetry, actually, it comes naturally. I do have hidden depths if anyone cares to find out. Shall I recite you another one of my little ditties? ... It goes like this ..." Bungy's voice trailed off into the distance as Tal forged ahead, his long, muscular legs covering three times the distance of his podgy companion. He smiled. Get Bungy on one of his favourite subjects ... himself, and everything else was forgotten. Tal made a mental note to change the subject, perhaps food next time – another favourite diversion.

Arriving at the back of the farmhouse the friends peeped cautiously through a gap in the fence, Bungy strategically positioning himself between Tal's front legs right under his nose. They couldn't believe their eyes. The hen house, usually sat peacefully within a spacious grassy run, now resembled a storm battered island marooned in the middle of a large brown lake behind a wall of sludge, which had apparently appeared out of nowhere.

"What on earth has happened?"

"Must have been the rain ..." Bungy's powers of deduction never ceased to amaze Tal.

"Really!" replied Tal sarcastically. "You don't say ..."

"It's a pond all right but not the sort I'm interested in ... If the chickens are trapped that means the angry spy is too ..."

"Hmmm ... I'm sure he's capable of tackling the mud if he's desperate enough ..."

Just as the words left Tal's mouth a large, bulky shape

appeared behind the chicken mesh – Samson evaluating the situation and deciding on the best means of escape. The large man cradled a pair of heavy leather boots close to his chest in one hand above the sludge line – they were looking distinctly grubby; Samson was looking extremely cross.

"Looks a bit angry to me ..." whispered Bungy nervously.

"Well, what a surprise ..." *Another nugget of wisdom,* thought Tal. "How would you feel if you were trapped, 'cooped up' even ... Ha ... Ha ... with a load of stinking chickens, had to breach a muddy wall and negotiate a swamp before you could reach the water trough to clean your favourite boots which had suffered the gross indignity of drowning in a sea of slurry ... *eh ... eh?*"

"Okay, *okay,* Mr Smart Alec ... one nil to you ... can we get back to the task in hand or my sister will keep me in solitary confinement for a month and feed me dry cream crackers!"

Distracted, they failed to notice that Samson had already got the door to the hen house open and was stepping out into the freezing brown lake rippling across the chicken run. They could hear him cursing under his breath as the chill slimy water enveloped his feet.

"As soon as I've got these blessed boots cleaned up I'm out of this hell hole once and for all!" The boots looked hurt. Samson turned to look over the fence inches from the ends of two terrified noses quivering on the other side. The dreadful smell oozing from Samson's cloak and the disturbed sludge was overpowering. A combined aroma of sweaty socks, mouldy cheese and ammonia assailed their noses stinging the back of their throats. Tal and Bungy held their breath against the stench and prayed Samson would look where he was putting his feet and not over the fence. Feeling terribly light-headed, Bungy started to sway, sure he would keel over at any time and the game would be up. Tal, seeing him start to wobble, nudged him encouragingly with his nose. Samson, judging that the coast was clear, turned away and waded towards the flimsy wire gate of the run. After considerable amounts of coaxing the gate juddered open parting the water with a gentle slooosssh masking the sound of Bungy letting out a strangled gasp.

"*He's going out!* Going to clean his boots just as I predicted," whispered Tal. "Now's our chance."

"You've got to be joking," hissed Bungy. "If you think I'm paddling through that muck you can think again – everyone knows cats hate water!"

"It's our only opportunity. You heard, he's no intention of going back in there."

"He's left his helmet and gun behind, see … he won't leave without those." Bungy had a better view of the straw bales piled in the corner.

"That means we don't have long. As long as it takes to clean a pair of muddy boots."

"*Big* muddy boots."

"Okay, big boots, more cleaning. We've still got to move quickly. I can't go cos the hens will see me sooner and raise the alarm. At least you're nearly the same colour as the swamp so less likely to be seen."

Bungy looked at Tal indignantly. "I *will* be the same colour of the swamp by the time I get to the other side …"

"Even better …"

"Oh, let's just get this over with …" Bungy picked up

the crumpled map, slipped round the edge of the fence and crept towards the murky lagoon as Samson disappeared in the distance round the hay barns towards the water trough. Taking another deep breath he strode bravely into the brown sea which lapped alarmingly against his chest, almost up to his chin. "*Yukkkkk,* I can't believe I'm doing this … I deserve a medal … or a big, fat, juicy piece of fish, always been partial to a bit of haddock but only had the pleasure once …" Talking to himself, being 'Zen' as Tal would call it, he made it to the door of the hen house. Dozens of pairs of bright, startled eyes, shining pinpricks piercing the gloom, fixed on him. Puffing and blowing he clambered over the mud wall as the hens shrank into the shadows. Strange, so far they'd not uttered a sound. *Probably in a state of shock after their close brush with a tidal wave,* he thought. Approaching the stack of bales he spotted more castaway chickens clinging desperately to their hay refuge, apparently frozen in fear. Midway up the makeshift island on a dry ledge lay Samson's heavy carbine and round metal helmet – *just like a pudding basin*, thought Bungy. The idea of the solid giant of a man, Samson, blustering around with a baking bowl glued to his head tickled him and he stifled a giggle as he paused to decide where to position the map. *Hysteria's setting in – I need to get out of here.* "Place the map somewhere not too obvious, or he will smell a rat." His sister's command rang in his ears. That was all well and good but the options were distinctly limited – he would have to make an executive decision. Shouldering the helmet sideways accompanied by lots of grunting, he placed the map close to its rim then pushed it back towards the weapon. The map obligingly wedged itself between the two objects, but stood out like a sore thumb.

Exhausted, he took a few moments to scan the coup for an alternative location, but this was the only dry area he could see. If the map got wet, the ink would run and it wouldn't make sense … it didn't really make sense anyway, but a least you could make out the words. Focussed on his mission, Bungy failed to notice the hens who had daringly escaped the island, were now gathering quietly round his feet. The leader of this rebellion, a cranky old rooster, puffed out his chest, stood to attention then sounded the charge with an ear-shattering crow. Before he knew what was happening, Bungy found himself surrounded by chickens, pecking his legs, chewing his tail, screeching and cackling with delight. "*Aaaaaargh!* Ger off, you murderous lot … *owww* … leave me alone." He thrashed around in the melee trying to bat them away, a confetti of feathers flying in the air and clinging to his damp dripping fur, but he was outnumbered.

Hearing the commotion Tal cleared the fence in one giant leap, forded the vast puddle and barged into the hen house scattering chickens in his wake. His entrance momentarily surprised the angry mob which scrabbled frenziedly back up the stacked bales to safety leaving a dazed, bedraggled creature staggering in circles at the bottom. "What hit me …?"

"Come on, come on, we have to get out of here … Samson will be on his way having heard that racket." Tal grabbed Bungy gently in his jaws by the scruff of the neck and headed for the door.

Down the yard Samson scrubbed vigorously until his fingers ached. Intent on his work, mind wandering elsewhere, the shrill screeching and ensuing hullabaloo shook him rigid. "*What* the heavens …" Yanking the dripping boots from the trough he strode quickly up the yard, wincing as his bare feet struck the rough concrete. The clamour increased as he approached – something had really upset the confounded chickens this time. A flicker of movement behind the mesh caught his eye, a red flash. He quickened his pace.

The chickens relished a good scrap and were not about to let it end so soon. Tal was trapped by a feathered blockade, more chickens gaining courage gleefully joined their friends in the scrum. He had a dilemma, to bark or growl at them would mean dropping poor Bungy into the throng. At this volume the spy would be wondering what was happening and be arriving any minute, then they really would be in trouble. Bungy yowled adding to the din; it was lost in the clamour. That's it, they were both doomed, thought Tal grimly.

Samson, stepping gingerly on the cold concrete, rounded the hay barns. From this distance all he could make out was a blizzard of feathers and occasional streaks of red. Perhaps a fox had happened upon the open chicken run and made the most of his luck. *Why am I bothering to find out when I have more important things to do?* The wet boots slapped against his thigh as he strode up the yard.

Sitting under the apple tree in the cottage garden, enjoying the warm sunshine, Amos and Pie heard the din reverberating across the field behind them. It came out of nowhere, harshly interrupting the peace of the moment. They exchanged looks then, without a word, hurtled towards the source of the noise, Amos struggling to keep up as his cloak helpfully wrapped itself around his legs.

"Stop wriggling. Keep still will you." At least that's what

Bungy interpreted from the muffled grunts Tal was making. It was impossible to know what was happening in the bedlam. All Bungy could think about was being squashed by a pair of large, smelly boots attached to Samson's sweaty feet. Judging by the size of his boots he had the kind of feet which were capable of covering the ground at great speed, which meant he would be crashing through that door any second. *What was Tal playing at … why couldn't he deal with a few stupid chickens? I wish he would stop swinging me around like a yo-yo, I think I'm going to be sick.* Bungy shut his eyes to stop the floor spinning and tried to be Zen. It wasn't working – the piece of juicy haddock dripping with butter just made the nausea worse, in fact … *uh oh …*

Samson had reached the edge of the miniature lake and hitched up his cloak to avoid it dragging through the water. There were two shapes in the coup, something bigger than a fox and … wait a minute … the podgy, grey and white, now mainly all grey, whiskered creature he had so far been unable to capture. They seemed to be trapped. Perhaps fortune did indeed come from adversity after all. Samson smiled a cruel smile and stepped into the chilly water.

Behind the fence two pairs of startled eyes, one bright blue looked on in horror at the scene before them – a battle royal in the hen house and Samson on the verge of discovering more than the map. For once Pie was at a loss – no daring plan or bright idea sprang from her nimble brain; her brother called it 'brain freeze' after he had demolished a whole carton of ice cream in one go. She looked round for Amos but he had disappeared. With a frantic look back to the chicken run, she saw him rush towards the open mesh door with his cloak held out in front of him like a fisherman about to net a shoal of fish. In one quick movement Amos threw his cloak at the blur of chickens. The cloak hit the floor trapping the majority of frenzied birds underneath, and landed in a heap at Tal's feet. The brown shape writhed and pulsed with struggling, indignant chickens as if it were alive. "Quickly, my friends, escape while you can," shouted Amos over the squawking cacophony. Tal jumped over the seething, brown heap, shot out the door and galloped through the water past a surprised spy, spraying Samson's legs, and scattering dirty, brown droplets over the clean boots. Stunned and with goose pimples spreading over his flesh from the cold shower, Samson paused halfway towards the run. It was long enough for Amos to swiftly gather up his cloak and run as a flurry of flustered chickens scrambled upright, blinking at the light. Glancing back at the scene, Amos failed to see the wooden threshold, tripped, and fell full length into the waiting puddle. Samson couldn't believe his luck, the King's woodsman spread-eagled at his feet. *An appropriate place for Royalist scum – an even better prize! I fancy I have methods I can use to extract some useful information from this yokel; the whereabouts of the treasure will soon be mine.*

He relished the moment.

Amos struggled valiantly with his sodden cloak which clung stubbornly to his body with a vice-like grip, pinning him down, constricting his movement, but the more he struggled, the tighter the wretched thing became. Samson bore down on him, eyes glinting with satisfaction.

Amos closed his eyes, expecting the worst.

"Aaaargh!" Samson bellowed, recoiling as if stung by a wasp. "Something tears at my shoulder … *aargh* … what in the devil's name is this sorcery …!" The large tawny

owl lined up for another pass, swooping like an arrow towards the spy's curly hair. Sinking its talons into the heavy webbing of his cloak close to the shoulder clasp, it just missed Samson's ear. Shreds of brown fluff floated into the air. Landing gracefully on the gable end of the farmhouse the owl assessed his prey with quick eyes. Then, taking off with a mighty beat of its splendid wings, it stooped again towards the target, making a direct line for Samson's head. Amos watched transfixed as the magnificent creature dropped like a stone, its rich, brown, handsomely-marked plumage streaking past him so close he could feel a mighty down draught from the passage of air. Despite the predicament he was in, it was difficult not to marvel at this wonder of nature. In all his years as a woodsman he had never been this close to an owl, and probably never would be again.

Samson did not, however, feel the same way; the owl was far too close, close enough to catch a musky whiff of decaying trees, bark and a hint of sap as its feathers brushed the top of his head. Fleetingly, the owl's saucer-like eyes locked with those of his prey, steely, focussed, intense. An adversary like no other, Samson's training had not prepared him for such a contest. All he could do was duck and weave to avoid the aggressive passes, all the time losing interest in the stranded figure at his feet. Pie watching this spectacle from behind the fence couldn't stand the tension any longer. Jumping up to balance precariously on the narrow tips of the fence posts, she tried desperately to rally Amos to his feet while the spy was distracted. With a mammoth effort Amos eventually scrambled to his knees and shuffled away awkwardly, painfully slowly, inching towards the fence and freedom.

Tal kept running until the farmyard was a distant speck. His jaw was aching from maintaining a light pressure on Bungy's scruff. Flopping down in a sheltered hollow of Bluebell Copse, a small spinney just over a little wooden bridge swimming with ribbons of bluebells in the spring, he carefully laid his limp cargo on to a soft, grassy knoll. Bungy's head lolled sideways, what a sight he made. He was almost completely brownish-grey all over, all traces of white fur caked in matted mud. Multicoloured, downy feathers sprouted all over his body, interspersed by small tender pink areas of exposed skin where the chickens had left their mark. Ten out of ten for bravery thought Tal as the dishevelled shape stirred, starting to come round. Battle worn and weary, Bungy tried to sit up and promptly keeled over at Tal's feet mumbling incoherently under his breath.

"What is it, matey …?" Tal nudged him softly, feeling the weight of responsibility. If anything happened to his friend, how could he possibly face the others … he'd done his best to save the little chap from a nasty fate.

"That wen …"

"Try not to move, just sit quietly till you feel better," insisted Tal.

"That w …" Bungy faltered and fell silent.

Panicking, Tal shoved him harder with his nose. "What is it …? What are you trying to say …?" he urged.

With monumental effort Bungy mustered all his strength and whispered almost inaudibly, "That went well …"

23

Unexpected Surprises

An interesting concept – that of time, mused Elias. Take away time and our worlds fall apart. Time structures our days, our deeds and plans. It was time itself, right this moment, which was frustrating him more than anything. There was too much of it between now and the night of his mission, too many moons before the one moon he craved, of which he dreamed, hungered for. Everything was in place, meticulously planned. He had drilled the troopers well, enduring their endless bloodthirsty talk. His patience had been tried by their constant aggression, arrogance and disrespectful jibes. Timing would be his only ally. Administer the powerful potion at the right moment and all would go to plan. If he failed to drug the troopers in time, or misjudged the dose, he realised their strength of will and raging hatred of the Parliamentarian doctrines would wreck everything he had put in place – his time here would be lost time, never to be regained. By his reckoning, there were only three more moons before it reached its magnificence. September had been despatched in a volley of squally showers and October had arrived with a clammy chill. The mood in the camp had changed, become charged with a subtle electricity, no person was unaffected by this latent invisible force which altered temperaments, sparked heated exchanges from innocent remarks. Time was their master now and they could do nothing but wait for it to play its hand.

Pie had watched the numbers on the calendar march relentlessly forward and couldn't believe a week had passed since the hen house incident. Her poor brother's legs still bore the scars from his altercation, pitted all over with pink polka dots where his fur was missing, he was a pathetic sight. Even more spectacular was his tummy which had been plucked raw, almost completely bald. She hadn't mentioned this to him, but she had an inkling his undercarriage would probably remain hairless for the rest of his days. Well at least it would be a talking point, a trophy from his battle, something to show off, of which he would probably be quite proud, knowing him like she did. Thankfully his colourful 'plumage' had washed off in the rain as he and Tal had made their way home across the fields.

The week had helped them all to recover. Amos' knees looked like they had been rubbed with a scouring pad and it had taken days for his cloak to dry, hung dripping over the Aga much to Tal's disgruntlement – this had necessitated repositioning his bed away from his beloved cooker to avoid it being soaked. Pie had come off lightly, no surprise there, but it had been a close call for all of them; the memories of Samson's wicked expression would haunt her for a long time to come. Thank goodness they had thrown him off the scent. By now he should be far away, following their clues designed to lure him out of the village in the opposite direction to the one they would be taking in three days' time. Her instinct, however, was telling her otherwise.

Something niggled away in the back of her mind, a feeling of foreboding had been living in her conscience for the past few days; she had been unable to shake it off. As time went on the feeling had grown stronger. She had a premonition things might not go well. It was tough being leader, she felt the weight of responsibility, but what could they do – they had to *stick to the plan.*

The encounter with the owl had shaken Samson to the core. Apart from his shoulders smarting from the vicious nicks to his skin, he couldn't erase the sight of those crushing, unflinching eyes that had held his gaze, burned into his very being as the powerful bird swooped towards him – the look of a true hunter. Now he knew what it felt like to be the prey. Snatching his gun from the hay bales he had run quickly back outside to dispense with the enemy but the rooflines and tree tops were deserted. The owl had vanished like a phantom. The old man and his motley crew too had also disappeared without trace, another defeat, another disappointment. Would his luck ever improve? Slumping on to the dry bales, sweeping away the shell shocked hens, he noticed a battered piece of paper at his feet. Most odd, it certainly hadn't been there before the flood … or before those crafty creatures turned up come to think of it. Flattening out the paper with trembling hands, for the second time that day his eyes widened with incredulity as he scanned the page before him. It was a tatty square of paper frayed at the edges. An outline roughly in the shape of a diamond had been sketched in the middle of the sheet. Crazy squiggles here and there seemed to represent areas of woodland – at least that's how he interpreted the blocks of sticks in rows. Underneath and around the outside of the outline there was a curious mixture of neat, upright writing crowded alongside untidy, scribbled letters and laborious crossings out. There was, however, no doubting its purpose – it was a map … a *treasure* map.

It read …

Ye Olde Doorsteppe Walk … 'Doorsteppe Walk' had a line through it and had been replaced by the words … Treassurre Mappe. Underneath the title there was a short introduction followed by what looked like a number of clues. The spelling was atrocious, the words a haphazard jumble typed over the top of the print underneath. He could just make out … hisstorric woodlannd, maggnifficennt duvcotte, legend off the Grreen Laddy. The clues were slightly easier to read. The first one said something about 'Peace' and 'Grace'. As he read on it occurred to him the clues were giving him directions, plotting a route. He sat engrossed reading and re-reading the clues, reciting them under his breath as if this would make his brain work more quickly in calculating the answers. The more he studied the rambling clues the more intrigued he became, but his suspicions were also growing. Someone, something … had wanted him to find this map – but why? What could the *treasure* be and how did this *someone* know about his mission? Or could it be that the hand of fate had a last been kind to him? His training had taught him to follow every lead but also to exercise caution. It was too good an opportunity to miss and was the purpose he had been looking for to escape this hellish existence – perhaps it was, in the words of the old saying, time, at last, to start counting his chickens.

"But *how* do we know for sure that Samson will take the bait?" asked Bungy again. Each time he'd asked this question he had not received a convincing reply. He couldn't believe, didn't want to think, that his nightmare experience might have been completely in vain.

"The simple answer is we don't know," sighed his sister. "We've not been watching the farmyard; we've got no idea what Samson has been up to in the last seven days."

"No one in their right mind would believe that ridiculous invention you call a map was serious, no one with any gumption that is …" scoffed Tal who also shared Bungy's frustration.

"That's exactly the point," sneered Pie. "Samson doesn't have any gumption. He's stupid. He's the most bungling spy I've ever clapped eyes on …"

"Oh yeah … since when did you last inhabit the world of espionage …" came the retort as Bungy adjusted his tender pink tummy on the cool kitchen tiles.

"I'll have you know I've watched a great deal of spy movies and can tell you categorically that its always the brainless spies that fall for the dummy clues …"

"*Oooooh,* well, here's some news for you … THAT'S IN A FILM …THIS IS REALITY!!" Bungy stuck his nose in the air and went to investigate an open paper bag on the pantry floor.

"I'm telling you he's thick as two short planks, to coin a phrase. What's more he's full of his own importance so the chance to be a hero, however out of the ordinary it may seem, will be irresistible. He can't bear the thought that if the map is for real he would be missing out on some personal glory. Trust me; I know these things … it's called psychology. He will, in fact, probably has already, started to work out the clues. At least it will give his little bit of grey matter some exercise. I can hear the cogs whirring from here ..." She chuckled, highly pleased with herself, then, overbalancing, unexpectedly slid off the window seat with an ungainly bump. Feigning nonchalance, she focussed intently on cleaning her paws ignoring the others' howls of laughter.

Samson had indeed been working out the clues and had every intention of following the map. There was a reason it had been deposited in the hen house; he had been meant to find it, and the only way to discover why, was to see where the map took him – to see for himself the treasure he was meant to find. Who knows, it could seal his promotion from General Cromwell. The clues were a bit vague and seemed to veer away from the village out to the north-east not the south as he had expected. This could be a red herring to throw him off the scent but he was cleverer than that and could see straight through their little ruse. This was a trick – he was supposed to think he was being sent on a wild goose chase but his superior intelligence and spying instinct told him that it was in fact a double bluff and the clues would actually take him straight to the treasure. Hah! They thought he was stupid – well nothing was further from the truth; he knew what they were up to and he was on his way to fame and fortune! A smug grin spread over his hard face, it had turned out to be a much better day in the end, things were finally going his way.

"What's that crackling noise?" Pie looked at Amos.

"Sounds like something trying to fight its way out of a packet of crisps," Tal mumbled sleepily, trying not to get drawn into the conversation. Pie and Amos were carefully studying the ancient tree markings that Amos had carved on a

247

rough pocket-sized piece of wood, going over the route they were expecting to take in a couple of days, retracing their steps to the clearing where they encountered Elias, hopefully this time going beyond to find the actual village itself.

"This route should be accurate but you never know," sighed Amos. "The full moon can play tricks with the landscape. It may have some surprises up its sleeve."

"I've had more than enough surprises to last me for a very *loooooong* time," came a voice out of what sounded like a lot of static, like when programmes ended on the television and it makes a *shusssshhing* noise with white dashes and dots flickering all over the screen.

"What *are* you wearing!" exclaimed Pie to the white rustling shape that arrived and sat down squarely on Amos' wooden map. A pink and white nose splodged with grey was just visible inside the white funnel. As Bungy turned to look at her, his head disappeared sideways into the depths of the makeshift garment.

"What do you think to my prototype, anti-ghost apparatus then ... natty *eh, eh* ...?"

"Anti-ghost ... wha ..." Pie was speechless. "It's a common or garden carrier bag with the name of a well-known supermarket chain emblazoned all over it. Have you got a contract for advertising or something ... *tee hee* ...?"

"You know your problem, Little Miss Top of the Class, you have got NO imagination. This fiendishly designed outfit doubles as camouflage. I'm white, like the ghost – so it will think I'm another ghost and leave me alone ... but not only that Ladies and Gentlepersons, it will keep me dry if the Green Lady is not scared of ghosts and decides to drip all over me again. *So whaddya think to that!*"

"I think it's ridiculous and all that rustling will give the game away the minute we step outside the front door. Not only that but you might as well be carrying a big sign that announces ... HELLO EVERYBODY! LOOK AT US. WE ARE ON A SECRET MISSION." Bungy looked crestfallen. "You blend naturally into the darkness (apart from your white bits) cos you're nearly all grey ... and white." She finished the sentence in a small voice. "As for the dripping ... (we know who's the drip here) ... well, according to your report you could hear the flipping ghost coming miles away with all that wailing so you just need to hide and GET OUT OF HER WAY ..."

"I'm never allowed to use my initiative – I don't get any praise for being inventive just a load of sarcastic remarks, so far I've been the hero, most of the time in this, this ... crusade ... mutter, mutter, mutter ..." Rustle, rustle, rustle, rustle ... Bungy disappeared towards the dining room after another quick inspection of the pantry for comfort food en route – unfortunately there were no opened packets within a tubby cat's reach.

Amos followed his passage with twinkling eyes. "You know, I'm going to miss that little fellow – I shall never forget our first encounter in the garden and the misfortune the poor thing experienced. I'm going to miss you all," he said quietly stroking the top of Tal's head allowing his fingers to linger enjoying its warm silkiness. "Life will never be the same."

"You can say that again," Tal added rolling on to his back for a tummy rub. "Our lives will definitely be very dull after you've gone home." They all fell silent realising that the next few days, if Pie's plan was successful, were going to be the last they would spend with Amos.

Tal, Amos and Pie sat in silence by the long conservatory window watching the sun descend from the sky – it was one of the most beautiful sunsets Tal thought he had ever seen. As the sun disappeared it left a kaleidoscope of hazy streaks on the blue canvas; topaz, amber, light pink, crimson, purple and violet. Then they were gone, replaced by a cold, flinty greyness and the faint silver disc of the moon. "There are times when I wish I could paint," sighed Tal. A shared calmness bound them in this unique beautiful moment. Pie shivered although warmth from the waning sun still hung in the room.

"Well, this is it team, dusk is approaching and we need to prepare. Has anyone seen my elusive brother?" No one had seen him all afternoon – it seemed once again he was conveniently unavailable. "I have not got the time or patience to ferret him out from one of his obscure hiding places. We'll have to go without him – I can't believe he would let us ... Amos, down at the last minute!" Pie was hopping mad. Jumping off the windowsill, she flicked up the lid of her wicker box and disappeared in one quick movement. The lid crashed down with a decisive thump. A muffled "I'll meet you at the front door in an hour" could just be heard then complete stillness. Tal and Amos knew better than to lift the lid and made their way to the kitchen for a last warm by the Aga.

Time played its usual trick and shortened the hour to what seemed like only ten minutes. The three companions assembled at the front door. Pie, arriving early, had been pacing up and down the doormat for at least five minutes chuntering about her unreliable brother. "I'm very disappointed in him, and will deal with him later. I can't believe he wouldn't want to say farewell to Amos."

"If I may, I think he is feeling wounded by your sharp tongue – his disguise was quite ingenious," Amos smiled at Pie. "He is a sensitive soul – perhaps you should treat him a little more kindly ..."

"*Hmmm* ... Thanks for the advice, I'll think about that."

"Think about what, Sis ..." They all glanced down to see a black shape behind them on the mat.

"Where *have* you been ... what is that, that ... *thing* ... you have on ...?" She peered into the gloom. "Is that a bin liner?"

"It's anti-ghost jacket Mark 2," said Bungy proudly.

"Anti-ghost jack ... oh, I give in ..."

"It's a special no rustle formula. Just makes a slight swishing noise when I walk, you can hardly hear it ... but YOU CAN'T SEE ME, CAN YOU?!! Come on then, let's get this show on the road." And with that he stepped jauntily into the night with a graceful *swisssssh* and trotted down the path melting into the darkness.

24

Making History

The brilliant full moon hung low like a vast silver coin over the lake. It seemed to skim so close to the ground Elias felt he could almost reach out and touch its shimmering face. An eerie, phosphorescent glow spread over the water radiating off the surface, around him the tents of the small encampment glowed luminous white. A small band of troopers gathered around the remains of a campfire jostling with each other in high spirits, relishing the task ahead, eager for battle. Elias turned his back on them fingering the leather bottle in his pocket. It was time. Grasping his hazel rod he strode silently towards the waiting men treading lightly on the silvery grass. The rod quivered as it connected with the ground. Elias felt the natural energies surge swiftly through his body. *We are as one; my rod will guide me well tonight.* Never before had Elias needed so much the magical protection and inspiration from his tall hazel staff; he may even have to draw on its ultimate power of invisibility if things, as foretold, went badly.

"So, tracker, the time is nigh. We are ready to fulfil our duty to the King, show our loyalty, unlike some ..." Elias stumbled, surprised, caught off guard. One of the surly renegades eyed him directly. Could this man be referring to his own personal fall from grace? His heart stopped momentarily. Could the two surly infantrymen be those responsible for his own disfavour with the King? Could they be about to reveal his true identity and dispense with him to wreak the vengeance they sought over Cromwell and his party? Elias's rod shook violently in his hand, confirming his suspicions. He must act quickly, stay aloof and maintain his composure despite the quaking feeling in the pit of his stomach.

"Aye, trooper, there are some who would waver, 'tis true. But no man here tonight goes against the King, I am certain. Come; let us share a toast together to seal our unity. It is a tradition where I come from ..."

"And just where do you come from, tracker, you appeared out of the night ...?" The young rebel persisted, enjoying the interplay. Elias needed to bring it to a close and quickly; he was fast losing his temper. "There will be time enough for discourse when our task is done. Come; drink whilst the ale is fresh ..." Elias turned away to an upturned barrel he had set by the fire and poured four small flagons of ale, stealthily adding five drops of the vile-smelling potion into each one. The troopers were too preoccupied with their revelry to notice. He hesitated then added two extra drops into two of the vessels. Pouring a further flagon for himself he distributed the ale around the group making sure the two flagons with the heavier doses were taken by the young renegades who held his gaze mockingly as they seized the drinks. As he had anticipated, the two young men downed the ale with gusto in one giant swig. *Perfect,* thought Elias, *you are mine now* ... He drank his own ale relishing the bitter sweetness on the back of his tongue. It tasted particularly good – the plan was in play; there was no turning back.

"For God and the King!" he raised his tankard skyward, it was silhouetted in the white face of the moon. *"For God and the King!"* came back the chorus. The two renegades threw their empty flagons into the dying embers of the fire where they lay blackening. Picking up their muskets they followed Elias towards the silvered tree line of the long wood.

Swish, swish, swish, swish. "If I may suggest, I think your design needs a little tweaking ... erm, I'm not criticising, I think it's got potential ..." Pie looked at Amos who smiled and nodded recognising her attempt at tact and diplomacy.

"Hmm ... seems to be getting slightly noisier and it's starting to rub on my war wounds at the tops of my legs ... I might have to make a small adjustment. You keep going. I'll catch you up." Bungy trotted to the grass verge and flopped on to the cool, slate white grass. Tucking his chin under his chest he craned his neck to peer at his tummy. There was no sound in the air of any kind. It was deathly quiet. He felt incredibly small. The moonlight magnified everything around him. Gigantic moonshadows strayed across the lane – there was definitely something sinister about them. Deciding it was better to get on with the modifications and catch up, he scrunched up into a tight ball to examine the 'legs' of his jacket. A distant shuffling noise interrupted his concentration. Looking around there was no sign of anything to disturb the silence. A bunch of dry fallen leaves scuttled past driven by a gust of wind. *Ah, perhaps they were the culprit ... now let me see if I ...*

There it was again, some kind of rhythm ... *Crunch,*

crunch, crunch, crunch … a faint marching beat drifted towards him amplified in the dead of night. Bungy stiffened, his ears tuning in to the approaching sound – definitely a marching noise, a sort of *regimental* kind of noise. His stomach churned. And what makes regimental kinds of noises … *military* noises? Boots … *big* military boots.

Surely not … It couldn't be. He hardly dare look. Reversing into the hedge bottom he held his breath as the noise grew in volume. *Crunch, crunch, crunch, CRUNCH, CRUNCH, CRUNCH, crunch, crunch, crunch* … The sound receded down the lane in the direction of his friends. A cold draught of air swirled past his nose as Samson's cloak swept by. The tall imposing figure was swallowed by the shadows then gone. "Talk about déjà vu. I've been here before … this is not in the plan! What the dickens is that idiotic spy up to? I knew he wasn't as stupid as he looks. He should be over the hill and miles away by now. Instead he's on a collision course with us and he's going to wreck everything. I've got to stop him, raise the alarm, do something … if I could just get out of this ridiculous straitjacket …" Tugging and pulling with all his strength the makeshift coat refused to budge, instead in the struggle he rolled further and further into the hedge bottom. The more he wriggled the more the coat put up a fight. Eventually Nature intervened and the hedge took pity on him; the sharp barbs of blackthorn ripped at the flimsy plastic until it was in shreds – he was free. Now he must follow the spy and find a way to divert his attention.

Samson was livid. He'd spent a whole week puzzling over those ridiculous clues and where had it got him … nowhere. He was sick of dodging into doorways, hiding round corners and trudging up and down hills, all for nothing. He had followed the clues religiously and they had led him to a village miles away in the opposite direction. He had been convinced he would find what he was looking for but instead the trail had gone cold and he realised he'd been hoodwinked, and by a bunch of amateurs at that. So he was doubly cross. There was no treasure, and he had been particularly stupid – he would have to keep this one to himself. "Call yourself a spy Samson Strong?" You're a pathetic excuse for one. After days of arguing with himself he now wanted revenge.

For the last two nights he'd kept watch on the cottage. There had to be a reason why they wanted him out of the way. Sure enough, his vigil had been rewarded. Earlier that night the party, including the old man, had set out down the garden path as the moon rose, heading south past the duck pond. Samson kept them in sight waiting until they were out on the cinder track which wound from the village down towards the woods. He then followed from a discreet distance keeping his eager boots in check; they were overjoyed to be on the march once again. He had never seen the moon so immense. Its sharp light danced off glossy holly leaves in the hedgerow where they sparkled and flashed like jewels. There was something mysterious, hypnotic almost, about the moon tonight, as if those who dared to be at large, to walk in the night, were somehow bewitched, drawn helplessly into its dazzling depths – Samson felt its magnetic pull as he stepped on to the soft earthen path towards Long Wood.

Amos and the others had already entered the wood and trod carefully the same path they had taken a month ago.

Amos led the way checking his rough map of scratched signs against the tree waymarks as they went along. They were approaching the sharp right angle in the path which was close to the forbidding guardian tree, the gateway to the clearing. "Remember, my friends, focus on the ground, do not look into the sunken depths of this evil tree and all will be well." Tal and Pie needed no reminding and carried on with their eyes glued to the forest floor. As if to catch them out, a giant shadow cast by the tree was projected by the moon right into their path. "Keep going, keep going, do not look up," Amos spoke quietly but firmly. Safely past the tree Tal found he had been holding his breath. The trapped air escaped with a noisy *hissss* – he watched the warm, misty spirals float up into the canopy.

"We must be almost at the clearing. Hang on a minute, where's Bungy?" Tal stopped abruptly. Deep in concentration, no one had noticed his absence.

"He is a complete and utter *liability;* I wash my paws of him …" Pie was exasperated. "We will just have to carry on having come this far – he's managed to find us every other time he's wandered off, let's just hope he keeps his wits about him and his … his … *disguise* works …" Amos and Tal were about to remonstrate but something about the tone of her voice changed their minds. They exchanged a worried look then set off after their leader as she crept deeper into the wood.

Keeping to the densest part of the wood, staying off the paths, Elias led the small band of troopers in the direction of the Hall. Progress was slow; it was hard work ducking under boughs, stepping over fallen logs, getting snagged on clinging brambles which clawed at their leather breeches, the hefty muskets they had insisted on bringing weighing them down. The men were complaining, swearing under their breath. Elias moved easily, at home on this terrain, his stout hazel rod guiding him, feeling the way. He was not sure how quickly the potion would take effect and didn't want to have to conceal the sleeping forms when the men became overpowered; he would leave them where they fell and let the trees do the rest. He had to keep up the charade until the last man had fallen. By the time they awoke, he would have disappeared silently into the night knowing that Cromwell was free to fight on. It was hard to know if the stronger dose given to the two angry rebels would cause any permanent damage; the herbs and mushrooms were always unpredictable. He wasn't particularly concerned; it was time they were taught a lesson. Up ahead through the trees the impressive outline of Palladian columns bleached white against the thick, dark forest came into view; they were getting close to the sweeping drive; Cromwell's party should be arriving shortly; all he had to do now was wait.

Bungy slunk low to the ground, running then crawling commando-style in pursuit of the spy, his belly scuffing the damp earth. Several times Samson stopped and looked around as if sensing his presence. Bungy froze flattening himself to the floor, legs outstretched, nose to the ground to conceal the white patches on his face. After a few seconds the heavy boots set off again. Bungy's mind was racing frantically trying to think of a suitable diversion to draw Samson away from his quest. Try as he might he reached the same sorry conclusion every time – *he* was the diversion. He was somehow going to have to get ahead of the big man and surprise him, then run like the clappers. How long it would take the seven-league boots to catch up with him he had no idea – not long. So, he had his answer; there was nothing else for it. The lives of his friends and Amos' only chance of getting home rested on him. Where was the Green Lady when you needed her? ... Now that *would* be a diversion. He couldn't believe he was praying for a good old-fashioned ghost to appear, but despite his pleas, the bell on the stable clock tower at Langhald Hall stayed infuriatingly silent.

He realised they were very close to the clearing where they had encountered the 'tree man' as Tal called Elias; he recognised the fork in the path. He remembered there was a kind of junction coming up at the fork of two tracks; one going to the clearing and one he guessed would lead to the Hall. One route would jeopardise his friends, the other would take him straight to Cromwell and who knows what kind of treacherous skulduggery. His options were pretty bleak. Samson was almost at the junction. Bungy was close enough to hear the leather creaking with the spy's every step; he had to act now or it would be too late. Sprinting off the path through a tangle of brambles, the sharp thorns prickling his delicate legs, he managed to get ahead of Samson keeping out of his sight. A handy low-hanging bough of a nearby ash tree provided a useful platform to spring up to a much longer wandering branch halfway up its enormous trunk. Balancing carefully Bungy tiptoed softy over the gnarled bark right to the slender end of the branch which sagged dangerously, groaning under his weight. He was now suspended a little higher than the top of Samson's head directly over the path. The stark light of the moon illuminated the track like a beacon, it was positively dazzling – up in the thinning canopy Bungy was well shadowed, good positioning he thought – perfect. He had a basic strategy, half formed admittedly, but a strategy nonetheless – wait till Samson was right underneath then aim for his head. It was a proven technique; he had seen it work to great effect when his sister had launched herself once from the top of the coal shed on to the shoulders of the unsuspecting delivery man just as he was about to release his load. The poor chap was startled out of his wits and had dropped his coals all over the lawn. Bungy had felt for the old guy who had then spent an hour picking up the black nuggets by hand and had subsequently refused to deliver to the cottage ever again. Pie thought it was great fun but now had no one to terrorise. Samson would hopefully be equally surprised; what would happen after that was anyone's guess but it certainly wasn't going to be a lot of fun. The branch was feeling just a little too flimsy for his liking. It was creaking menacingly; *ignore it … it's just gently bobbing in the wind*. Samson's tight, black, curly hair was one step away; Bungy coiled his body in readiness, all his weight in his haunches for maximum lift. The creaking intensified. Then suddenly, a loud *crrrrrackk!*

Before he could say 'fish fingers' the branch snapped, whipped into the air and catapulted him at great speed on to Samson's mass of wiry hair. The startled man screamed in agony, arms thrashing wildly at his head as Bungy sank his claws into Samson's scalp for better grip – it was just like a rodeo, the cowboys of the Wild West riding a bucking bronco, thought an equally startled cat whose strategy had not quite worked out how he'd expected. For several agonising seconds the two were locked in a bizarre ballet of pirouettes and bows while the spy rocked back and forth, doing his best to unseat his assailant. After a terrifying few moments Bungy decided it was time to dismount before he was decapitated by one of the many branches whizzing past his head. Screwing his eyes up tight he released the pressure on his claws and let gravity take its course. He flew through the air landing neatly on all fours with a muffled rustle into a bed of early fallen leaves some way down the track to the clearing – the strange triangular waymarker flashed past him on the way down – destiny had decreed the direction he was taking.

There was an unsettling silence then Bungy heard Samson approaching, breathing heavily in short, snatched breaths. "That damned, despicable, callous brute adds further insult to my injuries. When I catch that vicious beast I will pull its hairs out one by one!" *You'll have to find me first,* thought Bungy relishing the moment from a dark hollow in a dead tree close to the man's feet. All he could see at this level were the hefty boots angled first one way then the other as Samson, seething, turned this way and that feverishly searching the area. The boots then scuffed around the roots of the tree lifting clumps of brambles, Samson bending to peer underneath. And all the while two beady, amber eyes inches away looked on from the shadows of the hollow. Boiling with frustration Samson swung a kick at the base of the tree then turning on his heels set off purposefully on the track which lead to the village.

"No!" Bungy let out a quiet squeak into the dark. "Not that way, oh flippin' 'eck. What do I do *now* to stop him …?"

"What yer gerrin' so worked up about, matey?" The voice

came unexpectedly out of the darkness. Bungy's hair stood on end. In the shadow he could just make out an exquisite set of small, straight, pearlescent white teeth grinning at him. "'E's headin' int' reet direction, no problem ..."

"Bruce ... is that you?"

"Depends who wants te know like ... frien' ... or foe."

"Frien' ... friend, you dumpling – we've already met, you remember my sister, the smart one with all the ..."

"Opinions ... aye, I remember all right ... once met never forgotten ..." he sniffed then spat on the ground.

"Eeeergh, Tal was right about you – you're a good-for-nothing 'street dog'."

"Mmmmm ... is that wha' he said 'bout me ... quite a compliment, he's right enough, laddo Lurcher. Come te think o' it, where is the rest of yer motley crew?"

"On their way to find the village – help Amos get home once and for all."

"Amos? Amos ... the *woodsman?*"

"Is there another Amos?"

"I knew it! I knew yous would 'elp me out ... took a bit o' gettin' there like but got there in't end ... Come on, mate, no time to waste, got to find yer frien's."

"But ... but what about the spy ...?"

"As I says to yer, pay attention, he's goin' t'right way. He's goin' straight fer t'village ... *Royalist* village ... 'e'll be reet welcome there, look after 'im good an' proper they will ... he's headin' reet fer t'enemy camp so there's nowt te worry abou' there ..."

"But what if he catches up with t'others, you've got me at it now ... what if he finds Amos? He's been hunting him down ever since you lot arrived."

"Stick wi' me, kid … I knows all t'back roads … and t'ancient waymarks. Amos will be following 'is nose an' will pick same tracks as meself so we should find 'em quickly, no bother …"

With that he hopped out of the hollow and skipped off joyfully down the track with Bungy in tow, eyes glued to Bruce's stubby tail beating a rhythmic tick … tock in time with his step.

25

Langhald

Negotiating a knotted mat of tangled roots the trio arrived at the edge of the once dry stream bed. It seemed a very long time since the hot summer afternoon when they had all stood perplexed on the river bank looking out over an empty hazy meadow and a single evergreen oak tree. Tonight the view was surprisingly different. The dry baked bed now teemed with a busy little brook that, swelled by the recent heavy rain, rushed down the wood disappearing towards the lake. Over the brook through the trees a scattering of canvas tents could be seen fluttering gently against the glassy backdrop of the lake, mirrored by the moon against the lake's dense shadow, the tents appeared like small yachts bobbing on the water, masts fully rigged. Behind the camp up on a small rise, the mighty oak tree stood in solitary splendour watching quietly over the village and its inhabitants. The three friends stood in awed silence. It wasn't some clever enchantment or illusion, mirage perhaps, the village did exist – three pairs of eyes all saw the same sight; they couldn't all be hallucinating.

"This is the place you came with Bruce?" Amos turned to Tal who was looking extremely anxious.

"Yes ... but ... but, when I last came there was nothing

here, no sign of life until we went over the stream. It was like walking through a mist not being able to see what's in front of you and when the mist cleared the village was there. But ... but tonight, it's a living breathing place, as if the moon has brought it to life ..."

"Thankfully there is no one around, everyone's asleep ... hopefully," added Tal trying to reassure himself. "What do we do now?" Tal hoped fervently that Amos would decide to go from here on his own, after all, their part of the bargain had been to find this place and get Amos here safely, which they had done – surely it was up to Amos now ... and besides they had to find their own way home before the full moon waned taking the path with it, or they could end up wandering around disorientated for days. The memory of meeting Bruce deep in the wood at the last full moon flashed into Tal's thoughts. There was something Bruce had said that he needed to remember, something vitally important, but every time he tried to think what it was his mind went blank as if someone had flicked a switch, the moon perhaps, causing interference with the signals to his brain. It was getting beyond a joke – all he knew was he must remember tonight or it would be too late.

Pie sat quietly, studiously examining every inch of the landscape, surveying the encampment, stroking her whiskers as she carefully and methodically appraised the scene, analysed the situation and computed the next steps.

"Hmmm ... it's not ideal but we will most likely have to go into the camp and rouse someone to introduce Amos, ask if he can join them and explain he needs to travel back with them to his time ..."

Tal found himself staring at the magnificent oak, unable

to drag his eyes away, an unexpected urgency invaded his body, a pressing, agitating feeling which grew in strength as he stared at the tree across the moonlit field – could the tree be trying to communicate with him, surely not ... *I've spent too much time with Amos,* he thought shaking his head, flapping his ears violently to rid his body of the feeling, willing it to go away. But there it was again, an insistent, persistent irrational urge to look at the tree; the tree ... what was it about the dratted tree ...

The small group of infantrymen were becoming more spread out, several of them now stumbling and weaving, ricocheting drunkenly off trees as they tried to keep up with Elias. The potion was taking effect. The two more weedy men at the back of the group suddenly dropped to their knees, their eyes glassy. One of them fell forwards heavily, smacking his face on a waiting tree root, bloodying his nose; the other collapsed silently deflating into a shrivelled heap. Two down, two to go, Elias didn't look back. He sensed the rebels were still on their feet but slowing noticeably. Pausing briefly, listening in the stillness, nerve endings taut, he felt his tracking instincts sharpen, then take control. A faint jingle of bridles and harness, the stamping and snorting of horses could be heard somewhere not far away. The rebel troopers staggered up behind him swaying but still standing. "What's afoot, tracker ...? There is a foul smell in the air, our Parliamentarian friends must be close at hand ..." the words slurred struggling for coherence followed by a drunken guffaw. "We must make ready ..." The rebels fumbled awkwardly with their muskets, clumsily scattering gunpowder around their feet, fighting the heaviness dragging at their muscles, as they went through the well practised drill in increasing slow motion.

"Stand down your weapons, you idiots," Elias snapped in a hushed whisper, incredulous at their apparent ability to fight the effect of the powerful drugs. "There will be no combat – we use stealth and guile … neither quality you possess," he spat in disgust.

The jingling grew louder accompanied by the drumming of hoof beats announcing the arrival of Cromwell's party.

"We have more guile, tracker, than you would ever realise." The arrogant glare cut Elias deeply. "You are, at last, exposed, a traitor … your scheme will fail … *long live the Ki* …" The unfinished word hung in the air as the young soldier's knees buckled and his unsupported body crashed to the floor. His accomplice turned with great effort to face Elias struggling to focus, his vision blurred. The young man's arms sagged as he tried valiantly to hoist the armed musket to his sightline, instead it pointed directly at Elias's stomach. The trooper's finger searched aimlessly for the trigger as his body began to crumple gently towards the floor. Elias froze, willing the potion around the soldier's bloodstream, the muzzle of the musket a foot away from his body. The young man wore a bemused, dazed expression; another force far away had taken over his faculties, controlled his movements. With a supreme effort the trooper's finger curled locking on the trigger – fighting drowsiness the man willed his muscles to contract, to release the spark, ignite the gunpowder. Cromwell and his men were feet away on the path oblivious to the drama unfolding within the trees. Elias panicked shaking his staff, muttering an incantation to unleash the ultimate power of the hazel rod, to vanish from sight. The rod responded instantly quivering; tremors rippled through Elias's thick arm. Looking down all he could see was beaten earth where his shovel-sized hand had been.

Booooooooommmmm. A deafening shot blasted into the empty hollow blackness. Wreaths of acrid, stinging smoke belched into the air, the musket recoil was enough to unsteady the young man who rocked violently backwards coming to rest motionless on a carpet of leaves.

Bungy's eyes were smarting from peering into the gloom after his scruffy little guide who was covering the ground at quite a pace. The stumpy tail going ten to the dozen keeping time with Bruce's jaunty trot, punctuated every fourth step with a back leg hop. *What is it with dogs … they have to overcomplicate the simplest things like going for a walk …* Tripping over a tree root, Bungy ran squarely into Bruce's rear end not noticing he had come to a halt by a wide stream.

"Well … we's 'ere. Village is yonder, just over t'beck."

"But where are the others? And just where exactly is this mythical *village*?" Bungy was still highly sceptical that the village actually existed.

Bruce sniffed the air, a welcome scent of dry earth mingled with sap and freshly sawn wood hit his nose. "My guess is them be jus' downstream from 'ere." he nodded in the direction of flow. "Can't see t'village fer trees … but ten ter one yer mates are lookin' at it right now." Bruce hopped over the offending root and set off again into the dark.

"Hey! Hang on, wait for me." Bungy scurried to catch up.

The ride came to an abrupt halt. Six sturdy horses, coats gleaming with sweat, steaming in the cold, waited impatiently ears pricked, heads high, veins standing proud on their skin, alert to every nuance in the atmosphere around them. The ear-splitting sound had rent the air shaking the party from their good-natured banter and anticipation of a few days' relaxation before the long slog of the march south. The horses, startled, became skittish. They shied at shadows and pranced nervously on the spot, anxious to flee this scary place. The moon's rays piercing thick branches crept their way over the path, glancing off the row of ugly, round metal helmets. Despite being a social visit, Cromwell had insisted on full military uniform refusing to lower his standards. His only concession had been to keep their colourful pennants tightly furled under leather straps attached to each saddlebag; the procession, conspicuous in full battle regalia stood stock-still as statues, waiting. Feeling the tension increase the horses pawed restlessly at the ground snorting, circling anxiously, tossing their manes, grinding the bit between their teeth. A scout was despatched to ride ahead to the stables. He returned hastily with news of a body discovered close to the path apparently half-dead, that wasn't the only news; the body was that of a Royalist trooper. Alarm spread quickly through the party. In disarray, Cromwell's soldiers tried as one to turn their horses back the way they had come, straight into the path of an oncoming horseman.

"Sire! This way ... sire ..." the horseman's voice funnelled by the trees echoed loudly over the thrum of his galloping horse. "Follow me! We must make for safety ... I know a place where you and your men will not be discovered," the man urged. He was a youthful man wearing riding breeches with a brown, woven, cloth tunic secured over them by a thick leather belt. He sat confidently astride a stocky, bay horse with hogged mane on a worn but well-cared-for saddle, the leather supple, highly polished, had clearly been cleaned with pride. The horse was well groomed, its coat sleek, lovingly brushed. "I am Sir Randolph's head groomsman; I was sent to meet your party when a shot was heard. You must come this way with all speed." The young man spun the big horse round on its hocks with acrobatic ease, headed back up the track then cut off into the wood out of sight. Cromwell and his men had no choice but to trust the youth as it was clear danger lurked in the other direction. The soldiers swung their reins sharply against the necks of the prancing horses eager to join the gallop and set off in the wake of the groom, Cromwell leading at the front. The party galloped through the trees emerging on to a wide driveway which swept in front of a palatial columned mansion. As they thundered past the building the bell on the stable clock tower tolled once.

Bruce led Bungy along the bank of the swollen stream which gurgled and splashed its way down the gentle incline to the lake. Bungy eyed the stream warily and tried to keep well on to the shore – why was it things always ended up leading somewhere damp. There had been a lot of new experiences over the last few months and being wet was one he would definitely not want to repeat. "Not much further, me ol' son … what's up … freetened o' watter …? What a proper wuss …" Bungy looked hurt and decided to save the long explanation about the hen house incident for another time. Bruce was beginning to get on his nerves, Tal was right; he was a cocky little blighter.

Bungy thought he caught a glimpse of Tal's red coat glowing in the moonlight. They must be nearly there.

The only obstacle to be negotiated was a huge hollow tree which looked like some giant ogre had scooped out its insides leaving a smooth, perfect arc the full length of the trunk; it was big enough for a man to stand up in thought Bungy. This feature was in fact being demonstrated by a frighteningly large man standing within the hollow tree who stepped out straight into their path from behind the curving bark. Before Bruce could say "Aye up ..." the large man had gathered them both into his arms, similar to tree trunks, thought Bungy, and hoisted them into the air, level with his dark, glittering eyes.

"How nice to see you, my elusive little friend," Samson's stale breath wafted over Bungy's face. Cringing he shrunk back against the man's chest which felt like a brick wall.

"Who the flippin' 'eck are thee ...?" Bruce barked, wriggling furiously in the iron grasp. It was Samson's turn to recoil from the pungent smell oozing from Bruce's matted fur.

"He's the enemy spy ... not a very good one either," yowled Bungy, trying to free his paws to scratch the man but Samson's grip tightened around his middle until he could only just breathe in short laboured gasps.

"Tha'll be sorry, tha greet lump ... *gerroff* me, tha's no idea who tha's messin' wi' ... t'King'll deal wi' thee ... I has frien's in high places ... gerroff!!" Bruce took a deep breath and howled balefully into the darkness. The ominous, eerie wail echoed into the wood rising to the tree tops, out across the field and over the lake. For a small dog he could make a lot of noise thought Bungy astonished. The howl died away. Bruce looked at Bungy and winked taking in another deep breath *ooooooooowwwwwwwwwoooooooooooooooowwwwwwwoooooooo*

... the sound carried high into the air and swept down the stream to the three friends huddled together against a tree. What fearful monster could possibly make such a dreadful haunting noise – Pie and Tal cowered behind Amos' cloak shaking. Amos, however, was less perturbed – in fact he was positively elated. He knew exactly the source of the noise, his heart leapt. "Bruce – dear, faithful Bruce ..."

Somehow Bungy understood what Bruce was trying to do, the wink said it all. As the howl reached its crescendo Bungy felt Samson's grip momentarily relax, the spy was becoming extremely agitated trying to get his fingers around Bruce's snout to shut him up. It was Bungy's cue to sink his teeth into the back of the man's hand. Samson yelled in pain dropping Bungy like a hot cake. At the same time Bruce snarled ferociously snapping at the clenched fingers, inches away from the spy's nose. But Samson wasn't going to lose both his prizes. He hung on to Bruce with an outstretched arm holding the wiry terrier at a safe distance, keeping Bruce dangling unceremoniously, legs whirling round like he was furiously pedalling an imaginary bicycle.

Bungy hit the floor, shook himself and raced off in the direction of the others. Samson turned and ran after him still hanging on to Bruce, who, legs flailing, snapped wildly all the time trying to connect with the man's leathery flesh. Bungy ploughed blindly along the path not looking left or right, just heading straight for his friends. Darting in and out of bushes he zigzagged along trying to shake off the spy but to no avail; Samson was right behind him. *I can't put my friends in danger I have to lead Samson away,* he glanced quickly through the trees and saw, for the first time, the Royalist camp nestled at the lake side.

"It *does* exist." What was it Bruce had said – *"Samson would be well looked after"* – that's what he'd do; he would lead Samson right into his enemy's hands. With no more idea than saving his friends, not sure what action he'd take or what danger he may face, Bungy swerved sideways towards the stream which bubbled angrily in thousands of small eddies, churned by the tree roots below. *Here goes* … Taking a flying leap he fell just short of the other bank landing with a splosh in a belly flop, dunking his bottom and tail in the icy water. *Brrrrr, that's woken me up*, he thought as he pelted on towards the circle of tents.

"Surely my eyes do deceive me," whispered Amos breaking the silence. The others followed his gaze and gasped simultaneously. Illuminated in the moon's unflinching light a small dark shape could be seen hurtling across the wide expanse of the field rapidly approaching the encampment. The shape was really motoring, achieving an astonishing speed for a chubby couch potato cat, a fact that hadn't escaped Bungy who noticed his short legs had put on a spurt as if they had a mind of their own and were showing off to the incredulous onlookers hidden in the trees. For a moment he was a lone figure in the vast white expanse of the moon bleached meadow, then the reason for his desperate flight became obvious. Breaking out of the tree line having leapt the stream bed in one gigantic step, a tall, black, hulking figure entered the searchlight in determined pursuit.

"Samson!" cried the astonished friends in unison.

"What's *he* doing here? He should be miles away … and how has my stupid brother got himself into yet another pickle *and* managed to throw a spanner in the works at the same time ...?" exclaimed Pie. "All that planning and effort for nothing," her head dropped dejectedly.

"On the contrary, my dear," Amos interjected quietly. "Your brother has done the opposite; he has put his companions first and is drawing Samson away from our hiding place, leading him straight into the Royalist camp to almost certain capture. He is, where I come from, a hero."

It was true, she knew, her 'stupid' brother had used his brain for once but was now in grave danger. She watched as his shadow grew smaller and smaller receding into the distance. She willed him on with all her might but the large, menacing figure was gaining on him propelled along by his faithful hefty military boots which were having the time of their life, enjoying the thrill of the chase.

"If he can just reach the tree and get up high in the canopy, he should be safe." Thinking out loud she put her paws over her eyes not daring to look.

"Yes, he will be safe if he can get above Samson's reach, we have to pray he gets to the oak before Samson catches him up," agreed Amos. "He's only a few paces away, look ..."

The three friends watched the scene play out as if it were a film. Tal watched horrified, a growing dread creeping through his body. The meeting in the clearing with Bruce filtered through his mind, his brain sifting through the conversation for something crucial he had to remember.

"The *tree!*" he snapped suddenly making the others jump out of their skins.

"Yes, the tree should save him ..." reassured Amos.

"*No! ... no ...* he *mustn't* go near the tree, the moonlight ..."

"Have you lost your senses?" Pie glared at him from between her paws.

"When I met Bruce he told me about the path, the waymarks ..." He gabbled on. "He also gave me a warning. I remember now, I've been trying to remember but it's as if something's been blocking the memory ..."

"Well ... spit it out ... for heaven's sake."

"Do ye fancy life in 1642, lad ... cos that's where ye'll be ... wi' no way back ..." Bruce's words came tumbling into Tal's head.

"We mustn't go near the oak tree, pass under its branches, whilst the moon is full or we will end up back in 1642 ... and ... won't be able to return ..." His voice trailed off. Tal looked solemnly at Amos who looked back at him flabbergasted, not knowing whether to rejoice at this news or be alarmed as it seemed his friend was innocently, unexpectedly on a collision course with a new life, one, almost certainly, that he would not survive.

They stood stock-still, stunned by this revelation as the drama unfolded in front of them. Samson was bearing down on the exhausted cat who was visibly flagging but feet away from the base of the enormous tree. The friends watched in horror craning their necks, eyes trained on the tiny receding dot as Bungy ploughed on oblivious to the waiting disaster. Samson was now within reach of Bungy's tail, folding his large frame towards the ground he put out a massive hand to scoop up the tiring creature. With a monumental effort Bungy accelerated towards the tree sensing security and disappeared out of sight.

The Evergreen Oak

Bungy raced on, heart hammering, lungs about to explode, the sanctuary of the tree was only moments away. How on earth he was going to manage getting on to the lower branches with legs like jelly he had no idea, but would have to find strength from somewhere, the alternative was too awful to contemplate. The cold night air nipped at his nose transporting a subtle, familiar tang of ripe warm leather his way, the military boots were closing in covering the ground swiftly and surely; driven by Samson's piston-pumping legs they gleefully ate up the ground.

The stately oak tree loomed ahead, growing in majesty each step of the slope that Bungy's tired legs climbed – he had never before seen such an impressive and beautiful tree, its grand, symmetrical, flowing proportions and graceful tracery of branches silhouetted in the moonlight. One sturdy low branch grew out horizontally from the thick trunk some considerable distance before curving gently skyward to form a perfect cup-shaped refuge for a desperate cat. This would be his target. If he took a big leap towards the trunk, aiming for as much height as possible, then quickly shinned up the tree he should make it to the branch. The sweeping arms of the splendid tree seemed to be beckoning, calling, reeling him in on an invisible thread, helping him on his way – just a couple more strides and he was safe. Psyching himself up for a life or death leap he slowed slightly, pausing to make a split second calculation measuring the height and distance, priming his muscles for a 'superhuman' effort, all the time aware that Samson was breathing down his neck. Poised on the point of take-off he made one further adjustment then pictured himself high on the branch watching the top of Samson's head go charging past – it was a satisfying thought, enough to fire the adrenaline.

Samson's puffs and pants grew louder. Bungy could almost feel the hot laboured breath on his body; he didn't look back, just tried to focus … focus … *focus* … Crouching, eyes peering for the grainy whorls in the bark, he sprang in the air with all his might. All four paws were airborne. The exact moment he left the ground the shadows shifted, thickened, as a dark blur swept directly into his path buffeting his body with a strong current of air, knocking him off course. Bungy sensed a large black shape streak past. Then he was travelling sideways, instead of clinging to safe refuge; he was tumbling head over heels in the opposite direction. Jumping up slightly dazed he turned to face the tree determined to try again. Out of nowhere came a swift, black, formless shape lunging at him again, another blast of air inches away then a gentle but firm blow, a strange soft, downy kind of blow, as the arc of a large wing struck the back of his head. *Eeeaaaaak! Eeeeeeak!* A deafening screech as the owl soared past a foot off the ground. *Eeeeaaak! Eeeeaaak!* … It was shooing him away from the tree, back into the open.

In the commotion Bungy had no idea what had

happened to Samson, he had no choice but to keep running out across the field towards the lake with the huge bird right on his tail, beak outstretched, wings flapping furiously.

The military boots were in their element, stampeding straight for the oak with no intention of stopping, this was the most fun they had had in ages and the pull of the tree was magnetic. Samson felt a rush of elation, jubilation; he would soon have that infuriating animal in his grasp then he would enjoy extracting information from both his prisoners, putting his interrogation training to good use. The small, smelly creature tucked firmly under his arm was becoming a real nuisance but, he had to admit, it had admirable spirit – nipping and wriggling, constantly trying to get free, he'd cheerfully have dropped the vicious little hound way back but two captives would give him double the information, it was worth the effort.

Bruce was fed up with having his snout stuck under a disgustingly sweaty armpit, fragrance was not one of his own virtues, but no hound of the King's household should have to endure such a degrading experience. The burly soldier was incredibly strong; it would take a miracle to escape the iron grasp and Bruce was all out of ideas. They were gaining on the cat. Bruce felt for the little guy who was not exactly the athletic type but was putting on a commendable turn of speed. It was only a matter of time before they caught up; in fact it was then Bruce felt the big man alter his balance, check his stride and stoop towards the ground ready to gather up the unfortunate creature. Ah well, poor kid, there was nothing he could do to save him.

Huddled together on the river bank Amos, Tal and Pie watched open-mouthed in disbelief as the tiny dot disappeared completely from view. Dumbstruck they stared out over the moonlit field; eyes searching desperately for a tiny black pinprick in the sea of white, but the lonely outline of the tree stared hauntingly back at them. They each shared the same thought but none of them wanted to be the first to say it aloud. The stocky frame of Samson was careering full pelt towards the tree, his massive bulk casting a terrifying moonshadow; they watched, hardly daring to breathe, as the giant shadow also disappeared, swallowed up by the dark depths of the sweeping branches.

Moments passed like an eternity as the three companions, thoughts teeming wildly, tried to make sense of what they had just witnessed. Not wanting to believe what their eyes had shown them, unable to register the consequences of what had occurred, how life had just changed, all they could do was stare into the shadows hoping fervently that Bungy would survive his new existence. They each could not believe they would never see him again.

Pie broke the suffocating silence her head falling heavily to her chest. Turning her back on the camp she mumbled slowly, her words an emotional jumble of deep distress, frustration and incredulity, "My idiotic ... stupid ... infuriating ... *wonderful, heroic ... irreplaceable* brother ... how could this possibly happen ... *he* was the one trying to find a way to get Amos home, not the one who should actually be *going* there ..." She looked at Amos distraught. Amos did not reply but walked away from the group into the surrounding forest, head down, limp and dejected. Tal sprinted after him.

"*Do something!* ... You're the tree expert, undo the magic spell, ... *anything* ... I don't know ... talk nicely to the tree! ... *GO AND GET HIM BACK!* ..." Tal's hysterical, anguished cries bounced around the wood reverberating in the still air.

Amos kept walking and did not respond. Tal streaked through the trees in a flash and stood squarely in Amos' path. The old man stopped, refusing to lift his head as if carefully inspecting Tal's paws, then, Tal heard a quiet strangled sniff; tears were streaming from eyes deadened, no longer dancing and bright, down the weather-beaten face, running on to the extravagant moustache and dripping solemnly off the curly ends on to the floor. "My dear friend ... if only it were that simple ... I'm afraid it's impossible ... I believe Bruce is correct, once in 1642 that is where he will remain. I can do nothing to reverse what has happened ..."

Swiping blindly in the shadows, Samson's bare knuckles dragged on the sharp stubble of the field instead of connecting with Bungy's tail. He swiped again in the opposite direction but nothing other than shadowy air ran through his fingers. Despite the full moon, the shadows under the tree were impenetrable, blacker than black. Perhaps the creature had managed to climb part way up the tree but it was impossible to see even his hand in front of his face in this sooty darkness. Wandering around the base of the tree he put his arms in the air feeling for the long horizontal branch he had seen as he sped across the field. Sensing the spy's distraction and not one for passing up the offer of a morsel of tasty flesh Bruce sank his teeth into the thick, hairy wilderness of Samson's armpit with relish. The big man screamed and released his grip dropping the terrier to the ground with a bump allowing a relieved Bruce to scamper away in the direction of the lake. Rubbing furiously at the smarting skin under his arm he thrashed about madly in the deepening shadows. "Where can that confounded creature have got to ... he must have kept going passing under the tree." Starting again to jog, much to the delight of the boots which rapidly gathered speed, Samson headed out the other side of the oak tree and fell flat on his face. *"What in heaven's name ...!"* Rising to his knees he looked round in anger expecting to see a large protruding root as the culprit. Instead, the shiny blade of a vicious-looking sixteen-foot pike winked cheerily at him in the firelight. The pike rested against the leather-clad thigh of an imposing man squatting by the fire feeding a log to the glowing flames. *"Who ...? What ...? Where ...?* Have you perchance seen a fat grey and white cat, sire ...?" Samson asked falteringly, looking around in bewilderment at the rough timbered dwellings and small canvas tent next to the burly man with close-cropped, dark, curly hair and flashing black eyes.

"And what pray would a spy of General Cromwell want with a cat?" asked the man slowly in a menacing tone which made Samson's spine tingle. "In these parts cats earn their keep as mousers or are fed to the working dogs." The man did not look up; there was something familiar about his voice. "So tell me, brother, how is life in the elite world of spies these days ... word is you have been assigned a special mission ...?" the mocking voice continued.

"*Will? Will Strong?* It cannot be ..." The head of matted black hair turned upwards to face Samson and he saw himself in the deep, glittering eyes that stared defiantly back at him.

"Not such an elite spy as you would have everyone think, Samson. My Royalist friends will look forward to hearing of your escapades ... with your cat!" He laughed and jumped lithely to his feet knocking Samson back on to his haunches. Before the spy had time to move his hands were tightly bound with a leather tie and he was dragged roughly to his feet. The two men faced each other inches apart, exactly the same height and build; it was like looking at a mirror image. Not exactly the triumphant ending to his mission Samson had envisaged – taken prisoner by his own brother.

Hearing the galloping hoof beats Elias lay motionless behind a large, dead, fallen trunk which had long since given up its journey to the sky. Decrepit and decaying on the woodland floor, home to a myriad of invisible forest dwellers, the trunk lay stranded like a beached whale, encrusted with tiny ribbons of fungi and vivid mustard splashes of creeping lichen. The musty smell of the rotting wood clung to his nostrils but was a calming, welcome scent, reminding him of time spent rooted in the copse, feeling the sap rise through his veins.

It had been a close shave. His physical body had melted into the background, vanishing to become one with the trees just as the trooper had squeezed the trigger, the musket rounds whistling past his ears. He would never forget the look of amazement on the young man's face as the kick of the recoil drove into his shoulder sending him crumpled to the floor. The hoof beats faded into the distance carrying their mounts to safety. Elias stared peacefully up into the deep, inky vastness of the sky through a lattice of black branches dusted silver, stars flashed and twinkled across the heavens like scattered diamonds, the beauty was incomparable. He sighed heavily feeling the tension of the past few hours drain from his muscles. Cromwell lived to fight another day; his task was complete. Peering gingerly over the dead trunk Elias scanned the woods listening keenly, hearing only sounds of the night, an owl screeching somewhere over by the lake. The bell on the stable clock tower chimed once then fell silent. Slowly he raised his enormous frame off the floor; it was like the dead tree coming again to life. There was just time to collect his few meagre possessions from the camp then he would disappear, evaporate into the night as if he had never existed.

"I can't believe it; I just can't believe it," said Pie over and over shaking her head. They were all numb, deeply shocked at what had happened. Tal sat bolt upright on the edge of the stream, back turned away from the others, gazing out across the encampment focussing on the oak tree as if he could use the power of his mind to reverse the dreadful sequence of events. The whole situation was unreal, incomprehensible, yet he had watched helpless as the small, round blur, his best friend, had disappeared, forever. He had waited patiently for over an hour, expecting, willing, hoping, for a sign that it was all an illusion, but none had come; the vast field stretched before him empty and bare like a bar of silver sand alongside the lake, the scattering of tents like boats waiting for the turning tide.

"He was so brave, courageous – a true hero, despite his annoying little habits," sobbed Pie. "Meal times will never be the same again – I think I've permanently lost my appetite; *nothing* will ever be the same again. No one to chase me up the woodpile, no one to rescue from ridiculous situations … no one to curl up with at night …" She wandered away to the foot of the nearest tree and curled into a tight ball wrapped up in her own sorrow.

Amos remained quiet, pensive. He wished a large hole would open in the ground and swallow him forever. He would never forgive himself for bringing such distress into the lives of these unique, innocent companions. There was nothing he could do that would help, except for him to go away, become a hermit, and live out alone the existence dealt him by Fate. He had caused enough heartache.

"Could you just repeat the bit about being brave ... and the bit about being a hero ... I didn't quite catch it cos I was out of puff and breathing hard ... you can leave out the bit about annoying habits ..."

Amos looked down at his feet in the direction of the sound. There, large as life, preoccupied with removing twigs, brambles and clods of mud from his fur sat Bungy, bedraggled, almost unrecognisable after a marathon trek trailing through undergrowth, fording streams and traversing fields. The scruffy ball of fur looked up at Amos and the lopsided clownish grin was clear to see.

"In all the heavens, I cannot believe what my eyes present to me!! My dear, dear fellow, *is it really you* ...?"

Bungy looked around. "Well, there's no one else here ..."

"It is you!"

"Er ... I am me, yes ... is this a new game or something ...?" He chewed furiously at his tail. "It's going to take days to get rid of this bloomin' mud ... have I missed anything? It's been a bit of a roller-coaster ride tonight ..."

"I am not familiar with this 'roller coaster' turn of phrase of which you speak ..." Amos replied stupefied.

"Let's just say there's been lots of ups and downs," mumbled Bungy, legs splayed, tongue methodically rasping over the exposed pink skin of his ample belly.

"I must find the others."

"Yeah, where are they, those slackers …? Let's get on with the real business, before you know it the sun will be up …"

Amos bent and shook Pie gently.

"Leave me alone …"

"But … but there has been a miracle …"

"I'm not interested …"

"But Fate has been kind to us …"

"I doubt it … what are you rambling on about …?"

"What's this then, Sis … sleeping on duty, can't be bad, taking a nap whilst the lackeys do all the work …"

"I am NOT asleep …"

"You're doing a good impression …"

"Is nothing sacred? Can't I grieve in peace without having insults thrown at me by an ignorant scruffy hound, one with no social skills whatsoever, you're as sensitive as a brick …"

"I doubt you're related to Bruce, although stranger things have happened, it's *me* you fruitcake … I 'aven't got another sister …" Bungy nudged her with his wet nose. Pie opened her eyes and blinked in amazement.

"Wha' .., I … *Where did you come from* …?"

"Oh great, what happened to 'hello my *wonderful* brother, my brother the *hero*'," Bungy winked at Amos.

"You're *here* … not there …"

"Er … yeeeeesss … mmmmm …"

"You're not … you know …"

"No, I don't know … what's come over everyone? … how come I'm always the last to find things out? … can't get any sense out of anyone ..." with that he turned and shuffled off towards Tal whose outline shone fluorescently picked out by the moon's white glow.

"Ey up ... matey ..." Bungy flopped down beside Tal. "Beautiful, in't it ..."

"Depends how you look at it ... what you see ..."

"Very poetic my friend ... something strange has happened to you lot. I leave you for an hour and what happens? ... I find ... you've gone all ... all ... *Zen* on me ..." he chuckled, pleased with his choice of words. Bungy cleaned his paws for the third time, oblivious to the astonished look on Tal's face.

"Look like you've seen a ghost pal ... now me, I've seen a *real* ghost ... did I tell you about my encounter with The Green Lady? ... well ... I ..."

All Tal could do was stare. He stared long and hard at Bungy as if he was seeing him for the very first time, yet so much about him was so wonderfully familiar. Bungy rambled on and on with Tal hanging on every word; it was music to his ears. When Bungy finally ran out of steam Tal turned towards the dishevelled cat and butted him on the head gently with his long, elegant nose. Bungy returned the gesture; all was well again.

"We better get a move on ..." Pie was coming around and assuming her 'I'm in charge' mode dispensing orders brusquely to the group. "We have to find someone in the camp to help us before sunrise, come on ... Amos make sure you have all your belongings."

Amos smiled inwardly, happy to be bossed around, happy his friends were once again as they should be. The small party readied themselves to cross the stream towards the encampment. Bungy was not impressed at having to wade again through the freezing water but was not allowed to stay behind – the others wanted to keep a close eye on him. They lined up on the edge of the stream which sped by swelled by rainwater which had run off the fields. Standing waiting Bungy realised the full extent of the torrent that he had crossed earlier fuelled by adrenaline; he was amazed at his own bravado.

"Ahem, I'll have to take a run at this," he announced, taking several steps back. From behind him came a loud *Crrrackk.*

"*Sssshhh,*" they all chorused.

"It's not me," he whispered. "Not a twig in sight just here, it's all mud ... *eeeergh.*"

Crrrackk.

"D-d-d-d-d-don't l-l-l-l-l-look ... n-n-n-now b-b-but one of the trees is coming to life ..." Tal's teeth chattered in fear. "Amos, do something! ... Talk 'tree' or whatever it is you do ..." Tal backed into Amos' legs as he spoke trying to avoid the lumbering shape emerging from the gloom. Turning to see what all the fuss was about Pie and Bungy shot behind Amos' cloak terrified by what they saw. Only Amos stood his ground surrounded by his petrified companions. To their astonishment Amos put out his hand. "It's been many moons, my friend," he said to the swaying shape as it came into view.

"Too many," came a low guttural reply. The words sounded as if they travelled from the deepest depths of the soil, the very roots of the trees. A long, sinewy arm stretched towards the old man and a hand the size of a shovel engulfed the one that was offered. Tal found his snout confronted by the shins of the one person (if that was an appropriate description) in the world he wished to avoid.

"Strange times, my friend," Amos continued.

"Strange indeed," countered Elias. The exchange was strained, a game of cat and mouse with words – neither party wanting to give anything away.

The others watched in silence as the two men eyed each other warily.

"You, like I, have felt the hand of Fate and also find yourself trapped in this halfway existence – some other force controlling our destiny."

Elias gave the old man a puzzled look. "On the contrary, Amos, I am master of my own fate, a free man, trapped nowhere, and now my work here is done."

"We know all about your 'work' as you call it ..." a sudden outburst rose defiantly upwards from the floor splintering the tension between the two men. Pie, adopting her most confident pose, planted herself at Elias's feet and projected her voice forcefully in the direction of his ears which were a long way away. The grizzled man bent his thick neck like a supple bough caught in the wind to peer downwards, his eyes widened in amazement. "An impudent interruption from one so scrawny – the last time I saw such a creature it was satisfyingly stone dead in one of my more devious traps ... a fiendish invention which never fails, I may have one in my sack ..." He lifted the soft leather flap of the satchel slung across his body and rummaged around. Pie gulped nervously but stood her ground.

"Amos and I know exactly what you're up to ... don't we ...?" she looked up to Amos for support. "We know you're out for revenge ..." Tal and Bungy open-mouthed looked from Amos to Elias, Elias to Amos and back again, as if they were watching a game of tennis and Pie were the umpire.

"Hmmm … it's got guts this one … I'll say …" mocked Elias giving a low chuckle which crackled like the sound of snapping twigs.

"My companions here are all most brave, daring and honourable … I'm not sure I can say this any more of my oldest friend." Amos gave Elias a sad but pointed look.

Elias looked at the ground evading Amos' searching blue eyes. Amos stared at the crown of the tatty felt hat; Elias feeling his direct gaze went on the offensive. "You mean to tell me that two cats, one the size of a piece of damp nettle rope, the other as fat as a cannonball and … and …" his eyes travelled over Tal's body. "*Aaaahhh …* the incredible disappearing hound, handsome fellow, good muscle tone, sharp nose, an asset to any tracker worth his salt … we meet again, for a third time, luck, as the saying goes, is on my side …" The hazel rod twitched as Elias bore down towards Tal's scruff. "You have strange companions, my old friend; it baffles me how such small beasts, little more than fanciful play things can be of any use, but the noble hound here is a different matter. It is fortuitous we have met and you at least keep some good company …" Elias continued to look piercingly at Amos as his knobbly hand made to close round Tal's muzzle. Tal's lip began to curl baring gleaming white incisors. In a flash Tal launched snarling at the dinner plate-sized palm, sinking his teeth deep into the leathery skin. Elias doubled over in agony dropping the hazel rod to cradle his injured hand. Amos quickly retrieved the gnarled stick feeling at once a foreign life force flood through his body.

"As I said, my friends are courageous." The hazel rod burned in his grip; it was almost too hot to hold. "It is time for truth, my friend, for honesty. Let us put difference aside." Knowing the power hazel could yield over him Amos threw the staff back to Elias; it landed in his grasp with a loud smack. The anger burning in Elias's eyes faded as he slumped to the ground.

"You are right, Amos, always the wise one. Tonight I have stared death in the face and now I fight with my oldest friend. The omens are ominous, against me. My faithful rod warned me of danger and ill deeds around the evergreen oak at the time of the full moon; I must heed Nature's wisdom. Come, speak of your plight, tell me of your adventures and perhaps together we can make amends."

"I will do so but we must make all haste. Once the moon wanes our futures, or perhaps that should be our past ... will be in jeopardy." Amos glanced anxiously at the sky noting a real but almost imperceptible lightening towards the east.

Seated on a fallen log beside the rushing stream Amos and the others recounted a hastily abridged version of events, conscious all the time of the approaching dawn. When they described the local history meeting Elias's face became a mask of guilt. "It is true I sought to wreak vengeance on the King and almost lost my life in the process. This I did not expect, neither did I expect that despite the success of my plan my anger would not be quelled, my resentment would still burn. I was doomed to live with the injustice, the slight to my character festering inside for eternity – until that is, I met you in this unlikeliest of circumstances."

"See ... I told you there was a reason why we were all intended to meet here on this night ..." Pie looked smug.

"A cat with brains ... I must be wary of my prey in future ..." Elias gave a gruff laugh and tousled the top of Pie's head. Pie looked extremely uncomfortable but tried not to show it as the massive hand almost knocked her over.

They reached the end of their tale as the incandescent moonlight began to slowly lose its intensity. Amos scanned the sky distractedly.

"My noble friend here, ahem ... the 'handsome hound' ... tells us he has it on reliable authority that anyone or anything that passes beneath the branches of the evergreen oak when the moon is full will find themselves in the year 1642, with no way back ..." Amos paused to let Elias digest this information. "We have no way of knowing if this is true but your 'friend' Samson Strong took this path some hours ago in pursuit of our hero Bungy and has not been seen since."

Elias looked at the shadowy outline of the majestic tree on the horizon.

"It seems we are indeed well met this night. So it is true, the oak really does hold the power to open doors into new worlds, to allow passage into different realms."

"It would appear so, my friend, it would seem at last we can ... go home." Amos swallowed trying to stifle the lump rising in his throat. A momentary heaviness descended on the small band of friends as reality hit home.

"Wot's with the long face ... as I said to the 'oss ... Ha! Ha! Ha!" Trotting large as life out of the trees, cocking his leg on their makeshift seat, Bruce turned three circles, two clockwise and one anticlockwise, before flopping on to a pile of leaves at Amos' feet. Amos stared in disbelief at the dirty ball of tangled, wiry brown fur, singed black on the ends.

"You don't half pick your moments ..." Tal cast his eyes heavenward. "Can't you see we're having a conference, a serious, *important* discussion, but then serious isn't in your dictionary, is it *mate* ... you come along here, interrupting ... with the audacity to tiddle on our ..."

"I think, laddo, if it's all the same to ye, I knows exactly when to mek an entry ... I knows all about, ahem ... *timing* ..." Bruce rolled on to his back all four legs in the air inviting Amos to tickle his tummy.

"Bruce ... it's really you ...!" Amos' eyes shone with delight. It was Tal's turn to be speechless.

"By my reckonin' we have less than 'arf an hour before t'sun weks up. We need te gerra riddle on, I've gorra lot a rattin' to catch up on ..." With that Bruce made his way to the brink of the stream took a deep breath and jumped in. He stuck out his jaw keeping his head just above the surface while his stubby legs kicked rhythmically into a jerky dog paddle propelling him towards the other side.

"Time is upon us, and will wait for no man as the saying goes." Amos started to gather up his heavy cloak above his knees; Elias followed him to the crossing point, the feathers in his hat band ruffling in the breeze like a weathervane.

"It is perhaps for the best that time presses, saving us all from a long, painful goodbye." One by one Amos bent and gently stroked the heads of the three forlorn figures by his side. "You have my heartfelt thanks, my unique guardians of time ..., whenever I see a full moon I will be thinking only of you. Now I must catch up with my faithful friend Bruce or we will be parted again, this time forever ..." his voice shook with emotion. "Come, Elias, when we return I will speak with the King in your favour and we will let history take its course as it should."

With one last look back to his companions he waded through the freezing water and strode alongside Elias, Bruce skipping jauntily at his heels, across the field climbing the gentle slope crowned by the mighty tree. Turning briefly to raise his pike in salute, the blade flashing white in the moonlight, the two men walked in slow motion into the deep, sweeping shadows and disappeared from view.

The rush of water was the only sound; the stream burbled and danced in the fading moonlight, a mirror for the tumult of emotions washing mercilessly over three lonely friends. Shades of violet coloured the edges of the sky and flecked the rim of the moon. "It's getting light. We have to go ... NOW!" Tal took control nudging the others unceremoniously on the bottom with his wet nose.

"Do you *mind,*" grunted Pie indignantly.

"Come on, come on ... shake a leg." Tal jumped over the fallen log searching for the ribbon of light indicating the path. "Do hurry up, Mr Slow," he gave Bungy another ungainly shove. "Do you want to spend the foreseeable future out here with your drippy green mate? If we leave now, we should just make it back in time for breakfast."

"Good idea ..." yelled Bungy, suddenly registering a vast empty feeling in his tummy, "I'm famished."

Epilogue

An unrelenting, bitter winter gives way to a ripening spring; the seasons, following Nature's rhythms, coax the hedgerows into an overture of white froth, new blackthorn, new beginnings – the tilted earth turning slowly, revolving faithfully with time, counts down the days in a new year. A brown, furrowed sea of ploughed fields now wears a shimmering mantle of green shoots and vibrant yellow flowers. The house awakens, comforting daily routines are restored and a gentle stirring of the blood nudges drowsy hibernating souls from all-consuming sleepiness. A new normality beckons, and a queue forms at the pantry door.

Nature has spring-cleaned the countryside, thinks Tal, drawing in a deep revitalising breath of fresh crisp air, enjoying the feeling of warm sunshine on his back. Bowing elegantly into a long-legged stretch he surveys the garden, marvelling at the riot of spring colours that dazzle his eyes after the pervading greyness of long, dark winter days. Splashes of yellow, nodding daffodils jostle alongside cornflower blue muscari. Blood-red tulips open their scarlet mouths wide to drink in the sunshine, and all around drifts of heady scent from white, blue and pink hyacinth spires tease his nose. A skylark sings joyously overhead heralding another sparkling day. Time to escape and feel the earth under his pads rather than the fireside rug – the lanes and tracks are calling. Tal ventured further each day from the cottage, deeper into the woods; he didn't like to admit that he was looking for Bruce, but knew he was. He found himself loitering casually near oak trees, but the only passing encounter had been with a funny little fellow, remarkably a miniature version of himself, with a coat of burnished red, same white markings and the good old-fashioned name of Stanley. Either by chance or design on this lonely chap's part their meetings had become more frequent. Trotting in synchronisation together through the trees they made an unusual pair. Tal discovered more each time about the little chap's background – he had not had a good start in life. Abandoned as a youngster miles from home, timid, even frightened of his own shadow, Stanley had had to learn to survive all alone in a busy, noisy town. Gradually, escaping the tarmac he had drifted further and further away to where the air was clean and the spaces wide open. He was a sad little thing and seemed to enjoy Tal's company, listening attentively to Tal's detailed scouting instructions. Thoughts of Bruce soon faded into the background as Tal and Stanley became firm friends. Today he would show the young fellow Fox's Folly Wood and the evergreen oak ... and perhaps tell him their story.

With a rusty creak the wicker lid of the tatty box lifted slowly. Two bright eyes blinked hard at the sharp sting of sunlight streaming into the conservatory from all directions. Warmth enveloped Pie's slender frame as light diffused by the weave plaited a chequerboard pattern on her fur. Pushing the lid fully open with her nose she hopped sleepily into a large pool of sunshine and rolled luxuriously around on the warm wooden floor. Lying on her back, all four legs in the air, she lingered whilst the sun bathed her tummy in glorious heat. Nonchalantly studying the tiny, puffy clouds through the glass roof a thought occurred to her, meetings began again at the village hall today, time for some serious windowsill eavesdropping. After a quick wash she sauntered to the notice board to check the programme. 'The Art of Cupcakes' with Mavis Miggins was today's subject, hmmm … more up Bungy's street, but next week's talk caught her eye, 'The Ancient Folklore of Trees' with Oliver Twigg. She realised her fur was tingling, a sudden chill despite the warm spring sunshine, a pang of yearning stabbed deep inside, perhaps I'll learn something, or … *perhaps I'll just make the most of the warm lead flashing up on the roof. I wonder what my lazy brother is up to …*

The hunger clock seemed permanently set to 'eat'. Bungy's appetite threshold had quadrupled since his exploits with Amos, his reasoning being that from now on he could never quite be sure when he would get his next meal, so it was essential to keep 'topped up'. His food to activity ratio, however, after a long winter was completely out of kilter and the lithe, superhero feline of last summer had once again become the chubby moggy of past times. Making it on to the windowsill had become a challenge so it was time for action, because this was a big problem. Religiously, every evening throughout the winter, at the time of the full moon, Bungy sat motionless, hunkered down on the windowsill, eyes riveted on the garden scanning the silvered trees and lawn, staring into the depths of creeping shadows, searching for a sign. And, every evening, subdued and withdrawn, he had slunk off to his bed to let sleep heal his longing. He was finding it harder every day to believe the adventure ever happened. Where was the magic in the moonlight – had it been an illusion? Flopping once more into his bed, tired and emotional he struggled to find a cosy spot; his brain fighting his urge to sleep. Turning round and round clockwise then anticlockwise he slumped against the soft edge of the bed. Nuzzling deep into the cushion, welcome waves of sleep began to wash over him; he felt the tension draining from his limbs. Rolling over on to his expanding stomach something sharp dug into his tender pink flesh. Springing to his feet in alarm he saw the glint of something buried deep under the cushion – it was a beautiful golden brooch in the shape of a tiny braided knot.

– The End -